HONOR

in the

DUST

HONOR

in the

DUST

A WINSLOW BREED NOVEL

GILBERT MORRIS

HOWARD BOOKS
A DIVISION OF SIMON & SCHUSTER
NEW YORK

Our purpose at Howard Books is to:
- *Increase faith* in the hearts of growing Christians
- *Inspire holiness* in the lives of believers
- *Instill hope* in the hearts of struggling people everywhere

Because He's coming again!

HOWARD Fiction
A DIVISION OF SIMON & SCHUSTER

Published by Howard Books, a division of Simon & Schuster, Inc.
1230 Avenue of the Americas, New York, NY 10020
www.howardpublishing.com

Honor in the Dust © 2009 by Gilbert Morris

Wordserve Literary Group

Library of Congress Cataloging-in-Publication Data
Morris, Gilbert.
Honor in the dust: a Winslow Breed novel / Gilbert Morris.
p. cm.
I. Title.
PS3563.O8742H658 2009
813'.54—dc22   2009016663

ISBN 978-1-4165-8746-0 (pbk)
ISBN 978-1-4391-6837-0 (ebook)

10 9 8 7 6 5 4 3 2 1

For information regarding special discounts for bulk purchases,
please contact: Simon & Schuster Special Sales at 1-866-506-1949
or business@simonandschuster.com

The Simon & Schuster Speakers Bureau can bring authors to your live event. For more information or to book an event contact the Simon & Schuster Speakers Bureau at 1-866-248-3049 or visit our website at www.simonspeakers.com

Edited by David Lambert
Cover design by The Design Works Group
Interior design by Jaime Putorti

This novel is a work of fiction. Names, characters, places, and incidents either are the product of the author's imagination or are used fictitiously. Any resemblance to actual events, locales, organizations, or persons, living or dead, is entirely coincidental and beyond the intent of either the author or publisher.

To Johnnie—
Thanks for sixty wonderful years!
You have been the joy of my life
and the best wife on the planet
(or anywhere else, for that matter!).

PART ONE

The Prodigal

(1497–1512)

1

May 1497
Sussex, England

Claiborn Winslow leaned forward and patted his horse's sweaty neck. "Well done, Ned." He had pushed the stallion harder than he liked, but after so many months away he was hungry for home. He straightened in the saddle and gazed with pleasure at Stoneybrook, the Winslows' ancestral castle. It had withstood siege and battle, and it bore all the marks that time makes upon structures as well as upon men. There was nothing particularly beautiful about Stoneybrook. There were many castles in England that had more pleasing aspects. But Claiborn loved it more than any other.

The spring had brought a rich emerald-green growth to all the countryside, and verdant fields nuzzled against the very walls of Stoneybrook. If they were any indication, the summer's harvest would be good, indeed. The castle itself crowned a hill and was dominated by a formidable wall, outside of which a small village thrived. Even now, late in the day, people and carts and horses moved in and out of the central gate, and on the battlements Claiborn saw the banner of Winslow fluttering in the late-afternoon breeze, as if beckoning to him.

"My heaven, it's good to be home!"

He laughed at himself, adding, "I'm talking to myself. I must be worse off than I thought." His mind cascaded back to the battles he had seen, rare but fierce, and the men he had encountered. Some dreaded battle, feared it and could not force themselves forward. Others found joy in the clash of weapons and the shouts of victory when the battle was over. Claiborn was one of these, finding a natural rhythm to battle, a path from start to finish that seemed to be preordained for him. When the trumpets sounded and the drums rolled, his heart burned with excitement. God help him, he loved it. Loved being a soldier. But this, returning to Stoneybrook, had its own charm.

"Come on, Ned." Kicking his horse's sides Claiborn guided the animal to the village gate, and as he passed through, he ran across an old acquaintance, Ryland Tolliver, one of the blacksmiths who served Lord Edmund Winslow and the others of the family as well.

"Well, bless my soul!" Ryland boomed. "If it's not the soldier home from the wars!" He was a bulky man, his shoulders broad, his hands like steel hooks from his years at the forge. He laughed as Claiborn dismounted. "Good to see you, man. You're just getting home. All in one piece, I see."

"All in one piece." The two men shook hands, and Claiborn had to squeeze hard to keep his hand from being crushed by the burly blacksmith. "How are things here? My mother and my brother?"

"The same as they were when you left. What did you expect? We'd fall to pieces without you to keep us straight?"

"No, I'm not as vain as that. I'm sure the world would jog on pretty well without me."

"Tell me about the wars, man."

"Not now. I need to go see my family. But I'll come back later. We'll have enough ale to float a ship. I'll tell you lies about how I won the battles. You can tell lies about how you've won over the virtue of poor Sally McFarland."

"Sally McFarland? Why, she left here half a year ago."

"I thought you were going to marry that girl."

"She had other ideas. A blacksmith wasn't good enough for her." He looked at Ned and said, "Not much of a horse."

"He's a stayer. That's what I like. He needs shoeing, though. I'll leave him with you. Feed him something good. He's had a hard journey."

"That I'll do." He took the reins from Claiborn. "What about you, master? What brings you home at long last?"

Claiborn glanced back at him, and a smile touched his broad lips. "Well, I'm thinking about taking a wife."

"A wife? You? Why, you were made to be a bachelor man! Half the women in this village stare at you when you walk down the street."

"You boast on my behalf, but even if it was God's own truth, I'd not have just any woman."

"Ah, I see. So have you got one picked out?"

"Of course! Grace Barclay had my heart when we courted and she has never let it go."

"Oh, yes, Grace Barclay." There was a slight hesitation in the blacksmith's speech. He opened his lips again to speak, but then something came over him, and he clamped them together for a moment.

"Ryland, what is it? Grace is well?" Claiborn said, his heart seizing at the look on the blacksmith's face.

"She is well. Still pretty as ever." Ryland had ceased smiling, and he lifted the reins in his hand. "I best go and take care of the horse. He must have a thirst."

"As do I. I'll return on the morrow. Give him a good feed too. He's earned it."

⚬⚬

The servants were busy putting the evening meal together, and as he passed into the great hall, Claiborn spoke to many of them. He was smiling and remembering their names, and they responded to him well. He had always been a favorite with the servants, far more than his brother Edmund, the master of Stoneybrook, and enjoyed his special status. He paused beside one large woman who was pushing out of her clothing and said, "Martha, your shape is more . . . womanly than when I departed."

The cook giggled and said, "Away with you now, sir. None of your soldier's ways around here."

He grinned. "You are expecting a little one. It is nothing shameful, I assume."

"Shush! Mind that we're in public, sir. Such conversation is unseemly!" Her face softened and she leaned closer. "I married George, you know. A summer past."

"Well, good for George. With a good woman and a babe on the way, he must be content, indeed. What's for supper?"

"Nothing special, but likely better than some of the meals you've had."

"You're right about that. Soldier's fare is pretty rough stuff."

Passing on, Claiborn felt a lightness in his spirit. There was something about coming home that did something inside a man. He thought of the many campfires he had huddled next to in the fields, sometimes in drizzling rain and sometimes bitter-cold weather, dreaming of the smells and the sounds of Stoneybrook, wishing he were back. And now, at last, he was.

He turned to see his brother, emerging from the central door. "Edmund!"

He hurried forward to meet Edmund and said, "It's good to see you, Brother."

"And you," Edmund said, holding him at arm's length to get a good look. "No wounds this round?"

"Nothing that hasn't healed," Claiborn returned.

"Good, good. Mother will be so relieved."

The two turned to walk together down a passageway that

would lead to their mother's apartments. Claiborn restrained his pace, accommodating his smaller, older brother's shorter stride. "All is well here, Brother? You are well?"

"Never better. There is much to tell you. But it can wait until we sup."

A servant had just departed, after breathlessly telling Leah that her son had returned. Lady Winslow wished she had a moment to run a brush through her gray hair, but she could already hear her sons making their way down the corridor. She rose, straightening her skirts. How many nights had she prayed for Claiborn's return, feared for his very life! And here he was at last.

The two paused at her door. Leah's hand went to her breast as she surveyed her sons. Claiborn's rich auburn hair with just a trace of gold; Edmund's dull brown. Claiborn's broad forehead, sparkling blue eyes, high cheekbones, determined chin, generous lips that so easily curved into a smile. Here, here was the true Lord Winslow, a far more striking figure than his sallow, flabby brother. Her eyes flitted guiltily toward her eldest, wondering if he read her traitorous thoughts.

But Claiborn was already moving forward, arms out, and she rushed to him. He lifted her and twirled around, making her giggle and then flush with embarrassment. "Claiborn, Claiborn!"

He laughed, the sound warm and affectionate, and then gently set her on her feet. "You are still lovely, Mother."

"You are kind to an old woman," she said. She reached up and cradled his cheek. "The wars . . . You return to us unhurt?"

"Only aching for home," he returned.

He took the horsehide-covered seat she offered and Edmund took another. A servant arrived with refreshments and quickly poured.

"Are you hungry, Son?"

"Starved, but this will tide me over until we sup."

"Well, tell us about the wars," Edmund said.

"Like all wars—bloody and uncomfortable. I lost some good friends. God be praised, I came through all right."

Edmund let out a scoffing sound. "Don't tell me you've turned religious!"

"Religious enough to seek my Maker when facing death."

Edmund laughed. Leah frowned. He had a high-pitched laugh that sounded like the whinnying of a horse.

"Not very religious when you were growing up. I had to thrash you for chasing the maids."

Claiborn reddened and guiltily glanced at Leah. "I suppose I troubled you greatly."

"You were young," Leah put in. "Now you are a man."

"She forgets just how troublesome you were," Edmund said.

"You might have been the same had you faced manhood and the loss of your father in the same year. You were fortunate, Edmund, to be a man full grown before you became Lord Winslow."

Edmund pursed his narrow lips and considered her words. "Yes. I suppose there is a certain wisdom in that, Mother. A thousand apologies, Claiborn," he said, with no true apology in his tone.

"None offense taken. So tell me, what's the feeling here about the king?"

"Most are for Henry. He's a strong man—but it troubles all that he seems to have a ghost haunting him."

"A real ghost?"

"No, but it might be better if it were," Edmund said with a grin. "Henry Tudor defeated Richard III at Bosworth, and he claimed the crown. But he's always thinking that someone with a better claim to the crown will lead a rebellion and cut his head off."

"Do you think that could happen?"

"No. Henry's too clever to let that happen."

Leah fidgeted in her seat, wondering when Edmund would

tell his brother what he must be told. Would it be up to her? She kept silent for ten long minutes as the men continued to speak of Henry VII and his various campaigns. When they were silent, she blurted, "Has Edmund told you of his plans?"

Edmund shot her a quick, narrowed glance but then turned to engage his brother again.

"Plans?" Claiborn's bright blue eyes lit up. "What is it?"

"I'm to be married," he said, uncrossing his legs and crossing them again, studiedly casual.

"Well, I assumed you were already long married. Alice Williams is your intended bride, I suppose."

Edmund's face darkened. He took two quick swallows from his cup and then shook his head. "No," he said in a thin tone. "That didn't come to fruition. She married Sir Giles Mackson."

"Why, he's an old man!"

"I expect that's why Alice married him. She expects to wear him out, then she'll be in control of everything."

"I didn't think Alice was that kind of woman."

"Come, now, most women are that kind of woman. Apart from our dear mother, of course." He reached out a hand to Leah and she took it. He held it too tightly, as if warning her. "You truly haven't learned more of women as you've traveled?"

"Not of what you speak." His eyes moved to his brother's hand, still holding their mother's. "Well, who is it, then? Who is the future Lady Winslow?"

Leah couldn't bear to watch her handsome son's face. She stared studiously at her lap, waiting for the words to come.

"Obviously, I've considered it for some time," Edmund said, releasing their mother's hand, setting down his cup, and rising to stand behind her chair.

Claiborn frowned but forced a curious smile. Why was he hesitating? "Cease toying with me, Edmund. Who is she?"

"I have selected Grace Barclay."

Claiborn's fingers grew white as he gripped his cup. With a

shaking hand he set it down before he crushed it. "Grace Barclay," he whispered.

"Yes. She's comely enough, and I've come to a fine arrangement with her father. We shall obtain all the land that borders our own to the east. That'll be her dowry. We'll be able to put in new rye fields and carry more cattle. It'll add a quarter to the size of Stoneybrook. You know how hard I tried to buy that land from her father years ago. Well, he wouldn't sell—never would, I thought, but when he mentioned the match, I thought, well, why not? It's time I married and produced an heir for all of this. I'll show you around the property tomorrow."

Claiborn said nothing further. He felt frozen in place. Edmund prattled on about the new land that would soon be added, how it would benefit them all, and finally turned to the door and said, "Come along, you two. They ought to have something to eat on the table by now. You can tell us about the wars in more detail, Claiborn, now that you know all that's new here."

"Edmund, may I have a word with your brother?" Leah said quietly.

Edmund stared, as if he had forgotten she was there. After a moment's hesitation, he said, "Certainly, Mother. I shall see you both in the dining hall." Then, straightening his doublet, he exited the room.

Claiborn struggled to speak. At last he asked, "When will the marriage take place?"

"The date has not been set, but it will be soon." Leah turned warm eyes on her son. She reached out to touch his arm, but he flinched. She had stood idly by! Watched this transgression unfold! "Claiborn, it is a business arrangement. Nothing more."

"But she was mine. He knew I courted her."

"And then you left her. She has been of marriageable age for some time now. For all we knew, you could have already died on foreign soil. Like it or not, life continues for those of us left behind. Grace needed a husband; Edmund needed a wife. It was a natural choice."

Claiborn rose. "What of love? What of passion? Grace and I shared those things."

"Years ago, you shared those things. Now you must forget them. Your brother, Lord Winslow, has chosen."

"Chosen *my* intended!" Claiborn thundered, rising.

"You did not make your intentions clear," Leah said quietly, pain in every word.

"I could not leave Grace with a promise to marry. It was a promise I could not be sure I could keep. Too many die on the battlefield . . ." He turned away to the window, running a hand through his hair, anguished at the thought of never holding Grace in his arms, never declaring his love, enduring the sight of *her*, with *him*. His brother. His betrayer.

His mother came up behind him, and this time he allowed her touch on his arm. Slowly, quietly, she leaned her temple against his shoulder, simply standing beside him for a time in solidarity. "I'm sorry, Son. But you are too late. You cannot stop what is to come, only make your peace with it. It will be well in time. But you must stand aside."

Claiborn went through the motions of the returned soldier through the rest of the evening. He was not a particularly good actor, and many of the servants noticed how quiet he was. Edmund did not, however, continuing to fill the silence with endless chatter.

After the meal was over, Claiborn said, "I think I'll go to bed. My journey was long today."

"Yes, you'd better," Edmund said, mopping the gravy from a trencher with a chunk of bread. "Tomorrow we'll look things over, find something for you to do while you are home. Will you return to the army?"

"I'm not quite sure, Edmund."

"Bad business being a soldier! Out in the weather, always the danger of some Spaniard or Frenchman taking your head off. We'll find something for you around here. Time you got a profession. Maybe you'd make a lawyer or even go into the church." He laughed then and said, "No, not the church. Too much mischief in you for that! Go along, then. Sleep well, and we'll discuss it further on the morrow."

※

As Claiborn rode up to the property owned by John Barclay, he felt as if he were coming down with an illness. He had slept not at all but had paced the floor until his mother had sent a servant with a vessel of wine, which he downed quickly and soon afterward fell into a dream-laden sleep. As soon as the sun had come up, he had departed, only leaving word for Edmund that he had an errand to run.

Now, as he dismounted in front of the large house where Barclay lived with his family, a smiling servant came out.

"Greetings, sir. Shall I grain your horse?"

"No, just walk him until he cools."

He walked up to the door, his eyes troubled and his lips in a tight line. He was shown in by a house servant, and five minutes later John Barclay, Grace's father, came in.

"Well, Claiborn, you're back. All safe and sound, I trust?"

"Yes, sir. Safe and sound."

"How did the wars go? Here, let's have a little wine."

Claiborn's head was splitting already from the hangover, but he took the mulled wine so that he might have something to do with his hands.

John Barclay was a small man, handsome in his youth, but now at the age of forty beginning to show his age poorly. He pumped Claiborn for news of the wars, passed along the gossips of the court and of the neighborhood. Finally he got to what Claiborn had come to address.

"I assume your brother has told you that he and my girl Grace are to be married?"

"Yes, sir, he did."

"Well, it's a good match," he rushed on. "She's a good girl and your brother is a good man. Good blood on both sides! They'll be providing me with some fine grandchildren. A future."

Claiborn did not know exactly how to proceed. He had hoped to find Grace alone, but Barclay did not mention her, so finally he said, "I wonder if I might see Miss Grace? Offer my future sister-in-law my thoughts on her impending nuptials?"

"Certainly! She's out in the garden. Let her welcome you home. She'll tell you all about the wedding plans, I'm sure."

"Thank you, sir." Claiborn knew where the garden was, for he had visited Grace more than once in this place. He turned the corner, and his first sight of her stopped him in his tracks. She was even more beautiful than he remembered. A tall woman with blond hair and well-shaped green eyes and a beautiful smile. He stood there looking at her, and finally she turned and saw him. She was holding a pair of shears in her hands. She dropped them and cried out, "Claiborn!"

Moving forward, Claiborn felt as if he were in a dream world. He came to stand in front of her and could not think of what to say. It was so different from how he had imagined seeing her for the first time after his long absence. How many times had he imagined taking her into his arms, turning her face up, kissing her and whispering his love, and her own whispered declarations . . .

But that was not happening. Grace had good color in her cheeks as a rule, but now they were pale, and he could see her lips were trembling. "Claiborn, you're—you're home."

"Aye, I am."

A silence seemed to build a wall between them, and it was broken only when she whispered, "You know? About Edmund and me?"

"I knew nothing until yesterday, when Edmund told me."

"I thought he might send you word."

"He's not much of a one for writing." Claiborn suddenly reached out and took her by the upper arm. He squeezed too hard, saw pain rise, and released his grip. "I can't believe it, Grace! I thought we had an understanding."

Grace turned a little toward him. "An understanding of sorts," she said quietly. "But that was a long time ago, Claiborn. Much has transpired since you left."

He couldn't stop himself. Gently he reached out his hand to take hers. "I'm sorry. I was a fool."

"You were young. We both were. Perhaps it is best that we leave it at that." She turned her wide green eyes up to meet his.

He frowned. "Is that all it was to you? The passion of youth? Frivolity? Foolishness?"

"Nay," she said softly, so softly that he wondered if he had misheard her. But then she repeated it, squeezing his hand. His heart surged. Her voice was unsteady as she said, "I did everything I could to get out of the marriage, Claiborn. I begged my father, but he wouldn't take no for an answer. He's determined—and so is your brother."

"I know Edmund is stubborn, but there must have been *some* way, Grace."

"No, both your brother and my father see a woman as something to be traded. I don't think my father ever once thought of what I wanted, of what you and I once shared, of what would make me happy. Nor Edmund. He's never courted me. It is purely an arrangement that suits well—on the surface."

Suddenly Claiborn asked, "Do you think you might come to love him, Grace?"

Tears came into Grace's eyes. "No," she whispered. "Of course not! I love you, Claiborn. You must know that."

Then suddenly a great determination came to Claiborn. He could not see the end of what he planned to do, but he could see the beginning—which would undoubtedly bring a period of strife. And yet any great battle worth fighting began in the same way. "We'll have to go to them both, your father and my brother," he said. "We'll explain that we love each other, and we will have to make them understand."

Grace shook her head. "It won't do any good, Claiborn. Neither of them will listen. Their minds are made up."

"They'll have to listen!" Claiborn's voice was fierce. "Come. We'll talk to your father right now. And then I'll go try to reason with Edmund. My mother will come to my aid, I am certain."

"I fear it will do no good—"

"But we must try."

She accepted his other hand and met his gaze again. "Yes," she said with a nod, "we must try."

"Grace Barclay, if we manage this feat, would you honor me by becoming my bride?"

"Indeed," she said, smiling, with fear and hope in her beautiful eyes.

"Come, then," he said, tucking her hand into the crook of his arm. "Let us see to it then."

The two of them went inside and found Grace's father eating an apple. Claiborn knew there was no simple manner to enter the discussion at hand, so he said, "Mr. Barclay, forgive me for going against you and your arrangement with my brother, but I must tell you that Grace and I love each other. We want your permission to marry."

John Barclay stared at the two, then hastily swallowed a mouthful of grapes. The juice ran down his chin, and his face was scarlet. "What are you talking about, man? I've told you, she's to marry your brother!"

"Father, I never cared for Edmund," Grace said at once. She held her head up high and added, "I've loved Claiborn for a long time."

"Have you lost your senses, girl? Sir Edmund is the lord of Stoneybrook. He has the money and the title. What does this man have? A sword and the clothes he has on his back!"

"But Father—"

"Not another word, Grace! You're marrying Edmund Winslow, and I'll hear no more about it!" Barclay turned to Claiborn, his face contorted with rage. "And you! What sort of brother are you? Coming between your brother and the woman he's sought for his wife! You're a sorry excuse for a man! Get out of here and never come back, you understand me?" He turned to Grace and shouted, "As for you, girl, go to your room! I'll have more words for you later!"

※

As Claiborn rode through the environs of Barclay Manor, he felt as if he had been in a major battle. He loitered on the way home, trying to put together a speech that might move Edmund after so utterly failing with John Barclay. When he reached the castle, he saw his brother out in the field with one of the hired hands. He was pointing out some fences, no doubt, that needed to be built, and he turned as Claiborn rode up and dismounted.

"Well, you ran off early this morning. What was so pressing that you could not even stop to break your fast?"

"I must have a word with you, Edmund."

His brother said something to the field hand and then turned to walk beside Claiborn. "Well, what is it? Have you given thought to your profession?"

"No, no, it's about Grace."

Edmund's eyes narrowed. "Grace? What about her?"

Claiborn faced his brother and said, "Grace and I love each

other. We have for a long time. Forgive me for this, but we wish to be married, Edmund."

Edmund's face contorted into a look of confusion. "Have you lost your mind, Claiborn? She's engaged to me! Everyone knows about it."

Claiborn began to try to explain, to reason, and even to plead with Edmund, but Edmund scoffed, "You were always a romantic dreamer, boy. But you are a man grown now. You must embrace life and all its practicalities, as I have. Think if it. The woman is handsome, yes, but what she brings to this estate is even more attractive. There will be another girl for you."

"Perhaps Barclay will still give the land as Grace's dowry if she marries me."

"Of course he won't! Are you daft? I'm the master here! Now don't be difficult about this, Claiborn. It's for the good of the House of Winslow. Let's hear no more about it."

⚘

The thing could not be kept a secret, and soon everyone at both houses knew what had happened. Edmund made no secret of his displeasure. Finally, after three days, he found Claiborn, and his anger had hardened, but he gave Claiborn one more chance to quit his pursuit.

"Look you now, Claiborn," he said. "You know you have no way to provide for a wife without me. And if you stubbornly pursue this one as your wife, I shall turn you out. What kind of a life would a woman have with you then? You know as well as I she'd be miserable. Grace has always had the best of everything. What would she have with you outside of the House of Winslow? Dirt, poverty, sickness, misery, that's what she'd have. You must see that."

"But Edmund, we love each other. If you'd help me fit myself for a profession—"

"I *will* help you! I've said so already. But I'd be made to look ridiculous if my own brother took my choice for a wife from me. A lord cannot be made to look the fool. It would bind me in every future arrangement I wanted to make. No, the die has been cast. You must live with what has transpired in your absence."

Claiborn had never asked his brother for anything, and he hated to beg, but he pleaded with Edmund until he saw that it was useless.

"You cannot remain here," Edmund said flatly. "Not feeling the way you do about my intended. Refusing to act as a man. Refusing the way of honor."

"I cannot be the man God made me, honor what he has placed on my heart, and do anything but this!" Claiborn cried, arms out, fingers splayed.

Edmund stared at him for a moment and said coldly, "I never want to see you again, Claiborn. You have betrayed me, turned away from all I've given you!"

"And you did not betray me? You knew I courted Grace!"

"Once upon a time, as a young whelp! How was I to know you fancied a grand return, a romantic reunion? No, I deal with a man's responsibilities, and I shall move forward as that, as a man."

Claiborn stared hard at him. "Mother will—"

"Mother will side with me. With the lord of Winslow. She knows her place."

"Just as Grace will know it, right? Pretty, and placed in a corner, until you have need of her in your bed."

"Get out. My bride is my family, my business. And you, you are no longer kin to me."

⚶

"Grace, I've hoped you'd show more sense," her father said. "You don't see life the way it is, so I can't let you make such a terrible mistake."

"It would be a terrible mistake if I married a man I didn't love."

"Nonsense! You've been unfairly influenced by those French romances. I knew I should not have allowed them in my house!"

Grace sighed. To be fair, she had placed him in a terrible position and had never challenged him on anything of note. Until now. "Father, I believe in *love*. Did you not once love my mother?"

"There was no nonsense. She understood how things progress between a man and a woman. She . . ." He colored, growing so frustrated in choosing his words that he shook his finger in her face. "My father and her father saw that there were advantages to our marriage, and we were obedient. We had a good life."

Grace lost her mother to the fevers when she was fourteen, just as Claiborn had lost his father at the same age, but she well remembered how unhappy her mother had been, how she longed for affection but got very little from her husband. John had loved his wife, just as he loved his daughter, but he seemed incapacitated when it came to showing it.

"I love Claiborn, Father," she repeated. "I beg you, don't force me to marry a man I don't love."

John opened his mouth as if to say something in fury, then abruptly closed it, turning away from her. He took a step toward the fire burning in the hearth and ran a hand through his thinning hair. "We shall discuss it no further. You are marrying Sir Edmund Winslow. I shall see to it myself."

※

"We'll have to leave here, Grace." Claiborn had come under cover of darkness to meet with her in the garden. The air was heavy, for the rain had come earlier and soaked the earth.

"Yes, we will."

"I have nothing to offer you."

Grace looked up. "But I have something to offer you. You remember my Aunt Adella?"

"She married an Irishman when we were but children, didn't she?"

"Yes, and he died, and now she's dead. She left the farm in Ireland to me. That's where we must go and make our life."

It sounded like a dream—an unfavorable dream, since Claiborn had no good opinion of Ireland. But it seemed they had no choice. Perhaps it was of God, this provision.

"This asks much of you, Grace. You'd have the life you were born to, here, if you married Edmund."

"No, my life would be tragic, living with a man I don't love and never again seeing the man I do love. There is no choice. Come for me in two days' time. I shall meet you by the side gate, when all are deeply asleep."

⚭

Two days later, Claiborn waited outside Barclay House in the dark gardens that bordered the building, nervously shifting from foot to foot. He had stolen away from Stoneybrook as soon as even the lightest sleeper was deep into his dreams. But if she didn't emerge soon . . . If Edmund discovered he was gone and he was here, or if Grace's father came upon them . . . His hand went to his sword. He would do what it took to get his intended away from here. But if anyone died as they departed, it would haunt them forever.

"Please, Lord," he muttered under his breath. "Make a way for us. Help us depart in peace."

Two men came riding along, and Claiborn ducked into a copse of trees just in time to avoid them. But the lads were too deep into the ale to notice him or that Ned's soft whinny greeted their horses. They trotted past, laughing so giddily that Claiborn wondered how they stayed astride their mounts. His eyes moved back to the side door, where he had sent word for Grace to meet him. "Make haste, Grace," he begged through gritted teeth. "Make haste!"

Edmund was not a fool. He was certain to have encouraged servants to keep an eye out for him and any suspicious actions of his within Stoneybrook. With each minute that ticked by, the risk of exposure increased. Claiborn's eyes traced the outline of the side door, willing it to open. Had she changed her mind? Or been intercepted? His mind leaped through different options to choose should she not emerge within a few minutes. Steal inside? Summon a servant and demand to see her? Or walk away?

But then, there she was. He hesitated for a moment, wondering if his mind was playing tricks on him. No, it was her. She had come! He hurried forward, wincing as Ned stepped on a brittle branch. Her head swung toward the sound, and she hurriedly shut the door behind her, turning a key in the lock and pocketing it.

He took her hands in his. "All right, Sweetheart. We'll find someone to marry us straight away, and then we'll make a life together in Ireland. Thank you for this honor. Thank you for trusting me."

"I'm trusting you and God, Claiborn."

Claiborn was well aware that he did not really know God in the way that Grace did. She had a firm faith in the Lord. His own religion was more of a formality. But now he put his arms around her and kissed her. "I hope you're right, Grace. At least we'll have each other."

"Yes." Grace smiled up, tears in her eyes. "We'll have each other."

2

February 1499
Ireland

Claiborn straightened and grunted as he lifted a square of soaked peat sod. With an effort he turned and dropped it into the two-wheel cart beside him. Then he paused and looked up at the slate-gray sky. It was late. He had been working since dawn, as he had for almost two years. The rain that had drenched the land earlier had stopped except for a cold drizzle that still poured off his hat and down his loose collar. He rubbed his hands together; they were stiff with cold. A sudden longing came to him for some of the sunny lands that he had soldiered in. Sighing deeply, he moved to the front of the cart and picked up the tongue, every moment bringing a protest from his tired muscles. The winter rain had turned the field into a morass of mud. It took everything in him to break the wheels of the cart loose from the peat that sucked at them. His feet sank deep into the muddy surface, and the effort to draw the cart forward drained all his strength.

"What I wouldn't give for Ned's return!" The words rasped from his throat as he thought longingly of his horse. He had been forced to sell him the autumn past to buy food. There had been no choice after their pitiful summer crop failed. He'd bought a donkey—an old beast past his best years but still better than nothing—but he, too, had died, so now there was nothing except Claiborn's muscles and a grim determination.

As he pushed forward, he was remembering their arrival at this place, their initial excitement over the sweet, rounded hills, the expanse of rich soil, the tall stone manor—small, but respectable—at the top of the hill. At first, they believed with everything in them that God had made a special way for them, a path, a future. He remembered how they had been delighted with the emerald green of the land, the azure-blue skies overhead, and the sparkling brooks that ran through this particular part of Ireland. Truly, in the drier times of the year, it was a land of beauty.

But as the months passed, they realized that this land was also a killing place, an estate that could only be managed with many servants and field hands. People they could not afford to hire. It only took a week to find out that there was no way adequately to heat the drafty house, which emanated cold from its very walls. A few more, and they knew that the stone walls bordering their property were in dismal repair. Their few sheep were soon gone, lost to thieves and other predators. Even the spring, their only source of water save the frequent deluges that poured from the skies, proved difficult, its position being more than a hundred yards from shelter. How weary was he, hauling every drop in buckets to the house!

Claiborn's feet sank deep into the mud and made ugly sucking sounds as he pulled them free, hauling him back to the present. He stopped, his breath coming short, and he thought again, *I should not have brought Grace to this mudhole of a place!* Claiborn placed his hands on his hips and stared across the bare landscape. An uncontrollable tremor shook his body as the freezing wind searched and numbed him. He turned his eyes away from the drab brown and colorless gray landscape.

"Ireland, you're a deceitful piece of ground," he muttered, "and I wish I'd never laid eyes on you!"

Claiborn recognized that his voice was dull, not his own anymore. He ran a hand through his hair and considered the difficulties of the past year, the struggle to stay ahead of the freezing cold and wrest a bare subsistence from the stubborn land. All his life at Stoneybrook he had watched laborers but had never once thought about the price they paid for bringing food from the earth. Well, he understood now; he would never be able to look at laborers in a field without feeling a keen sympathy for them. But he didn't wish to be one of their number any longer. If only there was a way! Another path for them! He glanced at the house at the top of the hill and hauled the cart toward it.

Soldiering had been hard but not all the time. Every day on this piece of ground was a struggle. He thought with longing now of those times he had enjoyed as a soldier, how easy it had been just to live and to locate good food one way or another. Good food, warmth, laughter.

He struggled to haul the dead weight of the cart, loaded with peat, over a rock. He had grown to hate peat, but the Irish lived on it. They built their houses with squares of it, and it would burn, after a fashion. Since there was little natural timber, it was the only heat that the land would provide. Claiborn longed for a fire such as they had enjoyed in every main room of Stoneybrook—a roaring blaze coaxed from good, solid links of oak, waves of heat, bright light dancing over the walls.

But that was not their lot. This was their lot. The faint, pathetic glow of Irish sod, burning reluctantly in the hearth, heating little more than a five-foot arc.

Only thoughts of Grace, of cuddling with her before the fire as they did each eve, brought any warmth to his spirit.

Reaching the front door of the house, he dropped the tongue of the cart and stood for a moment, preparing for his entrance. He had to make the best of things, never to let Grace see how discouraged he had become. He forced himself to play a role—like an actor, he supposed. When an actor came out on a stage, no matter what his sorrow, he had to laugh if that was the role.

Claiborn shoved the wooden door open. It gave reluctantly, shedding bits of ice around the frame. He stepped inside, and then, even in the feeble light of the lantern that lit the interior, he saw Grace. The light on her face and in her eyes, as always, was a miracle to him. How could any woman, fine-born and accustomed to the best that servants could provide—good food, warm clothing, and roaring fires in the huge fireplaces of a manor house—keep such a cheerful spirit in such bleak surroundings? She came to him and circled her arms around his neck. He gratefully pulled her into his arms. She kissed him quickly and said, "You're freezing, Claiborn. Come and get warm."

"A man can come home to you, Sweetheart, and just the sight of you warms his heart, his feet, and his whole body." He was aware of the smell of cooked meat and was equally aware that was impossible; they hadn't had meat to eat for months. Could she have somehow obtained a leg of lamb? His mouth watered at the thought, but he kept silent, not wishing to plant disappointment within Grace if he was wrong.

"Why, you're becoming a poet," she said. "The next thing I know you'll have a lute out there and start playing love songs to me."

"That would be a good idea, I think. You've had precious little of the fine things you deserve."

"I have what I need, Claiborn, in you. How many times must we go through this? Now come over and get those wet things off. Look, I put your other clothes out to dry."

Quickly Claiborn stripped off his soaked clothing. He pulled off his roughly made shoes and the woolen cloths he used for stockings, which were stiff with ice. He toweled off with a piece of rough sacking and quickly put on the warm garments. The warmth of the clothes and even the feeble light of the fire loosed his foul mood.

"I found some good peat. I'll bring it in so it'll dry and burn better."

"That can wait. We must eat first. I have a surprise for you. Close your eyes."

Claiborn smiled. His stomach growled. "And what might that be, darling?"

"I said close your eyes! Come." She led him to one of the two chairs. Feeling his way, he sat himself down. "Don't open them now," she whispered. He heard her moving around, and finally she said, "All right. Open your eyes."

Claiborn blinked. There on a wooden platter was a large rabbit, baked and sending off a delicious odor.

"A happy Noel, husband!"

Claiborn slowly turned his eyes to his wife. He had forgotten that it was Christmas Day! He reached out and touched the rabbit and looked at her with wonder. For months they had existed solely on potatoes. "Where in the world did you get this?"

"The dogs caught him and were going to tear him apart, but I got him first. I have another surprise." She turned and out of the single small box that served as their food cupboard she brought a bottle. "Good beer. I've been saving it for our Christmas feast."

Claiborn's conscience smote him. "I didn't get you a thing. I—I forgot it was Christmas."

"I don't want anything. We have a fine meal and each other. Now, the blessing."

Claiborn bowed his head but murmured, "You'd better say it. I'm too stunned to speak." He kept his head bowed while she said a pretty little grace, and he marveled that her steadfast faith could rise above the terrible circumstances he had brought her to. His own had been steadily dismantled with each terrible week they had spent here.

"Now, we eat!" She smiled, and her eyes sparkled.

Claiborn picked up the single sharp knife that they had. He cut off some of the best part of the rabbit and put it on Grace's plate, knowing she would protest.

"Oh, that's the best part. Take it for yourself."

"Not a bit of it, Sweetheart. You eat that. It'll make you fat and pretty, as I am."

She giggled, picked up a bit of the meat, and ate it.

"You know," he said, after he had taken his first bite, "the French have a new invention." The well-seasoned meat was the best thing that he had ever tasted, he thought.

"What kind of invention?"

"It looks like a very small pitchfork, small enough to hold in your hand."

"What do you do with it?"

"Why, you cut your meat up into small portions with a knife, then stab a piece with this fork. Then you bring it to your mouth."

"Doesn't it get dirty?"

He laughed. "They're washable, you know. I don't think anything will ever come of it. A knife and fingers, that's good enough for any Englishman."

They ate half the rabbit, saving the rest for a meal later on, and moved on to what they ate at every meal, baked potatoes. The savory white rabbit meat had filled him up for the first time in what seemed like a year. Well, not filled exactly, but as close as he was likely to come. As he ate his potato, wishing for more rabbit, he watched how daintily she ate. She had always been slender but lately had grown frightfully thin. How much longer could they make it here?

He turned away from his foul thoughts, not wanting to ruin

her Christmas. Once the trenchers were cleared, he pulled her down in front of the fire. They sat on some old sacks, and he held her tightly, pulling a blanket over them to preserve the precious heat. Staring at the smoldering fire, they grew sleepy, and Claiborn felt his wife relax in his arms, her breathing becoming slow and deep. He tried not to think of the next day, of fighting the gray earth again.

Grace spoke, surprising him. "It's been a good Christmas."

"Yes, it has. I wish I had gotten you something, though."

"You give me yourself every day, Claiborn. That's a Christmas gift year 'round." She lifted her head to look at him. Her eyes were enormous in the dim light, it seemed, and she said, "I wonder if this house is anything like the innkeeper's where Mary and Joseph sought shelter."

"Both his house and stable were probably warmer than ours."

Grace smiled at him and ran her hand across his broad chest. They sat there not speaking, and finally she said in a halting whisper, "I—I do have a gift for you."

"Oh, Grace, you don't! It makes me feel terrible. I haven't given you anything."

"Oh, but you have."

He stared at her. "What do you mean? I haven't purchased any presents."

"You didn't give it to me exactly today, and I can't give yours to you until—well, until spring."

Claiborn had grown sleepy. He held her tightly as they soaked up the warmth. She did not speak again, and for a moment he was puzzled by what she had just said. "I can't have it until spring? What in the world is it, woman?"

"Can't you think of a gift that takes a few months for a woman to prepare?"

And then with a rush it came to him. It took his breath away as cleanly as when a fellow knight struck him in the solar plexus.

He sat up, set her apart from him to get a better look at her, and saw that she was delighted. She squeezed his hand. "Merry Christmas, my darling. You've given me life, and I'll be giving you our son when summer is upon us."

"How long have you known?"

"For some time now."

He pulled her forward again and kissed her cheeks and then said, "How do you know it'll be a boy?"

"I just know. He'll be as strong and handsome and good as his father."

Claiborn felt a surge of joy. He saw that she wanted to be told that he was happy, and he was, indeed filled with a happiness such as he had never known. Even in the cold, dank, murky interior of that sod house his happiness was like a living thing. *A son. A boy who will be ours. He'll be me, and he'll be Grace too.*

He said these things to her, and he could see that she was reveling in their shared joy. Finally they rose and had another toast in the remaining beer. A toast for the son that was to come.

But even as he spoke the words of cheer and joyous intention for Grace to hear, his mind was saying, *I can't let Grace have our baby in this place!* He forced a smile and ran his hand over her hair. He was not a man of prayer, but desperation drove him to try. *God, give my wife a better place than this to have our son.*

3

*G*race stared helplessly at the cupboard. There was only the end of a loaf of bread, an onion, and a small sack of dried beans. "There's not enough even for Claiborn," she whispered. A thought came to her. She picked up the bread and took a bite of it. She chewed it, and hunger gnawed at her vitals. There was never enough to eat, and it frightened her to think that she was not eating enough to feed her growing child. She tried to calculate when the baby would come, but could only guess that it would be late summer. She looked at the small store of food and smiled. "Well, now I won't be telling a lie when I tell him that I've already eaten."

Quickly she put the beans in a pan to soak over the fire and sat down to wait. Claiborn had gone to town on an errand. He had not said what it was exactly, but she suspected that he had gone to bargain for something to eat. She knew that he felt terrible about not being able to provide for her or their baby, but what were they to do? She filled the echoing house with her prayers, fending off the spring cold and the fear with words of faith, as had become her daily custom. She prayed for the baby within her womb, for Claiborn, and for herself, of course. She pushed away thoughts of the life that she had had before she came to this place, begged God to banish them from her mind and heart. She knew that Claiborn was grieved and carried a burden because he had not been able to provide luxuries or even a simple livelihood for her. So she prayed again that she would never show her dismay. It had occurred to her more than once that he was doing the same thing, that both of them were pretending that the hardships, the hunger, and the cold did not matter.

Hearing an unusual sound, she went to the door and pushed it open. She gasped in surprise, bringing her hand to her mouth.

There was her husband atop a cart of sorts and driving a fine brown horse. She watched as he pulled the horse to a halt before the house, saying, "Whoa, there." He jumped to the ground and came at once to the door. She stepped back and pulled him inside.

"Where did you get the horse and cart?"

He put his arms around her and kissed her, his eyes alight with excitement. "They belong to Mr. Sullivan."

"Well, then, what are you doing with them, Claiborn?"

"Sweetheart, I have a found a way for us, a way to make things better for you. I've been trying for weeks now to think of a way to get you out of this place, and it came to me last night."

"Out of here? But where would we go?"

"Well, you know Mr. Sullivan's wife has been taken ill. He must attend to his business, and the poor woman can't move. She can't do anything for herself. You're going to go and take care of her."

"All right. But what about you?"

Claiborn hesitated for a moment, and then he said, "Let me tell you what you'll get. I've seen the house. You'll have a warm room, and you'll cook for Mr. Sullivan and his family, care for his wife. You'll have good food, Grace, all you can eat. You'll be warm and safe, and Mr. Sullivan has told me that when it is time for the baby, he'll see that a midwife attends you."

"Mr. Sullivan will see to it," she repeated softly. Grace was watching his face carefully. "Where will you be, Claiborn? What is it you have planned?"

"I had an offer, Grace. You know the Irish lords are having trouble with the Scots invading up in the north, or about to. There is one I've known a long while. We got along well. He's a good man. He sent word, asking me to come to his aid." He hesitated, then said, "He wants me to join his forces."

"Oh, no. You can't do that, Claiborn." Fear came to her then for the first time. "I can't be without you, especially with the baby—"

"Look, Grace, we can't go on as we have been. The baby needs nourishment, and you need a better place. I'll be an officer. It pays well."

"I don't want you to leave."

"It won't be for long. These little wars never last. I'll save my pay, and if we take prisoners, I'll get a leader's share of the ransom money."

He held her tightly and talked steadily, and she saw the hope that was in him.

"It's not what I'd like, but I can't stand seeing you hungry and cold. It'll help me, Grace, to know that you're in a warm house. Mr. Sullivan is a fine, Christian man. He's already promised me that he'll see that you get anything you need. And it won't be a hard job taking care of Mrs. Sullivan."

"Won't it look strange my being there with my husband gone?"

"No, Mr. Sullivan is an older man, and his two boys will be there. So you'll be housekeeper and cook. Not an unusual situation. He's a good, solid, kind man, and he means to do well by you. And he needs you, Grace. Their family needs you. By spring, summer at the latest, I'll return to you."

Grace grew fearful, but somehow she knew this had to be. The baby had to be cared for. "Your son will have a good place to be born. That's what's important. I'll be all right. Don't fret over me. Just care for yourself so you can return to us."

"With a fine boy coming and you awaiting me, I'll take better care than ever. Now, let's move your things, and tonight you'll be eating at a real table with real food, all warm."

"You leave this night?" she asked in alarm.

"I must report on the morrow, Grace."

"So soon," she moaned.

"The time will go quickly, you'll see. Pray for me, and hopefully I'll return in time for our son's birth or soon after."

He was leaving, leaving her. Leaving them. But they might come together again and begin anew. With hope. With a future. But he left for battle. What if he was injured . . . or worse? She clung to him, wanting to remember what it was to be in Claiborn Winslow's arms. Wishing he could hold her forever. Wishing there was another way. But knowing there was not.

⚘

The spring had come and gone in a single bound, it seemed, and as Grace stood at the window holding Stuart, who was six weeks old, she felt a wave of gratitude to God. The midwife had said, "That's the easiest first child I've ever seen born. You were made to have children, Mrs. Winslow."

She walked back and forth, stopping beside the fire from time to time to tend the supper she was making. It had been a good time for her. Mr. Sullivan was indeed one of the kindest men she had ever known. His two boys were quiet men who worked hard, always respectful to her. And Mrs. Sullivan had made tremendous strides in regaining her health; she was often back on her feet for hours at a time, working beside Grace. If only Claiborn were home, here to meet and adore his bonny son alongside her.

She stopped and stared down at Stuart's face. The baby they

had agreed to name Stuart, after one of Grace's grandfathers, had stolen her heart as clearly as his father had. "Your da will soon return to us," she whispered and kissed the fat cheek. The baby's eyes opened, and he made a bubble, which amused her. She wiped his chin and said, "How about a meal, then, Stuart Winslow?" She sat down, nursed the baby, and then she rose to lay him in his cradle. But as she did, she heard a voice calling her name. Her heart seemed to stop for a moment—for it was Claiborn's voice. She turned to the door as it burst open, and there he was, strong and hale-looking.

Claiborn embraced her and Stuart, but held them gently, reverently. He kissed her and said, "You're more beautiful than ever." But his eyes quickly moved to their son.

She offered the baby to him. "Our son, Claiborn. Stuart, as we agreed."

He took the small bundle awkwardly into his massive arms, as if the babe might break, and looked down upon him. "He has red hair."

"Like yours. And the same wonderful cornflower-blue eyes. I think he's you all over again."

Claiborn was still looking down into Stuart's face. He finally said in shock, "How can a man love someone so much that he has just met?"

His remark delighted Grace. "He's fine and healthy, and he'll grow to be a man as fine as you. Come, I'll feed you. You must be hungry after your journey."

She made him a quick meal. She asked him question after question about his service, but he made little of it. He ate, reluctantly giving up Stuart, and when he was through, he reached out and pulled them both onto his lap.

"You've done marvelously well, Grace. Given me a son like no other I've ever seen. And obviously helped the Sullivan household too. This place has never looked better. But I have to tell you that every day all I could think of was my returning to you. It kept me awake at night, missing you, Grace." He leaned his head against hers then.

Tears came to her eyes, but they were tears of joy. "What are we going to do now, Claiborn? Please . . . tell me you will not leave me again."

"Not for a while. I don't think my heart could stand it. I've found a good place for us, or rather Mr. Sullivan did. I'm guessing by what he said that Mrs. Sullivan has recovered?"

"Enough to get about, care for herself," she said quietly, knowing the old woman was somewhere about. "She can do some cooking. They'll get along all right."

"Good, good. You know that big farm over to the north that belongs to Mr. Howell? Well, he's been talking to Mr. Sullivan, and he's looking for a man to be an overseer. He's got a pretty rowdy bunch over there, and it takes a pretty tough fellow to keep them in line."

"You're going to work for Mr. Howell?"

"Yes, and here's the good part. It has a fine house furnished for the caretaker, and there's a garden already started. And the workers will furnish anything we need."

"What of my aunt's house? Could we not live there?"

His face fell. "I fear we might lose it, Grace. To pay our bills . . . I've borrowed against it."

She reached up and touched his face. "I know you have done all you could. Might we try—try and keep it? Stay ahead of the payments?"

"We can try. Widell's a fair man."

"Then I'm game."

"You'll like it, Grace. The house is far nicer than your aunt's. Far warmer, and I can't spend half my day riding to and from the farm. Howell needs someone there all the time. Listen, it's going to be an easier life for us, Grace. We can live together. I'll oversee the farm, and you'll take care of this lovely son of ours."

A bubbling joy came to her, and she felt a thanksgiving rising in her like a wave. He took her in his arms. "God be praised," she whispered. "He brought you back, as I begged him to."

"Yes, and he kept you and Stuart safe too."

4

"*T*hose bells are going to drive me mad!"

Sir Ralph Parrish grinned at Edmund in rueful agreement. The two men had come to celebrate the coronation of the new king. The old king, Henry VII, had died after a long illness, and now all England was waiting to catch a glimpse of Henry VIII, the man who would hold their future in his hands.

The London streets were packed to capacity, and indeed the bells of a hundred churches had been ringing since the day before the coronation. It was the custom for the new king and queen to ride in splendor from the Tower to Westminster on that day.

Edmund felt someone edging close to his back, and he turned to see a poorly dressed man with a red face, evidently drunk.

"Get away from me!"

"Come now, Winslow, you can't blame him much. He's been celebrating." Parrish raised an eyebrow. "If they don't come pretty soon, and if we keep on running into that tavern to drink, we ourselves won't be able to stand up for the coronation."

Edmund scowled and tried to think amid the deafening

noise. "The new queen, Catherine of Aragon . . . Wasn't she married to Henry's brother, Arthur?"

"Quite a while ago. They were pledged when they were just children. And when they did marry, Arthur wasn't much. He was always sickly, and he died five months after the nuptials." Parrish laughed and shook his head. "The gossips all said that Arthur never availed himself of his bride in the bed."

"That's hard to believe. From what I hear, she's a handsome woman."

"Well, Arthur was a strange fellow."

"It looks like they're coming," Edmund said. He stood on tiptoe to see, and then a question came to him. "But if she's his brother's widow, how can Henry marry her?"

"The whim of the pope is a fanciful thing indeed. Did you know I attended the wedding of Prince Arthur and Catherine? It was a pitiful affair really, not at all the sort of event you would expect from royalty. She's lasted it out, though. After all these years she'll be queen—look, they're coming now."

Indeed, the new king and the queen neared, and the narrow streets, choked with shouting onlookers, greeted them. Girls in white dresses held wax candles and waved them as the couple passed. Members of each craft and guild stood rank on rank along the procession route along with the Lord Mayor and the aldermen. All the clergy of the city had arrayed themselves in their most gaudy costumes and some bore great jeweled crosses before them. When the king and queen passed, they swung silver censers and blessed them.

In the midst of a sea of cloth of gold and silver, the embroidered velvet of the king stood out as the most splendid of all. He wore scarlet robes of the richest velvet furred with ermine. Sewn into his golden robe were diamonds, emeralds, pearls, and other precious stones, which splashed and sparkled.

"He cuts quite a figure, does he not? And he's a big fellow, isn't he?"

"Oh yes. He is large. Fine-looking chap too. If any man ever looked like a king it's our Henry."

"Catherine is a vision as well." Surrounded by ladies-in-waiting all dressed in their finest, the queen wore white. Her thick, dark-red hair hung down to her waist, and she wore a jeweled circlet atop her head.

The two men remained there until the parade had moved on and the crowd had begun to disperse. Then Edmund said, "Well, we've done our duty, cheering them on. Now let's fetch another drink."

The men joined the throngs making their way to a tavern, with Edmund's two servants following closely behind. He glanced back at them. Orrick, who was in charge of the field work, was a tall, rangy fellow with a thatch of brown hair falling over his forehead and a brown beard that covered most of his features. Nap, a stable hand, had not been at Stoneybrook for very long. He was a rotund, almost circular fellow.

"Look sharp, you two," Edmund growled. "If a cutpurse manages to steal my money or his," he said, nodding at Parrish, "I'll take it out of your wages."

"Yes, m'lord," Orrick said. "We'll see to it that you get to your beds this night safely with your purses intact."

Edmund and Ralph Parrish shouldered their way through the crowd until they found a table and sat down. The servants moved to the wall to stay out of the way but keep watch over their charges.

Parrish called out, "Innkeeper! Some wine here! The best you've got."

Edmund brought up his favorite subject: how hard it was to get workers. "It's all that fellow Luther's fault."

"How is that, Edmund?"

"Why, he does away with order, of course. Gives the foolish impression that every man is as good as another."

Parrish shook his head. "Well, that may do for the Germans,

but it won't do for Englishmen. The king would never admit that any man was as good as he is, and you'd never admit that Orrick was as good a man as you."

"I wouldn't!"

Two women approached, obviously prostitutes, and not in their first youth. One of them smiled, revealing bad teeth, and said, "You gentlemen seeking some comfort?"

"Not from you, Dolly," Edmund said. "Move along now."

The woman dropped her false smile and said under her breath, "Come on, Gwen, there ain't no life in them two."

Parrish drank deeply and called for more wine. "Too bad we're married men. We could find us a couple of dollies. It's a pity that marriage cuts down on a man's wenching."

Edmund stared at him glumly. "Mayhap our wives should encourage it," he said, "if they themselves don't enjoy the marriage bed." Edmund felt little need to pretend. It was common knowledge that he and his wife, Edith, did not get along. "It's not like I thought it would be—married life, I mean. A man ought to marry a young woman, a girl. A woman grown picks up notions, and those things aren't good for people."

Parrish studied the wine in his cup and then looked up. "I told you that before you married, Edmund. You should have continued your life as a confirmed bachelor. You were much happier company in those days."

Edmund shook his head, drained his cup, and slammed it down. "I needed a son, Parrish, an heir. You know that."

"You and King Henry. Trying to sire a male heir."

"If only Edith was as comely as Catherine."

Parrish smiled ruefully. "Think what a pickle England would be in if the old king hadn't had Henry as well as Arthur. We'd have been stuck with a woman as our monarch."

The two men sat there drinking for hours, discussing one gripe after another. Finally Parrish said, "What about Claiborn?

The title could go to him if you don't get a son from Edith. Have you heard from him?"

"No, and I'd better not!"

"Come now, Edmund. He's your brother. I suppose you know he's serving as a mercenary again."

"I hope he takes an arrow in his eye." Edmund spat. "May he rot in the pit of perdition!"

"He might be your only solution in time."

"I'll have a son. You wait and see, Parrish." Edmund could feel the heat upon his face, but he couldn't help it. Hearing such words from his friend brought the betrayal back as if it were yesterday.

"You haven't forgiven him for stealing your woman."

Edmund sighed and cradled his forehead in his hand. "If he hadn't stolen Grace, things would have been different. That woman knew her place."

&

The Dowager Lady Winslow strode into the room with strength and purpose. "Edmund, I need to speak to you."

Edmund groaned, suffering from a hangover headache after his festivities in London. He knew from her tone and stride that he would not enjoy the conversation to come. "What is it, Mother?"

"I have heard that all is not well with Claiborn. He has been forced to assume a position as mercenary for the Irish."

"Hmm. Where did you hear such things?"

"Oh, a soldier from the next parish came back from the Irish wars, and he ran across your brother several months past. Claiborn sent a letter for me. He hoped to return to Grace and take a position as overseer for a farm near their land."

Leah stood directly in front of Edmund, but he could not summon the strength to meet her gaze. "Please, Edmund, set the past aside, forgive him. Bring them home, where they belong."

Edmund's face immediately flushed with anger. "I won't do it! I hate him, Mother! How can you even ask it of me? He stole the woman I was to marry."

"You didn't love Grace, but your brother did. In truth, he has as much cause to hold a grudge against you as you do against him. But you are Lord Winslow. It is your place to extend the olive branch."

"Let me alone, Mother. I'll never forgive him."

Leah's nostrils flared with barely disguised disgust. "Bitterness will kill as surely as a sword, Edmund. It might not be as quick, but it destroys as surely as poison or a dagger in the heart."

"Be that as it may," he returned, "my heart remains unchanged. Claiborn and his wife are not welcome here. Now depart in peace, Mother, and send a maid with some medicine for this headache."

෴

Lady Edith Winslow studied herself in a mirror. It was made of the finest polished metal and, unlike mirrors of less quality, managed to reveal something of a person's appearance. She turned and viewed herself from another angle, then moved her face close to study her features. For a woman of thirty-four years, she had few wrinkles, far fewer than many a younger woman.

"Ellen," she called. When the maid appeared, she helped Edith with her hair. She accidently jabbed her with a pin, and Edith cursed and slapped her face. The girl almost fell, as clumsy as she was simple. "Get out! Get out!"

The girl ran from the room and almost collided with Ives, Edith's nineteen-year-old son from an earlier marriage. He laughed. "Why don't you get a whip, Mother?" he said, leaning against the door frame. "You're going to hurt your hand slapping her face like that."

Edith glanced at her son, her mood lightening just from his presence. He was not tall but he was lean and had a fine head of dark hair. "If I had a whip, I'd use it on Edmund," she said quietly.

"Good. Give him a smack for me, will you? I'm tired of the fellow."

"Keep your voice down, Ives. What if he heard you?"

"Oh, he's hiding, Mother, or drunk as usual. Don't fret." Ives selected a juicy pear from a tray of fruit and bit into it. "A new dress?" he mumbled, appraising her from head to toe.

"Edmund is taking me to the king's court." She laughed suddenly. "But don't mention it, Ives. He doesn't know it yet."

Ives took another bite of the pear, still studying her with admiration. "You have certainly brought Sir Edmund Winslow to heel. Can't call his soul his own."

"It wasn't difficult. The man has the backbone of an eel."

"When will you force him to name me his heir?"

Edith turned back to the mirror and repositioned the comb in her hair before answering. "He still has visions of his own son, his own flesh and blood. But trust me, he'll never get him."

"You're not too old to bear a child."

Edith turned. There was a cruel smile on her lips. "I'm taking precautions." She came over and put her hand on Ives's cheek. "I'll say it again. In time you will be Lord Winslow. That's all you need to know."

Ives appeared unconvinced. "What about Grace, Claiborn's wife? You think Edmund's still in love with her?"

"It wasn't love spurned, Ives, it was a man's pride put down."

"It's been long enough. Perhaps he'll forgive them. That would put our plans in jeopardy."

"Oh, he won't ever forget what's been done. I'll keep his hate alive."

Ives studied his mother for a long moment and then asked, "Did he ever love you?"

"No."

"And you? Have you ever loved him in any way?"

"No, my sweet boy, I entered this marriage as he sought to enter into a marriage with Grace—as a benefit to my family, to me. As Edmund once said to me, love has no place in such arrangements. It only leads to disappointment."

5

Stuart Winslow's heart beat fast from the thrill of adventure and the deadly fear of being caught. The two emotions stirred him as he crouched in the high grass, watching Mead Oakes. Oakes was thirteen, three years older than Stuart. He had persuaded Stuart to come with him to snare rabbits. Stuart had snared rabbits before, of course, but never on Rolf Hyde's land, where it was clearly forbidden. He had refused at first to come with Mead, but the older boy had convinced him that there would be no danger.

"Old man Hyde won't be there, and we're heading toward his fallow land, anyhow. Nobody will see us."

Against his better judgment and without telling his mother, Stuart decided it was worth the risk. The two had left early in the morning, and they had snared three fat rabbits with little trouble. Now, however, with the sun coming up, Mead said, "I guess we'd best leave. You take one rabbit and I'll take two, since I'm the oldest."

"All right, Mead, but what about that other snare?"

"Let it go, Stuart. It's too dangerous."

"I thought you said Mr. Hyde was gone."

"He's got gamekeepers, though, ain't he? Anybody caught poaching will get the whip or be put in the stocks. Remember what it was like when they put Fred Jimmerson in the stocks? He had his head sticking out, and everybody pelted him with dead rats. Somebody threw a rock and knocked his eye out. No, it ain't worth it."

"You go on. I'll check and see if I got another rabbit."

"Better not." Mead shook his head doubtfully, then turned and made his way out of the field.

Stuart knew exactly where the snare was, and he wriggled through the tall grass until he found it. His heart gave a lurch when he saw that there was a rabbit in the trap. He broke the neck with one expert blow of the heavy stick he carried, shoved the rabbit into his sack, and felt a sense of victory and satisfaction. He played games with himself sometimes, and now he was pretending that he was a noble knight who had overcome some fierce mythical beast. Perhaps his mind was too much on that imaginary scene, for he was not aware of the man who stood before him until he was less than five feet away.

"Poacher, eh?" The speaker was a tall, heavyset man with cruel eyes and a twist to his mouth. "I know what to do with poachers. What's your name, boy?"

"Stuart Winslow."

"Come along. I'll go tell your people you'll face a poacher charge. You know what poachers get, don't you?"

Stuart could not even answer, he was so terrified. The man took him by the arm and dragged him along.

❦

Grace watched Rolf Hyde's eyes. They were a murky brown, and she read in them the lust that she had often seen in the eyes of men. She had heard that Hyde took advantage of his young female servants and also some of the older women at his country manor. He was a wealthy man, and now there was triumph in his look.

"So I caught him red-handed, and here's the evidence," he

said, lifting the two dead hares. "I'm going to take him to the sheriff."

"Please, Mr. Hyde, don't do that. He's only ten."

"That matters little. Poaching is poaching."

Grace forced herself to plead. She saw that Hyde was moving closer to her. Still holding Stuart with his left hand, he reached out with his right to trace her chin and said, "Of course, maybe I could forget some of the boy's lawbreaking—if you'd show a man some kindness."

Disgust swept through Grace. "There's nothing for you here, Mr. Hyde," she said in a determined voice.

Hyde's face flushed. "Then I'll take the boy down to the sheriff."

Grace watched them go, helpless. "If only Claiborn were here!" But he was not. Once again he had gone to serve with a small army that was engaged in one of the innumerable wars that the Irish seemed to carry on at all times. He'd promised to return to them here, at her aunt's farm . . . a month ago. "I don't know what to do. They can't put Stuart in jail or in the stocks. They just can't!"

⚶

The hearing was held in a relatively small room built for several purposes. Linton Stowe was the justice who was listening to Hyde's charge. Stowe was an older man with silver hair and clear blue eyes. He had the reputation, Grace knew, of being a fair man.

"All right, Mr. Hyde, what is your charge?"

"Well, I caught the boy red-handed, and there's the two rabbits he poached from my land. No excuse, Justice."

Stowe studied Stuart, and Grace followed his gaze, swelling with pride over her fine-looking boy. He was tall for his age, with a thatch of auburn hair and bright blue eyes. She thought she saw the justice's eyes flash with compassion.

Hyde threw a malevolent glance at Grace and said, "I went to tell his mother, and you know what she dared? She offered herself to me if I would let the boy off! Of course, I wouldn't do that. It wouldn't be right," he said with false morality.

"Mrs. Winslow, you may speak."

Grace stood on her feet. She faced the magistrate, her voice not loud but filled with certainty. "My boy did break the law, and I have the money to pay the fine. The vile thing that this man said of me is a lie."

"She's a whore and a liar!"

Stowe hesitated, then said, "In view of the youth of the young offender, I'm going to take the fine and release him to his family."

"She's naught but a whore!" Hyde roared. He turned and shoved his way out of the room. He was followed by a short man with hazel eyes who grabbed him by the arm and turned him around while he was still within earshot of Grace.

"Are you looney, man?"

"What are you talking about, Tillford?"

"You know who her husband is?"

"Some kind of a soldier fellow," he said dismissively.

"Claiborn Winslow. He's a demon with a sword, and when he comes home and finds the man who's called his wife a whore and a liar in public, why, he'll cut his heart out!" Tillford glanced back at Grace. "You'd better go back and make it right."

Hyde hesitated a moment. With a curse he turned and walked back over to her. The justice looked up, and Grace remained silent.

"Sir, I fear I let my anger get the better of my judgment."

"And how is that, Mr. Hyde?"

"Well, I said some things about the lady here that weren't true. I have a bad temper, and sometimes my mouth seems to have a mind of its own. So, Mrs. Winslow, I'll ask your pardon."

"Granted," said Grace carefully.

"Very well, then. I think it's wise that you made this right," the justice said. He turned back to Grace. "Take the boy and go home. But, Son, if I ever see you here again, it won't be as easy for you. Mind that you never appear before my bench again."

"Yes, sir. Never again," Stuart said.

Grace and Stuart made their way out, but she felt Hyde's eyes on her, and when she glanced at him, she saw that their family had a new enemy.

When they were outside, she said, "God was good to us, Stuart. It could have been very bad indeed."

"I'm so sorry, Mother. I won't ever do that again."

"That's good. I believe you."

"Will we have to tell Father?"

"Oh, yes, he would hear it anyhow. Better he hears it from you."

⚘

Grace was forced to hire men to hay when Claiborn had not returned in time. Worley, one of the men she had hired, came over to her. He wiped the sweat from his face and said, "That son of yours can do more work than some grown men."

Grace was pleased with that. "He is strong, is he not?"

"I thought Master Claiborn was due back by now. When do you expect him?"

Grace found she could not give a full answer to that, for indeed it was far past the time when Claiborn should have returned. She turned and walked into the house, and for the rest of the day repeated the man's words in her mind. *I thought Master Claiborn was due back by now.*

That night when Stuart came to the table, he saw that his mother seemed worried. "Are you worried, Mother?"

"A little bit."

"It's about Father, isn't it?"

"I wish he'd come home. He's been gone so long."

There had been no more trouble with Hyde, other than one unpleasant visit. He had come to the door and said, "I've bought the mortgage on your place from James Widell, the man who let 'im borrow on it. You'll make the payments to me now and not to him."

"Yes, Mr. Hyde, I'll tell my husband."

"Not home yet, I hear."

"No, not yet."

"How do you know he wasn't killed in battle?"

"He wasn't, Sir. I will tell him what you said about the mortgage." She shut the door, thinking, *He'll take our farm if he ever gets the chance.* She was not a woman who was greatly afraid of things, but this particular fear she could not put aside.

ॐ

A month after Hyde's visit, Stuart ran in. "It's a man in a wagon, mother! Somebody's in it!"

Grace's heart suddenly seemed to stop beating for a moment. She ran outside.

A small man with sunburned, leathery skin and only one arm was standing by a horse and wagon. "I'm looking for Mrs. Winslow," he said.

"I'm Mrs. Winslow."

"I'm Yale Wyatt. I done brought your husband home, Mrs. Winslow."

She hurried to the wagon. Claiborn was lying wrapped in a blanket on a bed of straw. "Claiborn!" Hastily she climbed into the wagon and knelt beside her husband. "Claiborn, it's me, Grace." His face was uncovered, and she could see that he was emaciated and flushed. His eyes were unfocused and he did not respond to her.

"What's wrong with him?" she asked.

"Well, besides his wounds, he's lain out in the open in the rain. His leg is pretty much healed up. We didn't have to cut it off like we thought, but he got lung fever or something. He ain't got no strength at all, ma'am, and for the last few days of our journey, he hasn't said a word."

Stuart climbed up on the wagon wheel to look down at them. The sight of his father's face frightened him. "He's so sick, Mother!"

"Yes, Stuart, but we'll see him back to health."

"I'll help you take him in, ma'am, if you'll show me the way."

"I'll go make a place in the house." She turned and went inside the house and made up the bed. She went back and saw that the soldier had pulled Claiborn upright. Claiborn's eyes were filled with fever, but suddenly he gave her a weary smile. "Well, I'm here, what's left of me, Grace."

Her heart surged with hope. "Claiborn, I'm so glad you're home!"

"Where's Stuart?"

"I'm right here, Father. I'll help you take him in, sir."

"That's good. Two of us can handle it. I lost my flipper in the same battle."

Wyatt and Stuart helped Claiborn stand. When the blanket fell back, Grace saw the dirty clothing hanging on him as though on a scarecrow. Her stomach turned as she considered the miseries her husband had endured.

They laid him on the bed, and she helped him put his feet up. He winced at the movement, growing more pale with every inch he crossed. But at last he was settled.

As for Stuart, he could not believe this was his father. Claiborn had left months before, the very picture of a strong, active, and healthy man. This scarecrow that had returned clearly frightened him. He hung back. But when Grace fixed a quick meal, and Yale sat and ate, telling how his father had been wounded, he listened intently.

"It was a bad battle. A cannonball landed near us. If it had been any closer, I think it would have taken the leg off. As it was, none of us thought he'd keep it. He laid out two days and nights with nothing to eat or drink. We didn't know where he was. Finally one of our men found him, and we got him back. The doctor, he done what he could, but it took a long time for that leg to heal, and he's still coughing a lot." Yale suddenly looked up and nodded firmly. "He was the best of us, ma'am. Always looking out for his men, he was, me in particular."

"Will you stay the night?" Grace asked.

"No, ma'am, I need to get back to my own family." He rose, and she followed him out.

"Thank you so much for bringing him home. It was kind of you."

"Well, he's a good man. He's talked about the Lord a lot, since he was wounded. He's got a good kind of religion, he has."

This puzzled Grace, and she questioned Yale more closely about it. As best as she could make out, her husband had indeed found a fellowship with God that he had not known when he left home.

"Well, I'll be thinking of your husband. You put me in your prayers."

"I shall."

Stuart was silent. When he went back, his father was in a fitful sleep. He sat beside him for a long time, looking as though he feared Claiborn would disappear if he didn't keep a close watch on him. Finally Grace pulled him away and said, "Let him sleep, Son. You'll see—it will be the best medicine possible."

⚘

Claiborn smiled at Grace. "I feel like a new man already. All washed and in nice, fresh, clean clothes in a nice, warm cottage with my wife and son."

"I'm so glad you're home. I prayed for you every day."

"Father, tell us about the battle," Stuart begged. He sat as close to Claiborn as he could get, and his eyes were lively.

"Not a pretty story, Son. We were outnumbered almost two to one, and I saw some good men die." Claiborn's eyes grew sad, but he continued his story. "I grew close to the men, especially a man named Mullins. We had some long talks. He'd wanted to be a minister, but his family was poor, so he received no education. He loved God with all his heart, and when he died, I wept for him."

"You cried?" Stuart was shocked. "Grown men don't cry!"

"Yes, they do. When the world falls in on you or when you lose something precious, you'll cry." He fell silent, then said softly, "Hawkins shouted for us to charge, and we did—right into the teeth of the enemy. The fire was so heavy our men were leaning into it, like men leaning into a stiff breeze. Men dropped all around me, shot to pieces."

"Was that when Mr. Mullins got killed?" Stuart asked.

"Yes. He fell, and I stopped to see if he was badly hurt. He was bleeding and knew he was dying. He said, *"I'm going to be with Jesus, sir. I hope to see you in heaven."*

"How awful!" Grace whispered.

"What did you do then, Father?" Stuart asked.

"What I had to do, Son. Hawkins was calling for us to charge, so that's what I did."

"Were you afraid?" Stuart asked.

"We were all afraid, Stuart. No shame in that. When men are about to possibly face God, they suddenly understand how fragile life really is."

"I prayed for you every day," Grace said.

"I know you did, Grace. And I'll have to tell you that something happened to me out there on the battlefield. I went down when a cannonball cut my leg from under me. You know, if it hadn't been for Wyatt, I'd have died. I was practically dead when they found me, but I had already called upon God. And I suppose you might know what I was saying to him."

"What was it? Tell me."

"I promised I'd serve him as best I could the rest of my life. I told him that I would follow Jesus no matter what it cost or where it took me. But you know, Grace, I didn't pray for a long time, because I thought it cowardly."

"Why would you think that, Claiborn?"

"It always seemed to me wrong that a man could serve the Devil all of his life, and then, when he was on the brink of death, try to make good with God. It just didn't seem the manly thing to do."

"But you have heard of the dying thief."

"Yes, the one that was crucified beside Jesus."

"And appealed to him and was saved," she whispered.

"Yes. I thought about that, and I called on God just like that thief did. *'Remember me, Jesus,'* I said."

Grace sat there enthralled, holding Claiborn's hand in both of hers. It was a bony hand, not at all the strong and vigorous hand to which she was accustomed. She felt her eyes fill with tears when he finally whispered to her, "I'm going to do exactly what I said. I'm going to serve our God."

The two sat there talking, with Stuart listening in. When Claiborn asked about the farm, how the crops were faring, she had to tell him about the new owner. "He's not a kind man, Claiborn."

"You're saying he would be hard on us if we didn't make the payments?"

"Oh, we'll make the payments. God will see to it. He's seen us this far."

"He must heal me so that I can work."

"Yes, but in the meantime, your son has been doing a man's work."

Claiborn turned to Stuart and smiled. "You're a fine lad, my son. I hate it that you must work so hard."

"I don't mind, Father."

Claiborn's weakness was evident in his drooping lids, and now he muttered as he dropped off to sleep, "God will take care of us. We're his now."

"He went to sleep so quickly," Stuart whispered.

"Yes, he's very weak. We'll have to feed him a little food at a time. Just broth until we get him on something solid. I'm afraid you'll have to do most of the work. We have little money to hire help."

"I can do it all."

Grace's heart suddenly filled with pride. She looked at Stuart and then pulled him forward and put her arms around him. "You're a fine boy, a true Winslow! Your father and I are very proud of you."

6

*T*he winter of 1511 brought blasts of cold air that swept across the barren landscape and closed like an iron fist on the land. Men stayed indoors close to their fire as much as possible, sitting out the cold weather and doing only work that was necessary.

Claiborn bent over to pick up a square of peat bog, and as he did, he swayed, for his leg had never recovered from the wound that he had taken in battle. He had prayed, and Grace had prayed, but Claiborn realized with bitterness that he was not the man that he had been—nor, indeed, would he ever be. He stood there for a moment looking over the gray, barren landscape, watching as the winter wind whipped across the fields and bent the dead grasses and weeds. It was about a dozen years since he had dug peat for a fire on Christmas Day and discovered Grace had come up with a baked rabbit for their Christmas dinner. That seemed long ago, but he noticed that the older he got, the quicker time seemed to pass. He stood there thinking long thoughts, his face stiff with cold and his hands raw from the work that he had tried to do.

Grace had taken care of him so well that physically he swiftly improved. She fed him good meals, saw to it that he did not do too much, and insisted that he exercised his leg regularly, keeping it from getting too stiff. Within a couple of months he moved from a crutch to a walking stick. Now he could do without that, except when he had to stand for long periods.

Despite the bitter cold, pride warmed his heart as he stood thinking about his wife and son. Stuart had been a help to him from the beginning, just as he was for his mother, doing anything he asked of him. He and Grace had had no more children. Although they were both young enough to have a larger family, it appeared that God had given them Stuart and then said, "No more." This thought troubled Claiborn for some time, but he had prayed, and God had given him great peace on the subject. It was as if God said, "I have given you a good son who will be a blessing to you and to many others. Pour yourself into him, and he will make the House of Winslow proud with his life."

This thought had come often to Claiborn, and he sighed heavily as he bent over to pick up another square of sod. How was this place to bring Stuart or the House of Winslow any glory at all? He pulled at the frozen sod. It tore at his fingernails, which were already bleeding. He tried to straighten up, but the mass of muddy, frozen earth that he held tenaciously clung to its birthplace and roots brought an abrupt halt. Claiborn, caught off balance, threw his weight onto his bad leg; it gave way instantly. He fell heavily to one side, and for a moment lay there panting like a dog. He knew his lungs had weakened and that they would never be what they once were. He was aware that he could never endure the hardship of a military life, and for a while this had been a grief to him, for it had been through his earnings as a soldier that he and Grace had managed to keep the farm together.

"Well, now, this is a pretty thing." His voice was raspy.

As he struggled to rise, he heard the sound of footsteps on the hard earth and looked around to see Stuart running across the field, concern on his youthful face. He was verging on manhood now, this son of his. Even as he lay on the ground trying to pull himself up, the warmth of pride returned to Claiborn as he looked up at his son's face. Stuart was wearing a doublet his mother had made for him out of old material. It was too small, and his wrists were out of it; his short breeches were made of wool and were patched. *The boy's growing like a weed. He may be as tall as my father. Surely as tall as I.*

"Father, are you all right?"

"Yes. I just slipped and fell, son. I'm fine."

Stuart leaned over him. Although his face was thin and his body was lean, there was good strength in the lad. Losing the roundness of childhood, he was poised on the brink of all the things that would transform him from boy to man. "Let me help you up."

"Thank you." Claiborn struggled to his feet and looked down into his son's anxious face. "Don't you worry, boy, I'm fine. Just slipped a little."

"Why don't you go into the house and get warm? I can get the rest of the peat."

"Suppose we do it together. I won't be much help but maybe can help you a tad. While we work, you can tell me what you've been doing."

Loading the cart, Stuart told his father of the fish he had caught in the river. "We're going to have it for supper tonight."

"When did you go fishing?"

"Oh, early this morning. It was still dark, and you were asleep."

"It was cold out on that river, wasn't it?"

"I pay it little heed."

Indeed, Stuart did not seem to be troubled by the temperature. Whether the weather was hot and others were sweating or it was freezing, and others shivered, he seemed to endure it without a qualm.

"Maybe you will go with me some morning, Father."

Claiborn knew that he would not, for the river was too far for him to walk on his bad leg, but he smiled and said, "I hope so. If not, maybe we'll try to catch us some fine plump conies." He smiled down benevolently. "Would you like that, Son?"

Stuart's face glowed for a moment, and then a thought passed through his mind and he dropped his head. "I did wrong, poaching on Mr. Hyde's land."

"That you did, Son, but it turned out all right." Claiborn reached out and clasped him by the shoulder. "Mind you, I believe it's just like stealing a man's money when you steal his game. Poaching is bad business. But we won't do any more of that, though, will we now?"

"No, indeed!"

The two continued to load the cart, with Stuart putting in two or three chunks of peat to his father's one. As they worked, Claiborn suddenly said, "You work too hard, Son."

"No, sir, I don't mind it at all."

"You need to have more time for the things that are fun."

"Oh, I go fishing and hunting, and I go to the village when there's a festival."

Claiborn was conscious of failing in some way. *He's missing his childhood. He seldom gets to have fun with the other boys his age. When I was eleven I was in every kind of game and sport there was. I must find a way to help him and Grace!*

"Well, that'll do enough for now. Let's go in and see what your mother has for us to eat."

Stuart at once took the tongue of the cart and dragged the wagon free. He was strong for his age and moved it easily over the hard ground.

Claiborn's mind was working hard, thinking of the future. The crippling blow he had taken had thrown his dreams out of order, and he could not see how they would make it. Money was scarce, and the payment on his debt would be due very soon. And Rolf Hyde was not known for his mercy.

❦

Grace sat beside a flickering candle that threw dim yellow light over her needlework. She made a little money by sewing fine things for the wives of the wealthy men of the village. It was not much, but every little bit helped, and as she sat there stitching, she thought how different her life was now from the one she had had before marriage.

In all truth, she had led an easy life as a young girl. There were no pressures on her to do anything except learn the things a young woman ought to learn. While her father was gruff and showed little affection, her mother had been a loving woman; until her death, she and Grace were inseparable. It was her mother who had taught Grace how to sew, and she remembered their cozy parlor, a roaring fire in the hearth, candles all about the room. Here it seemed there was a chill to her home the year round, and with winter closing in, it would become even more of a battle to ward off the cold.

Now, as always, when thoughts and doubts and fears came, she called out to God in her spirit. *Jesus, forgive my dour thoughts. You are the mighty Savior! Watch over us and keep us!*

It was little prayers like this that she prayed almost every hour. She could not understand those who at the end of the day when the body was tired and the mind was fatigued, could offer only a mumbled devotion, usually a memorized piece. To her, faith was a living, active, vital thing, and she had learned to send up little prayers many times a day rather than saving it all up.

Her neighbors had learned this about her. When one of them said, "Grace, I want you to pray for my son," they perhaps expected that she would go to church to pray, but Grace never waited. She would say, "Of course I will. Let's pray right now for James." And she would bow her head and often take the hand of the woman who had spoken to her. God did answer many of those prayers, but the act of spontaneously praying startled those who had asked. Yet it was a blessing to them, and she encouraged others to adopt this method of prayer.

She heard the sound of voices and put the sewing down. Opening the door, she saw Stuart and Claiborn pulling the cart full of sod. The wind was blowing, and the temperature was dropping. "There'll be snow soon," she said, and even uttering the words discouraged her. Life was hard enough without trying to survive the deep piles of snow that sometimes came and locked them in their home.

"Come on in. You're both bound to be frozen stiff."

Claiborn hobbled in, using his cane, and dropped into a chair. Stuart was right behind him. He said, "Mother, can I stir the fire up?"

"Of course, Stuart. We need to get warm." Grace took a pitcher out of a cupboard and poured a glassful of weak ale. She gave it to Claiborn, saying, "Drink this up. I think I'll make some hot punch out of the rest."

"That would go down well, indeed."

Claiborn sat while Grace fussed over him. He was exhausted from his struggle with the iron-hard earth. As he watched her busy herself, he thought that God had blessed him in a wife. He looked around and saw that the house was plain enough but Grace had made it warm and comfortable. Another thought ruined his first: *Rolf Hyde will be by soon—and he'll take this place if he can get it.*

Grace came over and sat down beside him. He said, "We must pray, Grace, that we'll have the money to make the payment on the land."

Grace was always happy when Claiborn expressed his faith. He was a praying man now. She reached over, as was her custom, took his hand, and said, "We'll pray right now. Lord," she began, without changing her tone, "we need your help. Actually, Lord, we need a miracle. You know all things. We're asking you to provide for us what we can't provide for ourselves.

Furnish us the money for the payment on this place. We will always remember your gracious kindness and your tender mercies in watching over us. I ask this in the name of Jesus."

Claiborn, as usual, took great pleasure in Grace's simple faith. "Amen." He turned and smiled. "God won't fail us. Nothing is impossible with him."

"That's true," Grace smiled too. "He can furnish a table in the wilderness."

⚸

As soon as Claiborn opened the door and saw Rolf Hyde standing there, a cold hand seemed to close around his heart. It was a disagreeable thing to feel fear, and he knew from reading his Latin Bible that the spirit of fear did not come from God. In battle he had known little fear and seemed to have courage that others lacked. But now, injured, with his family's welfare in the balance and Rolf Hyde standing at his door, he knew fear at its worst.

"Will you come in, Mr. Hyde?" he managed to ask.

"No, I'll not do that. I simply came by to remind you, Mr. Winslow, that the payment on the land is due in two days."

"I'm very much aware of that, sir."

"I don't want to be hard, but the payment must be made. You understand?"

"More than you can imagine." Claiborn paused and said, "I doubt you'd consider an extension, seeing that—"

"Indeed not! This is a matter of business. Nothing personal, but I must have my money or I will have to take legal action."

"You would put us out in the middle of a bitter winter?"

Hyde did not smile. His eyes narrowed, as if he was homing in on his prey. "As I say, it's a matter of business. Nothing personal. I'll be waiting. Unless you'd care to make the payment now."

"No, sir, I do not."

"You don't have it, do you?"

There was such triumph in Hyde's voice that hatred rose in Claiborn's heart. As a Christian he knew he was supposed to love his enemies, but if he had trouble doing that with any man, it was with Rolf Hyde! Claiborn had never forgotten that Hyde had called his wife a vile name in public, and though he had withdrawn it, Claiborn knew it was because he was afraid of his sword. He was not afraid now, for he had the upper hand. "I'll bid you good day, Mr. Hyde."

"Day after tomorrow. Not an hour after sundown."

Standing at the closed door, Claiborn knew there was a duel going on in his heart. One part of him wanted to believe that God would answer the prayers that he and Grace had uttered, asking for help to pay for the land—but part of him doubted.

That night after supper as the three of them sat around the table, he read to them out of the Bible.

Grace loved this. "I'm so glad your father made you learn Latin."

"I hated it. My master had to beat it into me with a cane."

"I believe you're the only man in the village aside from the priest who has a Bible."

"Why don't we have a Bible in English, Father?" Stuart was sitting with his hands clasped before him. His eyes had that inquisitive look that his parents had often seen. He was an imaginative boy full of questions and always interested in learning.

"Well, the leaders of the church feel that only the priests are able to interpret the Scripture."

"But that's not so!" Stuart protested. "I can understand it. It's easy when you read it to me and explain it."

"Perhaps I ought to go into the church's employ as interpreter." Claiborn smiled, for he knew nothing was further from his mind. The tragedy was that many priests could not read Latin, even if they had access to a Bible. Claiborn shook his head and said, "Someday there will be a Bible in English, but it will be over the protest of the church in Rome."

"What if we don't get the money?" Stuart asked, abruptly changing the subject.

"God will help us," Grace said. She reached over and patted Stuart's hand and then held it. "We have to believe God."

"That's right. You remember the verse I've read to you several times. 'Without faith it is impossible to please God.' When you come to God you have to believe that he exists and that he's going to provide the help that we need. That's what we're hanging on to, Stuart."

꧁

It was one thing, Claiborn had learned, to speak words of faith, but another to face harsh realities in a world that seemed to be filled with such things. He had been full of assurance when Stuart had asked his question, but when he'd gone to bed, doubts came trooping in like armed men, and he found his faith challenged. It took all of his spiritual strength to cling to what he believed was truth.

The day before the payment was due, there was still no money. No one in the Winslow household mentioned the deepest fear or the struggle with doubt. Each of them cried out to God. Claiborn spoke to God throughout the day and knew Grace did the same. It was harder to read Stuart, for he did not share everything. He had a depth, this boy who had had to grow up before his time. Claiborn often found it difficult to gauge Stuart's spiritual life. He was fascinated by the Bible stories that Claiborn read to him, but who could really know what went on in the heart of an eleven-year-old.

There was little work to do now. They had plenty of sod, and the cow had been milked. They had had an early afternoon meal, and afterward they sat around not mentioning the danger that they faced on the morrow.

Suddenly Stuart lifted his head. "Somebody's coming."

"You have the hearing of a horned owl, boy! I don't hear a thing."

"I think I can," Grace said. "Though I can't imagine who could be out in this kind of weather."

Indeed, it was bitter outside. The house itself was scarcely bearable, even with the peat burning at an alarming rate.

"He's stopping outside."

Claiborn heard hooves ringing on the iron earth. He hobbled across the room and opened the door before there was a knock. A man stood there. Claiborn did not recognize him. "Good day, sir."

"Mr. Winslow?"

"Yes, indeed."

"My name is Oliver Butler. You might have heard of me."

"I—I think I have, but I can't sort the memories out. Come in, Mr. Butler. You must be frozen."

Butler stepped inside. He was wearing a long, thick wrap lined with fur and a fur cap that covered his ears. His nose was red with the cold, but he seemed hale and hearty for an older man. His hair was silver, and the lines in his face spoke of years of life.

"I take it this is your good wife and son."

"Yes, sir. This is my wife, Grace, and this is my son, Stuart." Uncertain, Claiborn finally said, "Sit down, sir. My wife has been brewing a drink out of a root. She's the only one who knows how to make it, and you might take a liking to it."

"Something hot would be good." Butler sat down and smiled at Stuart. "How are you this morning, young Winslow?"

"I'm fine, sir."

"You'll never have to wonder what your father looked like. Just look in a mirror or in still water and you'll see his face."

"Most of my family are like that," Claiborn said, picking up the idle conversation. "There's always a family resemblance in Winslow men."

"Well do I know that. I knew your grandfather, you know, and your great-grandfather too."

Instantly a memory came back. "I remember you now!" Claiborn exclaimed. "I met you when I was a small boy."

"Ah, you remember that, do you? It was Christmas, if I remember, and I gave you a fine knife."

"I do indeed remember that."

"Well, I don't suppose you kept the knife."

"No, sir, I'm sorry to say it wore out years ago, but I kept it for a long time."

"Try this, Claiborn. See if it's to your liking." He handed Claiborn a knife from his belt.

Grace set down a cup of the root tea she had brewed. Butler picked up the cup, sipped it cautiously, then nodded and smiled. "This is very good."

Butler seemed to be studying Claiborn in an intense way. "You're wondering why I'm here in the middle of this bad weather. Well, I came at the command of an old friend of mine."

"Indeed, for what purpose?"

"To bring you something. Two things really. One is the good word from a lady named Leah Winslow."

"My mother! You are in contact with her, sir?"

"As much as possible. As a matter of fact"—a smile suddenly turned the weathered lips up at the corners, and his eyes seemed to sparkle—"I did my very best to persuade her to marry me instead of that rascal of a father of yours."

"You courted my mother?"

"With everything in me," Butler said. The memory seemed to please him, and he turned his head to one side. "If I'd had my way, you'd be a Butler instead of a Winslow. I would have liked that very much indeed."

"My mother sent you, then?"

"Yes, she did."

"Tell me all about Stoneybrook. What's happened in my absence?"

"Well, things are going well enough, I suppose . . ."

The three of them listened as he spoke of home. Edmund had continued to expand his holdings but had failed to produce an heir with his new wife, a cold woman by all accounts. Leah was as strong as ever, continuing to ride each afternoon regardless of the weather. Stuart had never seen Stoneybrook or known his uncle or grandmother, but he listened eagerly all the same.

"We don't get much news here. It's very kind of you to come and share it with us. What about the new king?"

"King Henry? Well"—a frown creased the old man's face, and he shook his head sorrowfully—"he's bound and determined to go to war."

"That's a mistake. With France, I assume?"

"Of course. He's heard the tales of Henry V going over the water and soundly defeating the Frenchmen. We lost most of the territory that he won, but now this Henry is quite a romantic. He jousts, and he knows all the stories of knights and fair ladies. He's quite a man."

"I'd like to see him."

"You'd be very impressed. He sings. He likes music. He dances. Now he wants to be a soldier, and he's determined to be a soldier. I expect that by the time I get back there will be some progress toward a war."

The old man sat silent for some time and finally said, "I have brought you this from your mother." He opened a bag that was tied to his belt and pulled out two items, one a paper folded over, the other a heavy bag.

"It's money!" Claiborn exclaimed.

"That it is. Your mother will probably explain, but as for me, I must be on my way."

"Won't you stay for a meal?"

"No, I am on my way to see one of my nephews, still a good

distance from here." He rose to his feet and despite their urgings would not stay.

At the door he stared at Claiborn and said, "You have the look of your father. He was quite a man. But your mother should have married me." He laughed. "I've been telling her that for forty years, it seems."

When they had sped Butler on his way, they opened the bag and counted the money.

"God and Mother be praised, this will see us through."

"See what the letter says," Grace said.

Claiborn pulled open the brief letter and read it to them. "'Claiborn, I hope this finds you well. God has told me that you must return to Stoneybrook with your family. I have been praying for you and feel that this is God's plan for you.'"

"Why does she say that we're to come to Stoneybrook?" Stuart asked. "That's your old home, isn't it, Father?"

"Yes, indeed, but I would not be welcome there to anyone but my mother." He returned to the letter. "'Please consider it. We will find a way for you to make peace with your brother. God will see to it, if it is his will. I would find much joy in your return and in meeting my grandson at last. Please, my son. Make haste and return home, where you and your family belong.'"

"We must fast and pray tonight," Grace said firmly. "We will wait on a word from God."

꙰

They did fast and pray through the night, though off and on they perhaps dozed.

The sun was coming up when Claiborn, who had been sitting at the table with his face in his hands, said, "Grace, I feel God has spoken to me."

"What did he say? I have a feeling about this too."

"I feel we must honor the word that my mother has received.

She always was a woman who could go to God and find out things."

"But how will we go? After we pay our debts, we won't have much left to reach Stoneybrook."

"But we'll have God. We'll go to my home again, my boy," he said to Stuart, who had just risen from his bed. "If my brother won't have us, at least we'll know that we were seeking to do God's will."

PART TWO

The Homecoming

(1512–1521)

7

*T*he shrill call of a cock somewhere in the distance drew Claiborn out of a fitful sleep. He had a sudden memory of his last meeting with Hyde, but bitter as it had been he felt suddenly as if he'd been delivered from a prison! At least it was over now. Their debts on the land had all been paid. He shivered and tried to burrow deeper beneath the thin bedcover, but the cold was penetrating and it seemed impossible to get any warmth in the frigid air of the small house. He slipped his arm around Grace who at once turned to him, and he saw that her eyes were open.

"Is it time to go?"

"Yes, it is." But he held her for a moment. The trip would be difficult, especially in winter, but they were committed. Throwing the cover back, Claiborn felt the cold attack his body, and he dressed as quickly as he could. "We'll build up the fire."

"There's no need if we're leaving."

"We'll have a fire," Claiborn said stubbornly, "and we've got enough food for a good breakfast. We'll need it today."

"All right. I'll fix us a good one. We have some bacon left and we'll eat all the eggs the hens have laid."

Grace slipped into her woolen dress and pulled on an outer garment sewn together from remnants of other clothes. She drew on stockings and shoved her feet into shoes made of un-tanned cowhide. They did little to keep the feet warm, but at least they protected her feet from sharp stones.

Then Claiborn called out, "All right, Stuart, out of bed." The boy sat up, his auburn hair tousled, his eyes half shut, groggy with sleep. "Is it time to leave?" he mumbled.

"After a fine breakfast, we'll load the cart and be off to Stoneybrook."

Stuart threw the bedcover back and his thin shirt revealed his lean body. *He looks like a skinned rabbit,* Claiborn thought. "You get the fire going, all right?"

"Yes, sir."

Claiborn smiled at the boy fondly.

While Stuart made the fire, Grace stepped outside. The day before, they had sold their goat and all but six of the chickens. These they would take with them to eat along the way. She stepped into the barn and quickly went to the familiar places where the eggs were lying. She found seven of them and mur-mured, "Thank you, Lord. This will be a good breakfast." Turn-ing, she went back into the house. "I've got seven eggs. We'll eat them all," she said.

"We'll need to take some," Claiborn protested.

"I have three dozen stored," she answered.

"You are as thrifty as you are beautiful, woman!"

She had milked the cow before they had sold her to one of the neighbors for two pounds, and there was a bucket half filled with milk.

Grace busied herself with making the breakfast. When it was ready and the room was filled with the smell of frying bacon, they sat down to a better breakfast than they were accus-tomed to.

"Lord, bless this food. We thank you for it," Claiborn said. "Be with us on our journey and keep us safe and in the center of your will. It is in the name of Jesus we ask it. Amen."

"Amen," Grace said. And then they attacked the breakfast. They ate until they were full, and then Claiborn said, "It's time to go. The cart is mostly loaded except for whatever food we're managing to take."

They put on their heaviest clothing and stuffed the rest into the cart, a two-wheeled affair drawn by a scrawny horse that looked older than Methuselah. His rather fanciful name was Reginald. They had been given him for nothing from a farmer who had shrugged and said, "He ain't worth nothing to me. Take him if you want him."

"I doubt this horse will make it all the way to Stoneybrook," Claiborn said doubtfully. "I fear Reggie's had his best days."

Grace laid her hand on the horse's scrawny neck. "God, please bless this animal and keep him strong and let him get us all the way home."

The word *home* sent something along Claiborn's nerves. Home for him for more than a decade had been a meager house in Ireland. Home now had become something else. He doubted his mother's belief that they could somehow make a way with his brother, but he had overwhelmed his doubts with protests of faith. *God, you've sent this word to my mother, and she sent it to us. We're acting on it,* he prayed silently. *Please make a way with Edmund for us.*

The feeble sun was just beginning to show itself in the east. It cast a watery light over the landscape as the three came out. "Well, we're bound for Stoneybrook. Are you ready, Stuart?"

"Yes, sir!"

"Then lead us out."

Stuart at once went up to the head of the horse whose name was Reginald. "Come on, Reggie," Stuart said and, seizing the bridle, led the horse forward. Reginald stepped out, and they all followed the path that led to the road. When they were about to turn onto the road, Claiborn stopped and looked back at the house for a brief moment. He turned to Grace, who was also looking back. "Are you afraid?"

"No, not in the least. God has told us to do this."

"How about you, Stuart?"

"We'll be fine!"

"That's the way to talk!"

So their journey began. As they took the road leading to the coast, where they would take a boat across the sea, all three of them were thinking private thoughts. Once in a while one of them would speak cheerfully to the others. Although they soon became stiff with cold, at least they were on their way to a place where God had told them to go.

✿

Grace had prepared a meal of sorts. It was their fourth day on the road, and they had consumed much of their provisions. She had roasted potatoes, the largest for Claiborn. She was saving the three chickens they had left.

"Watch this. It's hot," she said, handing Stuart his potato.

"I love potatoes," Stuart said. He took the knife from his father, split the potato open, and began nibbling at it. "Ow, it's hot!" he said.

"It's good, though. Put some salt on it," Grace said.

The three of them ate their potatoes. It was not enough, but at least it was hot and put some warmth in them.

"How much further can we go today, Father?"

"I think we'll be able to make the coast the day after tomorrow if Reginald holds out."

"He's doing fine." They had brought along some feed, which was carefully meted out, and Reginald acted as if better fed than he had been in his whole life. Under their care and food, Reginald seemed to be reborn, even with his heavy load.

They traveled until the sun dipped into the west.

Suddenly Stuart said, "Look, there's where we can stay!"

"Where?" Grace asked.

"There. See that cave?"

"Go check it out, Son," Claiborn said.

The boy was back in a moment. "It's just fine," he said excitedly. "It goes back a way, and if it rains, we'll be nice and dry. There's plenty of dead wood outside too."

"We'll cook one of our chickens," Grace said.

"That will go down well."

They made their way to the cave, and indeed it was the next best thing to their cottage. They put the cart in front of the cave. Claiborn unharnessed Reginald. There was some dead grass for him to graze on, and they staked him out.

"Now then, let's cook us a good supper," Grace said with a smile. "Anybody hungry?"

"Everybody's hungry," Stuart beamed.

An hour later they were sitting around a fire in the mouth of the cave. The chicken had been fried and half of it consumed. They could have eaten it all, but they spared enough for another meal. As they sat in front of the cheerful blaze, Stuart watched the yellow flames flicker. From time to time he would feed the fire, and finally he yawned and said, "I'm sleepy."

"Let's keep the fire going tonight," Claiborn said.

"I'll stay up and do that," Stuart responded groggily.

"No, you get some sleep. I'll wake you up after a while, and you can watch for a while then."

The boy crawled under one of the thin covers and was asleep at once.

"He's worn out," Grace said.

"So are you. So am I, for that matter. This cold weather saps a man's strength."

Despite their weariness, they sat enjoying the fire. Finally Grace said, "Are you afraid what it will be like when you face Edmund?"

"He won't welcome us, but we'll have done what we think God wants us to do. It'll be good to see Mother again."

"I always liked your mother. She was always so sweet to me."

"She could be sharp at times. I remember once she caught me picking some of her flowers. She just about wore my hide out with a switch, but she kissed me after she was done whipping me and said, "There, a whipping and a kiss." He laughed at the thought. "I always loved her."

"I'm anxious to hear more about the word she received from God." Grace leaned forward and picked up a twig. She stuck the end of it in the flame, waited until it caught, and then held it up like a candle. She watched it until it burned down and then tossed it into the fire and said, "Let's build the fire up and go to sleep. You need rest, Claiborn."

※

"Well, we're in England but we're broke." Claiborn looked at the boat that had brought them across the sea. Their passage had taken practically all the money they had. "But we're here in England, and we won't starve."

Those words came back to haunt him, for the days stretched out. The feed ran out, and Reginald was barely able to pull the cart at a stumbling walk. The weather grew worse. It was late one afternoon when Grace felt something touch her cheek. She glanced sharply up at the gray sky. She had been dreading this, as had Claiborn, and she wondered, *How will we get through a snowstorm?*

"It's cold, isn't it, Mother?" Stuart was now walking beside her while Claiborn led the horse.

"I'm afraid we're in for it," Claiborn called back.

And then it came, first in barely visible specks, shimmering ice on the wind, then in fat flakes. Two hours later the piled snow made for slow going, especially for Claiborn, whose bad leg was trembling under him.

"We'll have to take shelter somewhere, Claiborn," Grace called out.

"All right. We'll stop at the next place we see."

Thirty minutes later they saw the outline of a building. Claiborn advanced and called, "Hello, the house!"

Soon there came a reply. "Who be it?"

"It's me and my wife and son. We've been caught in the storm."

"Well, I guess you'd better come in."

Glad of the welcome, they moved forward.

A small old man, no more than five foot three, was looking up at Claiborn from the doorway of a small cabin, which was little more than a shack. Standing in the doorway, he stared at Grace and Stuart. "You don't be robbers, be you?"

"No, we're a Christian family journeying home."

"Well, come in and thaw yourselves out."

They went into the cabin. There was a fireplace and a crackling fire. A pot over the fire bubbled with something that smelled so good that it made Claiborn's jaws ache.

"Get over by the fire, lad, and thaw yourself out." He turned, and they saw that his neck had been injured so that he could not straighten his head. "Be you hungry?"

"I'm afraid we are. We've come a long way."

"Where you be going?"

"We're going to a place called Stoneybrook, my old home."

"Bad time to be traveling. Sit you down. You can have some of this stew if you want it. I call it my everything stew."

"Everything stew? What's in it?" Grace asked with a smile.

"Everything I trap or shoot goes in there. Just don't ask too many questions, and don't think about it too much. It's good."

Soon the three of them were eating the stew out of wooden bowls carved by the old man. It was very good.

"I like your stew, sir," Claiborn said. "It's fit for a king!"

"Posh, don't call me no sir. I'm just old Jeremy Watkins." He served them more stew, and they filled up on it. "Good to have a little company. Tell me about yourselves. I get hungry for talk. Since me wife died, there's nobody to talk to much."

They paid for their supper in talk, and the old man listened with his eyes glittering like a small bird's.

He said, "You be tired. I got plenty of cover. Lay yourselves down there in front of that fire. You can take my bed, lady."

"No, I wouldn't do that."

"Don't argue with your host! The bed it is for you. The rest of us can make out best as we can."

They all slept better than they had since leaving their cottage, and the old man gave them a good breakfast the next morning.

As they left, Grace said, "God bless you, dear friend."

"Why, that's kind of you, and God bless you too. I put some food up for you. I saw that you was traveling kind of light."

"I think you must be an angel sent to help us."

The old man suddenly giggled, a high-pitched giggle at that. "Nobody's ever called me an angel, but thank you, lady."

The snowstorm faded later in the day. The wind was still keen, but the sun came out and melted the snow, which left the road a thick, sticky mud. They traveled for three days, and each day got harder. The food was almost entirely gone. The chickens had been eaten, and they had only a few potatoes, and they ate them one morning for breakfast.

"We're not far from Stoneybrook now. I know this country," Claiborn said.

"How far is it?"

"No more than ten miles. We'll get there today."

Now that the time had come to face up to whatever reception would be given them, Claiborn had lost some of his assurance. He would be glad to see his mother, but from Edmund he expected nothing. He knew how stubborn Edmund was, how he found it difficult to forgive others, and as they plodded along, he prayed constantly that they would find favor.

When they stopped at midday to eat the last of their provisions, he said suddenly, "You know what I think of in the Bible that reminds me of us?"

"What is it? Tell me," Stuart said.

"Well, you've heard me tell the story of Jacob. How he cheated his brother and had to run away. Years later he came back, and he had a large family. Several wives, concubines."

"What's a concubine?"

"I'll let you explain that, Grace."

"It's just a woman who's not quite a wife."

Claiborn nodded. "That's as good a definition as any. Well, he started back, and when he got close to his home he grew afraid. He had wronged his brother, and someone had told him that his brother was coming with four hundred armed men, and there he was, just a shepherd really, with no skill in arms."

"What happened?" Stuart breathed, his eyes bright with interest.

"Well, he went out that night, I think probably to pray, and he met an angel."

"What did he look like?"

"The Bible doesn't say, but it says that Jacob wrestled with him."

"How could you wrestle with an angel?"

"I don't know, Son, but that's what the Bible says. It says they wrestled all night, and finally the angel said, 'Let me go.' And Jacob said, "No, I'm not going to let you go until you bless me."

"And did he bless him?"

"Yes, he did. That was the good Lord, I think, and he reconciled Jacob with his brother, and Jacob had a long and happy life."

"I wish we had an angel to go with us. Your brother sounds like a mean man."

Claiborn exchanged quick glances with Grace. The boy had picked up more than they had intended. Claiborn had no knowledge of how much Stuart knew about how he had stolen his brother's intended bride, but Stuart would no doubt hear the story if they stayed anywhere near Stoneybrook.

"I did wrong my brother. He's your uncle, you know."

"What did you do to him?"

"Tell him the truth, Claiborn. He'll hear it anyway," Grace said.

"Well, your Uncle Edmund was going to marry your mother, but she didn't love him. For some strange reason, she always loved me."

"And so you ran away with her, didn't you?"

"Well, I went to my brother and tried to reason with him, but he was angry and wouldn't listen. I suppose he had a right, but he didn't love your mother the way I did. So we ran off to be married and then settled in Ireland."

Stuart's eyes were fastened on the two of them. "Maybe he won't still be angry. It's been a long time."

"Almost fourteen years, but we'll have to find out when we see him. Now, let's go on. I'd like to make Stoneybrook before dark."

※

"It's so big!" Stuart said. He was staring at the castle and the town and the outlying fields. "This is all your brother's?"

"Yes, it is. Not nearly as big as some. Come along. Let's go." He heard his name called, and he looked up to see Orrick, who saw to the management of the fields, coming toward him, surprise washing across his face. He stopped in front of the three and grinned broadly. "Well, you're back again, Mr. Winslow."

"Yes, I am, Orrick. You're looking well."

"And you don't, if I may say so."

"Well, we've had a hard journey."

"Did your brother send for you?"

Knowing what was in Orrick's mind, he said, "No, but I need to see him. Would you go tell him and my mother that we're here?"

"Aye, I'll tell them. I'm glad to see you, Mr. Winslow," he said in encouragement. "Others will be too, regardless of how your brother responds. Will you wait here or come in?"

"We'd better wait out here."

๏

Edmund sat in front of a fire half asleep and frowned when Orrick entered his private parlor uninvited. "M'lord, you're wanted in the courtyard."

"What? Wanted by whom?"

Orrick looked down at the floor, as if unwilling to say what he must. "It's your brother, Mr. Claiborn Winslow, and he has his wife and son with him."

Edmund jumped to his feet. "What's the villain doing here?"

"He wants to see you, m'lord. I might say he looks pretty bad. Very much like a sick man. They're all pretty worn down."

Edmund scowled at Orrick. "That's none of my affair! In the courtyard, you say?"

"Yes, m'lord. They wouldn't come in."

"I should think not."

Edmund dashed out of the room. When he burst into the open air and saw his brother standing there, he could not speak for a moment. Indeed, Orrick had spoken the truth. Claiborn was not the same man. He was so changed that for a moment Edmund could not believe it was Claiborn, but the anger rose in him as his eyes fell on Grace and then on the boy. *That could have been my son*, he thought bitterly.

He stopped in front of Claiborn and said, "Why are you here? No one sent for you."

"Well, yes, someone did, in a way."

"Who took that liberty? Certainly not I."

"I got a letter from Mother."

Edmund could not answer for a moment. His anger was not flaring now; it was a dull, steady glow. "You can't stay here. Get out."

"Please, Edmund, forgive me. I know I wronged you."

"Oh, now that you're starving and have no place else to go, you're sorry! Where have you been with your sorrow all these years?"

"I would have asked earlier, but I didn't think it would do any good."

"It won't. You get out of here now."

"Very well. Come along, Grace."

They turned the weary animal around and started back to the courtyard gates.

They had just gotten outside when Orrick came rushing after them. "Mr. Winslow," he said, "your mother says I'm to take you to her summer house."

Life came into Claiborn's eyes. "Where is my mother?"

"She's in the castle. She said she'll see you later, but for now you go to her house and stay there."

"That's kind of her."

"I'll go along with you. I think there's plenty of wood. You could have a nice fire, and she said to bring you whatever food I can get from the kitchen. You look kind of lean in the shank, Mr. Winslow, if you don't mind my saying so."

"It has been a long, hard journey, but I'm mostly concerned about my wife and son."

"That's a fine-looking boy. Looks just like you."

Stuart heard this and smiled. "I am just like him."

"My name's Orrick, boy. What's yours?"

"Stuart."

"Stuart Winslow. Well, you're the spitting image of your father—" He almost said "as he used to be," but he broke off the words.

Thirty minutes later they were at a house lodged beside a small brook that gurgled as it passed. Orrick opened the door, and as they unloaded their possessions, he got a fire going in the large fireplace.

"I'm going to get some food from the kitchen. I'll be back with it soon."

"That's kind of you, Orrick. You always were kind to me, though."

Orrick stopped and chewed on his lower lip. Politics were part of his life. He had to get along with Edmund, but he had always had a warm spot in his heart for Claiborn. "I thought of you often since you've been gone, sir. It's good to see you back again and your lady and your fine boy." He turned then and disappeared.

"You see? God has made a way," Grace said. Looking around the house, which was small but well-built and snug, she murmured, "Do you suppose your mother will let us stay here?"

"I don't know if she can or not. Legally it might belong to Edmund, but somehow I think it will work out."

⚶

Lady Leah Winslow was in her room, sitting in front of the fire. She had watched Claiborn and his family arrive and leave.

She longed to go after them with Orrick, see them to her house, sit and talk with them, but first she had to deal with Edmund. Her son and Edith arrived as soon as Orrick departed.

Edmund burst out, "Well, Mother, have you heard?"

"Yes. Claiborn's home."

"He says you sent for him."

"That's right, I did."

"You must get rid of him," Edith snapped. "They have no place here. After what he did to your son, I'm surprised that you'd even think of it."

"God told me to send for him."

Both Edith and Edmund stared at her. She looked at them calmly and dared them to speak. Edith almost choked when she said, "God told you? He came to this room, and he spoke to you face to face?"

"God speaks through his Spirit."

"Well, he can't stay," Edith said. "Tell her, Edmund." When he remained silent, she circled him, glaring at him all the while. "We don't have any sons, Edmund. Would you hand all this to your betrayer of a brother?"

"I would never do that! Not after what he did to me!"

"Then be rid of him!"

Leah knew her son's marriage to Edith was hard and had only grown more difficult. Edmund turned to his mother. "I cannot allow them to stay here. I'm sorry, Mother."

"Well, you do what you must, Edmund. If you refuse to help your brother, I will. I'll use the land your father put in my name to help them."

Edmund blinked in shock, and Edith did the same. Leah knew they practically counted the days until her death, when her large tract of land adjacent to the present Winslow land would become Edmund's. Then he would have nearly twice as much land to till without having to pay her an annual fee.

"Now wait a minute, Mother—"

"No, that's the way it will be, Edmund. You make your choice. Either you help your brother and his family or I will."

Edmund glanced at Edith, then back to her. Leah returned their cold glare, hoping they saw her steely resolve.

"Very well, he can stay," Edmund said at last, ignoring Edith's start of surprise. "But he'll be under my authority. And they certainly cannot reside here. They must stay in that house."

"I'm sure one day you'll find charity in your heart for your brother, Edmund." Leah smiled. "For now it is enough. But please go and assure Claiborn and his family that you've changed your mind, that they are now welcome at Stoneybrook; I know he will not set foot again within the castle gates until he hears directly from you."

Edmund swallowed hard but turned and left the room. Edith stayed for a moment, but Leah simply shook her head with a frown, warning her not to say a word.

Edmund stood in the parlor of Leah's house, refusing to take a seat and carefully avoiding any glance in Grace's direction, staring instead at his brother. "You've been of little use since you were born, but our mother wants you to stay. Out of respect for her, I have chosen to allow it. She says you can use this house. In the meanwhile, you will take care of the hawks and the dogs. Surely you haven't forgotten all you knew about falcons." Indeed, Claiborn had always been good with hunting birds. "You and the boy can take care of them until I find somebody else."

With that, he left, and Claiborn sat down heavily, head in hands.

As soon as the door shut behind Edmund, Stuart blurted, "I hate him! He's horrible. Let's go away from here."

"No," Claiborn said. "No, Son, God led us here. And here we will stay until his reasoning becomes clear."

"At least here we have food, shelter, work," Grace said, putting a comforting hand on her husband's shoulder.

He looked up at her. "And maybe in time we will succeed in gaining my brother's forgiveness as well as his tolerance."

8

The care of the hawks was no work at all for Stuart, even though Sir Edmund had intended it to be punishment. Stuart, now nearing the age of manhood, loved the birds, and his father, he was convinced, knew more about hunting falcons than any man in England—even more than the king himself.

He held the bird named Sky on his wrist and felt the power of the talons as they clamped down. "There's a good bird," he whispered. The hawk was hooded, but when Stuart ran his fingers along its throat, it opened the wide beak, a signal that it waited to be fed. With his free hand Stuart got hold of a small fragment of meat and held it up. The hawk took it daintily enough but then gobbled it down.

Putting the hawk back on its perch and removing the hood, Stuart looked over all the birds. The mews had been in terrible shape when his family arrived, but Stuart and his father had worked to make it clean and suitable for the noble birds. Stuart then took over as much of the work as possible, giving his father time to regain his health.

"You have a gift for the birds, Son."

Stuart quickly turned. His father had come in silently, his feet making no noise on the litter—mostly sawdust and reeds—

beneath the bird cages. "You've taught me everything I know, Father."

"I am proud of your gift with these noble birds. It's the sport of kings."

"One day the king might take a liking to our birds."

"Well, you aim high. He has the choice of any birds in the kingdom."

"But ours will be the best, won't they?"

"I trust they will."

At that moment Sir Edmund came charging in. "You two are idling, as usual, I see. Can't get an hour's worth of work out of you!"

Stuart's temper flared, but before he could speak, Claiborn said quietly, "I'm sorry, Brother. We were just working a little with the hawks here."

"You were lazing about! That's what you always do. You must work harder."

"What, in particular, would you like us to do?"

"Go over and help with the horses."

"With pleasure."

"Go on and help with the horses," Edmund snapped. "Then I'll find something else for you to do."

"Right away, Edmund," Claiborn snapped back, suddenly at the end of his patience. Stuart clamped his lips shut as he walked beside his father. Claiborn was still limping pretty badly, but Stuart was glad to see the color in his cheeks and pleased that he had put some meat on his thin frame. He felt the weight of his father's hand on his shoulder, and it pleased him. He listened as his father kept up a running monologue about hawks and their training, care and feeding, how to breed them, things he already knew. But he didn't stop him; it felt good to walk with his father, listen to him. Even better to be away from Edmund. With each step, Stuart's racing heartbeat slowed.

Claiborn paused outside the stables and said, "You're taking in all I say just as if it came from heaven. Not many boys listen to their father as you do. I appreciate that, Stuart."

After they had helped with the horses, which did not take long, for there was really nothing to do, late in the afternoon Claiborn led Stuart back to the summer house. He pulled out a pair of foils from a rack and said, "How about a fencing lesson?"

"Yes!" Stuart cried. He loved fencing. He and his father took time to practice every day, whenever possible. He took the foil, which had a button on the end of it, and put his right foot forward, his left back. His left arm was curved behind his head.

"That's a good fighting pose you have there." Claiborn took the same pose and advanced. Soon the air was full of the clanging steel of the foils. Stuart's arms were not strong enough yet to push a fight, but in two more years he knew they'd rival his father's.

Stuart startled when a voice said, "Well, aren't you two the very picture of noble leisure." Stuart turned to see Lady Edith, who was watching them with cold eyes. She had come by, no doubt, to spy on them. Without another word, she turned and walked away, her head high.

"Why does she hate us, Father?" Stuart had learned to expect nothing in the way of kindness from the woman and watched her with something akin to hatred. It was not so much the way she treated him, but he could barely stand it when she showed cruelty to his parents.

"Well, that's hard to say, Son. I'd guess she has no gentleness in her, and if there is no gentleness, there is no love. Mayhap she hates everyone."

"Even Sir Edmund?"

"Even herself. Now then, let's see what your mother and grandmother have been doing."

They entered the house and found Lady Leah still there. She

smiled and held out her hand, and at once Stuart went to her and took it, leaned over and kissed it.

"Is that right, Grandmother?"

"Why, you've done as well as a courtier! I can't believe you have such grace. You are a real nobleman, Stuart Winslow!"

Stuart flushed. He liked his grandmother very much. She told him stories of her younger days, grand stories of when life at Stoneybrook was peaceful and joyful. Leah brought him small presents, and he knew that most of the food that came to their table was from her.

"Sit down and tell me what you'd like to hear today," she said.

Stuart sat as close to her as he could and said, "Tell me about the court and how the people act there."

"Well, it's a very wicked place, my boy."

"Oh, Grandmother, not really!"

"You have good morals, Grandson, but I hope you never get caught up in the king's court."

Stuart smiled and said, "You never can tell. Now then, let me show you what I've learned to play on this lute."

Afterward, she said, "Very good, Stuart. Very good. Now let me sing you a song." She sang in a thin, sweet voice:

Henry, our royal king, would ride a-hunting
To the green forest so pleasant and fair;
To see the harts skipping, and dainty does tripping:
Unto merry Sherwood his nobles repair:
Hawk and hound were unbound and free.

"Do you know who wrote that song, Stuart?"

"No, Grandmother."

"The king himself. Our sovereign lord Henry."

The news surprised Stuart. "I thought he was a warrior and a soldier."

"Indeed he is. They tell me he's outstanding in the arts of weaponry, with a lance, with a broadsword, the longbow. He's almost unbeatable, but he's also a good dancer and a good singer." She looked at Claiborn, who was sitting across the room, studying the two with a smile on his broad lips. "Are you still teaching the boy Latin?"

"Yes, he is," Stuart answered, instead of waiting for his father. "But what good is it?"

"Well, for one thing," Lady Leah said, "you can read the Word of God. The Bible. If there were no other reward, that would be enough. Learn all you can, Stuart. Do you know that the king speaks six languages?"

"Truly?"

"Truly. He's quite a scholar. That ought to encourage you."

"I want to be a soldier, and I want to be rich."

"The two don't often go together, Stuart. Ask your father about that." Lady Leah put her hand on Stuart's shoulder and added softly, "Be as good a man as your father, Grandson, and that will bring you far more joy than either soldiering or wealth."

Stuart looked up into his grandmother's face and felt a love for her that he longed to express. He said, "I'm glad we're here. With you."

"I'm glad too, Stuart. You make life cheerful for this old woman."

⚭

"Whoa there, Shannon!" Stuart cried. Ives, Lady Edith's son, had asked him to exercise his prize mare by walking her about the yard; she was always easier to ride if she'd had a brief jaunt. Stuart was leading the gray mare when the horse, a spirited animal, reared up, pulled the reins from Stuart's hands, and trotted off.

Stuart ran after her, but, of course, he could not catch her.

He knew he'd have to follow her until she let herself be caught—but he had no opportunity for that. A rough hand grabbed him. It was Ives, his eyes filled with fury.

"You bumpkin! You idiot, you let my horse get away!"

"I'm sorry, Ives, she jerked the reins—"

Ives suddenly slapped his face with an open palm and then brought his hand back and hit him on the other cheek. "I'll teach you to mistreat my horse!" He dragged the boy over to one side, and taking a pocket knife out from his belt, he cut a switch. "Bend over, boy, I'm going to teach you a lesson!"

There was no help for it, so gritting his teeth, Stuart bent over. He heard the whistling of the cane, and pain shot through him as Ives struck him across the buttocks. Again—and again—

Suddenly Ives fell away from him, jerked away by Claiborn Winslow. Never had Stuart seen his father look so fearsome.

"You will not thrash my son, Ives."

"*You* are giving *me* orders? You might have once been second son on this land, but now Mother is certain that I will be named heir."

"That hasn't happened yet, has it?" Claiborn said.

"No, but for now, you are servant and I, master. And you, Claiborn," he sneered, "have crossed the line."

"You crossed the line when you dared to strike my son. You will not do it again."

His words plainly infuriated Ives, who went to draw his sword. At once Claiborn pulled a knife from his belt. He did not threaten Ives with it. He simply held it in his hands.

Ives stared at him; everyone at Stoneybrook knew Claiborn Winslow was an expert with every sort of blade. He swallowed hard, rammed the sword home, and glared at Claiborn.

"Second thoughts are usually best," Claiborn said mildly.

Ives's eyes narrowed. "You'll hear from Lord Edmund about this!"

"I'm sure I will, but mark my words, if you ever touch my son again, know that it will be most unpleasant for you. Regardless of what Edmund thinks."

Ives walked away, his back stiff.

The entire incident frightened Stuart. "What—what will happen when Uncle Edmund hears about it? Lady Edith?"

"I don't know, but it wasn't your fault, Son. I saw the whole thing. Pay it no mind."

"I can get the horse now. She'll settle eventually if you don't chase after her."

"Good idea."

He watched as Stuart moved after the horse, quietly approaching her. When he was ten feet away, Stuart stood still, and after a moment the mare came over to sniff his hand. He took the reins, patted her on the cheekbone, and whispered to her.

Claiborn knew that Edmund's reaction would be severe. He was well aware that it was only his mother who stood between himself and his brother. If it were not for Lady Leah, he would not even be here. He would not have a home to offer Grace and Stuart. But would she be enough to keep Edmund at bay for long?

※

Edmund was not a fool. Claiborn was valuable to Stoneybrook, even though he was not the man he once was. He cost nothing, for Lady Leah paid all his expenses, and his expertise in falconry might one day bring Stoneybrook glory—and financial gain.

"The boy could be useful too," Edmund muttered, staring at the empty doorway through which Ives had just passed. He knew the man tended to embellish things.

Rising, he left the castle and sought Orrick, who had seen the whole thing. Regardless of how it had unfolded, Claiborn had no right to threaten one of his men. He charged down to the mews, where he found his brother.

"You drew your knife on Ives! What were you thinking, sir?"

"I took it in my hand, yes. He was pulling his sword out, and I had to defend myself."

Edmund glared at Claiborn and felt once again that which he had often felt, envy of his younger brother. Envy had always been there, for Claiborn had the romance, the daring, the ability that he himself lacked. He only had the fact that he was the elder brother. He made a lot of noisy threats, but when he turned away, he felt defeated.

Father Gibbons, the parish priest, came to visit Edmund, Edith, and Leah. A fat man, he never refused any of the food Stoneybrook's fine cooks set before him. He listened carefully as Edmund talked about his brother.

"He's not the man he used to be. He limps, and he hasn't gained his strength back, but I will say this for him—he knows hawks. My, how that man knows hawks! Mark my words, Father, one of these days we'll have birds that even the king himself will envy."

"I remember your brother. He was very literate, if I remember."

"Oh, yes, he can read Latin."

This surprised Father Gibbons. "Read Latin? Who tutored him?"

"Oh, all the tutors we brought in schooled him in the subject. He proved more adept at it than I. Somewhere, amid his travels as a soldier, he even obtained a Bible. He reads out of it to his family."

"That's unseemly!" Edith said. She, Ives, and Lady Leah were sitting across the table from the two men. "It should be stopped."

Father Gibbons nodded his agreement. "I'll have a word with him."

"Oh, that would be useless," Ives grunted. "He's a violent man and a rebel. Would you believe he pulled his knife on me the other day?"

Lady Leah shifted in her seat. "I believe that's a gross exaggeration."

But the priest leaned forward. "I am shocked. I'm sure he was properly chastised."

"No, my husband doesn't believe in such things," Edith said. "He let him off with just a warning. As if that will do any good!"

Sir Edmund said, "I told him that if he ever made a move like that again with a knife or anything else, he would wind up in the stocks!"

☙

Father Gibbons did not comment again, but the next day he went to visit Claiborn and his family. Invited in for a glass of ale, he said almost in passing, "I understand you read Latin."

"Yes, I do. It's a fascinating language, isn't it, Father?"

"How does it happen that you read it?"

"As a child, I had one tutor in particular who was a Latin scholar. I was interested in some of the Latin poets, so he taught me to read Latin."

"I don't suppose you've read the Bible?"

"Oh, yes. I have a Latin Bible."

"I trust that you don't use it for the wrong purpose."

"I don't understand you, Father. What sort of wrong purpose?"

"Well, you are aware of the church's position, that the Holy Father believes that only a priest can understand the Bible."

"I respectfully disagree. I believe I understand it."

As soon as Gibbons left, Grace said, "What a pompous man! Probably ignorant himself of everything that's not spoonfed by the pope!"

"Be careful how you speak of the pope, Grace. People have been put in stocks for less than that."

"I know, but I'm glad you're teaching Stuart Latin. Now he can read the Word of God for himself."

"I wish every believer could read the scripture for himself, but that day will be long coming. I understand the king has changed his mind."

"About what, Claiborn?"

"He was interested at one time in having the Bible translated into English, but the talk is now that he's decided that would be dangerous." He laughed suddenly. "Think of it, Grace! The Bible, dangerous! What a foolish thing to believe. Everyone should have the right to read the Word of God!"

9

Claiborn ran the plane along the length of clear maple and watched as a tiny curl of the wood rose up and fell to the ground. "This is a fine tool. I think my grandfather must have made it. It's been in the family as long as I can remember."

"Was he a carpenter too?" Stuart asked.

"A very accomplished craftsman. People came from miles around to persuade him to make things for them, but he only made new things that challenged him. He said he grew tired of making the same thing twice."

The two were in the shed that Claiborn had converted into a shop. Along with Latin lessons and instruction on falconry and weaponry, he was teaching Stuart how to use tools.

Claiborn watched as Stuart took the plane and moved it carefully. He thought how quickly the two years had passed. Stuart was now eighteen, no longer the thin boy who had come to Stoneybrook. And he was only a shade shorter than Claiborn himself. The shoulders had broadened, the muscles in the arms had grown not bulky but sleek and sinewy, giving the boy speed and grace in his movement.

"I've got something I want to show you, Father."

"You've been keeping secrets."

Stuart grinned. His skin was tanned from the outdoor air,

and there was a healthy look to his face, a glow. His eyes were the same blue as Claiborn's, but there was something almost magical about Stuart's eyes. They sometimes seemed to sparkle when he was excited or angry.

"What is this thing you've got now?"

"I'll show you."

The young man moved aside a piece of canvas and brought out a bow. "Here it is."

Claiborn took the bow and examined it. It was as smooth as anything he had ever seen. "You put a fine finish on this." He looked at it more closely. "What are these lines? I don't understand what you've done here."

"Well, you know when you take a piece of yew and make a bow out of it, that's the best bow that any man could make, the best wood, wouldn't you say, Father?"

"Yes, I believe so. Well, this is yew, but these darker streaks, what's that?"

"Ironwood. You see what I've done? What I thought was this. Bows made out of yew are flexible, but they're not as strong as some other woods. But woods that are strong are so stiff that they would shatter when crafted into a bow."

"So what did you do?"

"I sawed thin strips of different kinds of wood—mostly ironwood and yew but some maple too—and I glued them together."

"How did you learn to do that?"

"I went down to the cabinetmaker. He does it all the time. There are tiny pins that go all the way through. You see this? That's an ironwood peg. I drilled the hole and I put the glue on it that the carpenter showed me how to make and I let it set."

"Well, what's the advantage of it?"

Stuart grinned. "I'll show you. Here, string it up, Father."

Taking the linen string that Stuart handed him, Claiborn looped it over the notch at one end of the bow, turned the bow the other way, and put his foot beside it. He began to push the bow down. A look of amazement came over his face. "Why, this is impressively strong!"

"Very strong. It takes a good man just to string it."

Claiborn pushed down the upper part of the bow and managed to slip the loop on the free end of the string into the upper notch. The bow was strung.

"Now let's go outside. Here's an arrow."

Stuart said, "Shoot it as far as you can."

"All right." Claiborn tilted the bow at a forty-five-degree angle. When he pulled back he had to strain. He released the string and watched the arrow. It climbed and arced, and Claiborn was amazed to see how far it had gone.

"Have you ever shot an arrow that far, Father?"

"Never, nor has anyone else. Not with a yew bow." He looked at the bow as if there was some magic in it. He ran his hands over the smooth curve of it and studied it in wonder.

"Well done, Son! Well done. The king would be interested in a bow like this."

Stuart's eyes lit up. "Do you really think so?"

"I certainly do."

"I'm going to make an even better one, now that I've become accustomed to gluing, and then perhaps one day we can show it to the king."

Claiborn smiled. "Come on. Let's go and see if this arrow does as well shooting hares as it does on distance."

❀

"You there, boy. I want you to go pick up a load of hay from Sir John Walsh. You know where he lives?" Edmund frowned.

"No, sir."

"You don't know Old Sodbury manor?"

"I know where that is," Claiborn said.

"Well, I don't want you to go. Tell him how to get there.

Stuart, pick up the hay and tell him I'll send the money over to-morrow."

"I'll be glad to go for it, Edmund," Claiborn said.

"I wouldn't trust you. You'd drink it all up."

"I'll go get the hay and bring it back," Stuart said, swallowing the words he wished to say. It was no use arguing with Uncle Edmund. Best to do what was necessary and be done with him as soon as possible.

"And be sure you don't stop at a tavern on the way and chase after some wench!"

Stuart ignored him and went to hitch up the wagon.

Edmund told Claiborn, "You're wasting your time teaching that boy to read Latin. He'll never be anything but a hostler or something like that."

"Perhaps something more than that, Brother. And he'll be able to read our Bible. That's worth something to even a hostler."

"You," Edmund sneered. "You call yourself a Christian."

"Yes, I do."

"You know what you did to me. You ruined my life."

"I've apologized over and over, Edmund. You know I've always regretted bringing pain to you."

"You don't truly regret it." Edmund cursed and shook his head.

Claiborn said, "It's true. I don't regret marrying for love. But I will tell you again, Brother, that I'm very sorry for hurting you. And I'm grateful for your permission to stay at Stoneybrook. It's your kindness that gives my family a home and a place to work."

Edmund stared at Claiborn for a long moment. "Get to work," he grunted, then turned around and walked away.

Stuart got lost on the way to Old Sodbury manor, but after asking three different people for directions, finally found the proper road.

Seeing nobody in the yard, he walked up to the door and knocked sharply.

A young girl stood there. She had the lightest hair he had ever seen, yellow as gold, and a pair of eyes almost as blue as his own.

"I-I've come to pick up a load of hay," he stammered, "for Lord Edmund Winslow."

"Oh, begging your pardon, but my uncle isn't here. He'll be back shortly, I'm sure."

"I'll wait out here, then."

"You've driven all the way from Stoneybrook?"

"Yes, miss, I have."

"Well, you must be hot and hungry. Come in. I've been baking today. How would some fresh bread and a bit of mutton sound to you?"

Stuart smiled suddenly. "That sounds like a bit of heaven."

"Well, then, come in. What's your name?"

"Stuart Winslow."

"I'm Heather Evans. Come along."

Stuart smiled when they entered the kitchen. "That smells better than anything I can think of. Fresh-baked bread!"

"Sit down there, and I'll cut you some of this mutton." She sliced him a healthy portion and then took a loaf from a cooling pan and sliced off the end of it. "Here's some fresh butter, if you'd like it."

"Who wouldn't like fresh butter on fresh bread? Aren't you going to eat, Miss Evans?"

"No, I've already eaten. I'll just have something to drink here while you eat. Can you drink cider?"

"I don't know. I've never had any."

She stared at him. "You've never had cider?"

"No, miss. What is it?"

"It's made from apples."

"I love apples."

"Well, you'll like cider then. I'll have to go down to the cellar to get it. It stays cool down there. You go ahead and eat."

As she left, he noticed her trim figure and wondered how old she was. Not as old as himself.

Probably about twelve, I guess. Going to be pretty when she grows up. He took his knife, sliced off bites of the mutton, and spread butter on the fresh bread.

Heather came back with a pitcher, poured him a mugful, and said, "Try your first taste of cider."

Stuart tasted it, and his eyes opened wide. "That's the best thing I ever had to drink in my life!"

Heather laughed. "I'm glad you think so. I helped make it."

"You're the young lady of the house?"

"Not really. I'm the niece of Sir John. I live here with him and his family."

Stuart held back from asking about her own family, but she supplied the information anyway. "My mother died some time ago, and my father travels. He's Sir John's brother. So he leaves me here, and Mr. Tyndale educates me along with my uncle's two sons."

Stuart finished the mutton and would have eaten more, which she offered, but he thought it might be greedy. "I will take some more of that cider, miss. It sure is good."

Heather poured the cider, and then began to draw from him some of his own story.

Heather had heard of the Winslow family, of course. She had seen Lord Winslow, and she had heard tales of a younger brother who had gone bad. And this was his son. *He is so handsome and doesn't even seem to know it,* Heather thought. She soon found out that his father, once a soldier, had been injured and that his mother's name was Grace.

And then she remembered the old story about how Lord Edmund had been engaged to Grace but the younger brother and the woman had fallen in love and they had fled the country.

She was ready to hear more about it, at first hand—from their son!—when Mr. Tyndale came through the garden gate.

A tall man entered the kitchen, and Heather said, "Mr. Tyndale, this is Stuart Winslow. Stuart, this is Mr. William Tyndale. He's the scholar who teaches the children of the house."

Stuart stood up at once.

"I'm happy to know you, Master Winslow."

"And I you, sir."

"You live close?"

"At Stoneybrook. Lord Edmund Winslow is my uncle."

"Oh, yes, I believe I've met him."

"Won't you sit down and have something to eat?" Heather asked. "We have fresh mutton and fresh bread. Stuart can tell you whether it's good or not."

"Oh, sir, it's very good, and I've never had any cider before. I wonder if they drink cider in heaven."

"I'm not sure about that. In any case, I will have something to eat. I'm rather hungry."

"Sit down, sir. I'll fix you a plate."

The tall man sat down, and he began to question Stuart in almost the same manner as Heather had. But the subject matter was different.

"Are you a follower of Jesus, Master Winslow?"

"Yes, sir, I think I am."

Tyndale smiled. "Well, surely you know what you think about Jesus Christ."

"My father is a Christian and my mother and my grandmother."

"Well, that's good. I'm happy to hear it. But what about you?"

"I try to be a good man."

"We all try that, I suppose."

Stuart was trying desperately to think of something that he could offer the man, and then an inspiration came. "I can read the Latin Bible." He saw this caught Tyndale's attention. His eyes suddenly brightened and he said, "I read it every night."

"How did you learn to read Latin?"

"My father taught me. I'm not very good at it, but I'm learning."

"What do you read, Stuart?"

"Oh, just the Bible. That's the only book we have."

"Well, that's a good book."

"Mr. Tyndale knows all about the Bible. He knows more than the priests!" Heather exclaimed.

"You mustn't say that, child. That would offend the priests greatly. What part of the Bible do you favor most, Stuart?"

"I like the stories in the Old Testament about King David and Samson and the old warriors of God."

"Yes, a young man would be drawn to that. Are you interested in fencing and that sort of thing?"

"Oh, yes! My father's teaching me."

"So he's teaching you to read the Bible and to handle a sword. That is most intriguing."

Heather had brought the food, and for a while William Tyndale ate in silence. Finally he asked, "Do you know the most shameful thing about the Bible?"

"Shameful? I didn't think anything was shameful about the Bible."

"Well, it's not about the Bible. More about its current form."

"What do you mean, Mr. Tyndale?"

"I mean it's in Latin. How many Englishmen do you know who can read Latin? How many Frenchmen, for that matter, or Germans? The only people able to read Latin are the priests, and the pope has said that they are the only ones who are capable of understanding it—which I think is wrong."

"I think so too," Stuart said eagerly. "Why, I understand a lot of it."

"Do you? Tell me something you undertsand."

"Well, the Bible says that God made everything. That's the first verse, and I believe that."

"Good for you, young Winslow! You're on your way."

Tyndale finished the last of his meal and sat there talking until Heather's two cousins came in. They were reluctant scholars. Tyndale laughed. "Come on. I must pound something into your wooden little heads." He put his hand out. "I'll be expecting to hear more from you about this Bible you read. You know, some day the Bible will be in English, and every farmer will be able to read it for himself. Come back again, and we'll talk. And I'd like to meet your parents."

"Would you come and visit us, sir?"

"I will do that as soon as I can. You may expect me." He herded the boys into the next room for their lessons.

As soon as he was gone, Stuart said, "I've never met such an engaging and knowledgeable fellow. You're lucky, having him as a tutor."

"Indeed. The priests don't like him, though."

"I can see why. He's trespassing on their ground."

She stared at him. "What does that mean?"

"I don't know. It's just a thing people say."

Twenty minutes later Sir John came in, and as soon as Heather had explained the presence of the young man, Walsh said, "Oh, yes. Come along. I'll show you where the hay is. I'll have my man help you load it."

"Sir Edmund said he'd send the money over tomorrow."

"That will be fine."

Stuart loaded the hay, and it did not take long with the help that he received. He went back then to thank Heather. "It was as good a meal as I've ever had."

She smiled at him, and he said suddenly, "You're going to have lots of suitors, Miss Evans. Some day they'll be lined up just to touch your hand."

"Where did you learn such fine sayings? You sound as though you've been at court."

"Oh, no! I've never have been at court. My grandmother tells me they say things like that. In any case, thanks for the cider and for the mutton."

"Come back and see us. Mr. Tyndale will be looking for you."

"It's hard for me to get away, but I'll do the best I can. Good-bye, miss."

"Please call me Heather."

"Good-bye, then, Heather." He smiled, hesitated, and then she put out her hand. He took it and felt its warmth.

"Come back and visit," she repeated softly.

"I'll do that."

All the way home he thought about two things—William Tyndale and Heather Evans—in very different lights. She was the prettiest thing he had seen in a long time, and when she got to womanhood she would be a dream. And William Tyndale was a man of the mind such as he had never met.

10

Claiborn was puzzled but pleased by the new interest that Stuart took in the Bible. He saw that it was not just the language that fascinated the young man; it was the Scripture itself. Before, he had merely listened, but now he seemed to soak in the Scripture and its meaning. Claiborn had always translated into English, just to be sure that Stuart understood the words, but over the course of the last two months, he found it less and less necessary.

He was reading one evening with Stuart by the light of several candles. It was late and Grace had gone to bed, but the two had become interested in the interpretation of several verses.

Claiborn was about ready to go to bed himself, intending to end the evening reading with Psalm 7. Stuart read it in the Latin and then put it into his own words. He had done very well up to the fifth verse, but then he looked up at Claiborn and said, "I don't understand this next part."

"Well, let's see. The whole verse says, 'Let the enemy persecute my soul, and take it; yes, let him tread down my life upon the earth and lay mine honor in the dust.'"

"I don't understand that. It sounds like a terrible thing."

"Well, in the verses before, he said, 'If I have done evil . . . '"

So when a man does an evil thing he is going to have to pay for it."

"Well, what does 'lay mine honor in the dust' mean? That sounds like a bad thing to me."

Claiborn leaned back and closed his eyes, thinking of the possible answers. Finally he opened them and leaned forward, saying intently, "A man's honor is what he is. It's his word. It's what makes him trustworthy. Everything that's good. That's his honor. You understand that, Son?"

"Yes, sir, I know what honor is, but why would he lay his honor in the dust?"

"David wrote this psalm, and he didn't say that he himself was going to lay his honor in the dust. Look at verses three and four. Let me just give you the sense of it. 'O Lord my God, if I have done this; if there be iniquity in my hands, if I have rewarded evil unto him that was at peace with me, let the enemy persecute my soul. Let him tread down my life upon the earth and lay mine honor in the dust.'"

"I don't understand it very well."

"Why, David was so careful with his honor that he was actually saying to God, 'If I do a dishonorable thing, you can kill me, you can tread down my life upon the earth.' He was saying, 'If I lose my honor, I have nothing left. The most precious thing I have is in the dust.' That's a rather sad thing, Son. When you leave the law of God, you take your honor, which is a clean, pure, and holy thing, and you throw it in the dirt."

"Why would anybody do that?"

Claiborn shook his head. His face was full of pain. He said slowly, "Men do that. Remember Judas, who betrayed the Lord Jesus?"

"Yes, sir."

"He put his honor in the dust. And King Solomon. He started out as a good man, but then he made poor choices. He, too, put his honor in the dust."

Stuart was staring at his father. "I would never do that."

Claiborn leaned forward and put his hand over his son's. "Of course you won't. You're going to be a man of God, and you're going to keep your honor bright and clean, because when a man loses his honor, he loses everything. He may be rich. He may have a hundred horses. He may have a castle, but if he has no honor, he's nothing."

"I don't see how men could do that."

"I had a friend once. He'd gone wrong. I asked him how it happened, and he said, 'Well, Claiborn, I didn't wake one morning and say, "I think I'm going to be a bad man. I'm going to become a liar and a cheat." Didn't happen like that, Claiborn. I gave in on one little thing, and the next time it was easier, and easier the third time. So part by part and piece by piece my honor was gone.'"

Stuart shivered. "I don't like to think that might happen to me. It scares me."

"It's always scary to think about losing your honor, but you're not going to do that, Son."

"You never did."

"I hope not. Well, you ponder this tomorrow. That's why we have this Bible. It's full of wisdom and things we are to watch out for. So that's what we'll do, right?"

"Yes, sir. I hope Mr. Tyndale comes. We can ask him about this."

"I'm very anxious to meet him."

"He said he'd be here soon."

Claiborn suspected that young Miss Evans had drawn Stuart to Old Sodbury as much as the scholar, Mr. Tyndale, but he kept his suspicions to himself. He liked what his son's few visits to the Walsh household had encouraged within the boy, regardless of what inspired them—a maid or the mind.

Stuart got up, stretched, went over to his bed, rolled over, and seemed to go to sleep at once. *Ah, when I was his age, I could do that too, but not any longer.* Claiborn grinned at his own thoughts and went to bed. He'd persuade his mind to slumber; his body was more than ready.

⚘

". . . and so my father and I were talking about the seventh psalm, Mr. Tyndale."

"What did you decide?"

"Well, I didn't understand it until he explained it to me."

"You see? It doesn't take a priest. What did you find out?"

"He said that when a man does evil things, it's like taking his honor that's clean and pure and throwing it in the dirt or in the mud."

"A very good translation. I must remember that."

"Are you still translating the Bible into English?" Heather asked. She sat across from the two, hovering over Mr. Tyndale's own worn Latin Bible.

"Oh, I've only done portions, those that capture my interest the most. Someday I'd like to take the whole Bible," he said, stretching out his arms, "and translate it into English and put it in every home in England."

"I doubt they'd let you do that, sir. I hear the king is against such things."

"No, I doubt that he'd be in favor."

The three of them sat for a while longer, chatting, and after Tyndale and Stuart left, Mona, Lady Walsh's maid, came over and looked out at young Winslow as he mounted his horse.

"Ain't he a dream?"

Heather scolded her. "You ought not to be thinking such things!"

Mona was sixteen and full of dreams, mostly of young men. Heather was aware that she always found a way to be close by when Stuart visited. She said, "You ought not to be looking at men like that."

"Well, I choose to look, and I think he's the finest man I've ever seen in my life."

"He is a fine young man," Heather murmured.

Mona said with wide, excited eyes, "Look, the prince has returned."

Heather glanced out the door, and sure enough Winslow was dismounting and tying his reins to a post.

"Hello, I'm back." He smiled. Heather saw that Mona nearly melted at that smile.

"Mr. Tyndale got my mind in such a knot. You were going to show me the new ducklings. You forgot."

"Oh, I did, didn't I?" Heather said. "Come along. They're so sweet."

"I hope the turtles don't get them."

"So do I. I hate turtles."

"Well, God made the turtles just as he made the little ducks. I've never understood that, have you?"

"We'll have to ask Mr. Tyndale about that."

"I'm going to ask him too why the good Lord made mosquitoes and poisonous snakes. Doesn't seem quite right."

"You'd better not say that to Mr. Tyndale." Heather was skipping along.

Suddenly Stuart took her hand. "I can't tell you, Heather, how much these visits have meant to me."

Heather was very much aware of his hand holding hers. She knew he was not flirting with her, that he sincerely liked her. That pleased her a great deal.

"I've enjoyed your visits too, Stuart."

When they reached the pond, they admired the ducks that were paddling along in a line behind their mother like a small armada. They talked for a long time. It seemed that they could always find something to talk about.

"You know," she said, "I never could talk to anybody as I talk to you, Stuart."

"Well, I was thinking the same thing. Usually I'm tongue-tied when I get in the presence of a pretty girl."

"I've wanted to ask you something, Stuart, but I've waited until now so as to know you better."

"Go ahead. I probably don't know the answer, but try anyway."

"What do you want to do, once you're a grown man?"

The question seemed to stump Stuart. He ran his hand through his auburn hair; she saw that it had tiny flecks of gold in it. He rubbed his jaw and frowned. "What do you mean?" he asked finally.

"Well, you must think God has some reason for putting you here."

"Why, I never thought about it. I just do what I have to do."

"No, there's more to it than that."

"Well, what has he got *you* here for?"

"To fall in love. To get married. To have children. To be a grandmother. To grow old with a man who I love."

Stuart had never heard this idea phrased exactly as this girl had put it. He studied her thoughtfully. She had the clearest skin he had ever seen—it shimmered in the sunshine—and bright, clear eyes. "Well, I expect that will happen. You're certain to marry your choice of man."

"And you?"

Again Stuart thought hard. He said, "I'd like to be where things are happening."

"Not Stoneybrook?"

"Nothing ever happens there. I work with birds. I help with the plowing and the harvest. I'd like to be in a battle. I'd like to be in the king's army as my father was. Be a king's man."

"Do you think you ever will be?"

Stuart suddenly laughed at himself. "Not a chance, Heather. Not a chance. I'm the son of a poor man."

"You never can tell."

"I believe I can. Anyway, have you started learning Latin yet? You said you wanted to."

"Mr. Tyndale's teaching me. He thought it was wonderful that I wanted to learn."

"Perhaps we can study together if I can visit more."

"Oh, yes, please do! Come back every chance you get."

The two stood there for a moment and then they slowly walked back. As always, they talked all the way there. Before he mounted his horse he lifted his hat and said, "Good-bye. I'll see you soon."

"Good-bye, Stuart."

As she watched him go, Mona came out. "Did you see them blue eyes?"

"Mona, you're so silly!"

But all she could think of was his eyes. The color was beautiful, yes, but it was the tenderness she saw within them that had captured her.

⚮

Claiborn sat down beside Grace and took her hand in both of his. "Are you unwell?"

"On the contrary. I'm feeling wonderfully well. Just a bit . . . distracted." She looked at him and smiled a secretive smile.

"Why are you laughing at me?" he demanded.

"Because you're about to get the shock of your life, and I want to see how you'll handle it."

Claiborn stared at her. "I've had a few shocks in my life. Do you think this one is going to be good or bad?"

"I'll let you decide."

"All right. Let's have it then, Wife."

She took her hand from his and reached up to cup his cheek. "You're a wonderful father. I've never seen a better. You're making a fine young man out of our son."

"Well, he makes easy work of it."

"Yes, he does, but you have something to do with how he's turned out."

"And?"

"You're going to need all that practice."

Claiborn stared at her, puzzled. There was something like a smile playing around her lips, and finally she said, "You're not very quick today, Claiborn."

"Truly, I never am. What's the secret?"

"You're going to be a father again."

For a moment Claiborn could not understand her. Then he did. He blinked with surprise, swallowed hard, and grabbed her hand. "Is it possible?"

"Oh, you've made it very possible. I thought I was past the age of childbearing, but apparently the good Lord doesn't think so."

"How long have you known?"

"Not too long."

"Maybe it will be a girl this time, just like you. Wouldn't I love that!"

"I'd like that too, but it's as the Lord wills."

"Have you told anybody else?"

"Of course not. Who would I tell before I told my husband?" She laughed and said, "You're not thinking very clearly."

"Well, you've given me much joy. Truly." He drew her to him and kissed her. "An old man like me."

"You're not old."

"Beaten, battered, weary. How am I going to handle a baby again?"

"The same way you handled Stuart. You're the same man."

When Stuart came in and saw them sitting close together, holding each other, he was surprised. They were smiling. He said, "What has happened?"

"We have a surprise for you," Claiborn said.

"Is it a good one?"

"It is a fine surprise. You tell him, Wife."

Grace smiled a beautiful smile and said, "You're going to have a baby brother or a baby sister, Stuart."

For a moment Stuart could not fully comprehend what she was saying. He thought idiotically, *Maybe they've found a baby.* "Good. I hope it's a boy or a girl," he said, with a smile. A baby!

"A boy or a girl? Why, it'd have to be, wouldn't it?" Claiborn laughed.

11

Well, we're in for it now."

Stuart looked up at his father in surprise. "What do you mean, Father?"

"I've heard that the king's progress is about to descend upon us."

"What is a progress?"

"The king's court becomes a sort of traveling banquet. He has the idea that people want to see him, so he chooses this way to show himself to his people—along with half his court. They visit the estates of wealthy lords and stay there until the poor fellow is eaten out of house and home. Then they move on to the next victim."

"And they're coming here, to Stoneybrook."

"Here," Claiborn said, with one eyebrow cocked.

Stuart smiled. "Uncle Edmund must be so pleased."

"And unhappy. It'll cost him a thousand pounds a day. He'll be forced to take a loan simply to feed them. I hear tell Sir Edwin Backon purchased sixty sheep and nearly thirty pigs, as well as calves, oxen, and birds!"

"Could he refuse to house the progress?"

Claiborn cast him a rueful grin. "There is no choice in the matter. Even the neighboring villages will be forced to gather gravel and strew it across the road, simply so that the king will not be stuck in any mud en route to Stoneybrook."

Stuart rubbed his hands together. "It will be grand. Fireworks?"

"Most likely."

"Orators? Actors?"

"Most certainly."

"Musicians? Dancers?"

"I do so hope. I'd like to twirl your mother across the dance square, given half a chance."

Stuart grinned at his father. "Uncle Edmund's pain is our gain, as I see it. This is fortunate, indeed."

"Now, Stuart . . ."

�❧

The king's progress reached Stoneybrook at midsummer. Every servant was on needles and pins, and Edmund and Edith had been preparing nervously for weeks.

Finally the servant who had been sent out to reconnoiter came galloping up, his eyes wide. "They're coming! The king is coming!" He slid off his horse and gasped, "Lord Winslow, it looks like there are hundreds of them!"

"Lord help us," Edmund moaned. "This is worse than an invasion by the French!"

When the king arrived at the head of his entourage, however, the lord, his lady, and Ives were there bowing and scraping, and when the king dismounted he cried out, "No ceremony! No ceremony, Lord Winslow!"

"We are glad to welcome you to our house, Your Majesty."

The king was arrayed gorgeously. He had traveled under a heavily embroidered canopy of gold cloth. He wore hose and a striped doublet in tones of scarlet and crimson, and around his shoulders he wore a purple velvet mantle. This was tied on with a thick rope of gold and ended in a train four yards long. He carried a dagger with an enormous gem in the hilt and wore a gold collar bearing a round-cut diamond the size of a large walnut.

Henry clapped his hand on Edmund's shoulder as if they were equals. "We're imposing on you, Lord Winslow," he boomed. "I trust we'll be no trouble."

Edmund managed a smile and said with all the sincerity that he could muster, "It's an honor, Your Majesty, and my family is delighted that you have chosen to grace us with your presence." He hoped his face did not betray him; within, he thought the king and his company had descended upon poor Stoneybrook like the voracious swarm of locusts that descended upon Egypt.

※

The king's visit began that night with a royal banquet. Stuart was pressed into service to carry food into the great hall from the kitchen, and what a feast it was! He shouldered what seemed like mountains of food upon heavy trenchers and platters. The air was full of sounds: people talking and laughing, loud music from dozens of instruments, and singers lifting their voices. The great hall also hosted many dogs, so the room was filled with the sounds of barking and snarling when they fought over the bones that were thrown to them.

Each course consisted of at least a dozen dishes, and as best as Stuart and his father could count, entire carcasses had been consumed of cattle, sheep, hogs, and hundreds of chickens, to say nothing of the swans, geese, ducks, and conger eels. Piles of pears and apples went to flavor the meat and the fowl, and bread-making never stopped.

Finally Stuart stopped for breath and simply watched the nobility of England with King Henry VIII in all his glory. Between the courses came pageantry in foods: confections sculpted in sugar and wax in the shape of figures. Some of them were biblical, such as an angel announcing Jesus' birth to three shepherds riding in from the East. Wine, of course, came in an endless stream, washing down every dish.

Finally the banquet ceased, and the king was shown to the chamber of Lord and Lady Winslow, who had vacated it. Every room was filled with the nobility of England.

Stuart moved over to where Edmund was standing, his face pale. "Rather expensive entertainment, Uncle, isn't it?"

"He'll bankrupt me!" he said in a hoarse whisper. "As sure as the world, he'll bankrupt me! Why does he have to do this?"

"Hopefully he won't stay too long."

"I wish he'd go bless somebody else with his presence," Edmund muttered, misery in his eyes. He looked over the remnants of the food and shook his head. "They ate more food than we could eat in six months. Oh, that he would leave and all the rest of them too!"

❦

When the king was looking at the mews the next day, Edmund was pleased when he said, "Why, these are as fine birds as I have seen! I wouldn't mind having some of them in my own mews."

"Well, take your pick, Your Majesty."

"Oh, no. I can't take on any more birds right now. I had a good fellow, an old man, who took care of them. But he's stiffened up and died on me."

Sir Ralph Parrish was standing close by. He was Edmund's closest friend. He said at once, "Well, that's a shame, Your Majesty. These are the finest birds in the county."

"Who keeps them for you, Lord Winslow?"

Edmund said, "Oh, I do a great deal of it myself. But my brother does some of it."

"Where is he? I'd like to talk to him."

Claiborn was fetched, and the king carefully looked him over. "I'll be needing a man to help me with my birds. I'd like it to be you. You've done a fine job here."

"Your Majesty, that is such an honor, but as you see, I'm crippled. I was wounded in one of the Irish wars. I've never been able to get my strength back."

"Well, Your Majesty," Sir Ralph piped up, "his son is his equal."

Quickly Claiborn said, "He would be too young for the post. He's but seventeen, Your Majesty."

"Bah, old enough to take on a man's work, I say."

When Claiborn did not acquiesce, the king called for a contest at the butts—shooting the longbow.

All of the visitors came to watch, as did all the servants—in fact, Lord Winslow's whole household. Targets were set up, and soon bows were twanging and arrows were whizzing through the air and striking targets with loud thumps.

The king said, "Well, Kyd, you'll have to show these fellows how it's done."

Bartrum Kyd was the king's champion with the longbow. He was a boastful fellow, a large man with muscular arms and deepset gray eyes.

"I'd like to win a prize for Your Majesty if we could have a contest, but I think this day I could beat any man in England."

"I believe you have the truth of it, Kyd."

Parrish had listened to Kyd boasting and could stand it no longer. "Why, there is a lad here not come to full growth I'd put against you, Mr. Kyd."

"Bring him forth." Kyd smiled benevolently. "I'll bet you a hundred pounds that I can beat any man that you can put up."

"Yes, let's have it," the king said. "Who is this young fellow?"

"He's the son of the man you met, Claiborn Winslow, the keeper of the hawks."

"Hmm. Doubly intriguing, then. Send for the boy."

It did not take long before Stuart was brought before the king, his ironwood laminated longbow in hand.

Stuart was nervous, but the king eyed him favorably. "Fine-looking son you have here, Winslow. That's your bow?"

"Yes, sire, it is."

"All right. Let's see what you can hit."

The targets were set up, and men began to shoot. Obviously Kyd was an expert. He hit the center every time. Man after man did his best but was vanquished.

Finally the king said, "Well, young Winslow, you've stayed up with my master bowman."

"Sire, if you'd move the targets back another hundred yards, we could make it interesting." Stuart was in such awe of the king that he could hardly speak without stuttering.

The king looked surprised but then laughed. "Well, you're either a boaster or a better shot. We'll soon discover which. Move those targets back a hundred yards," he called.

At this distance it was all Kyd could do to get the arrow into the target, and several fell short.

"All right, young Winslow," King Henry said, "let's see you shoot."

"Yes, Your Majesty." Stuart notched an arrow, pulled it back, and it flew through the air and hit dead center. A cry went up.

"A hit!" the king cried. "I do declare a center hit!"

That was the beginning. Kyd hit the target at times, some-times missed, but it seemed that day that Stuart Winslow could not miss.

The king said, "You draw a mighty bow, young fellow."

"I made it myself, Your Majesty. It's a new way of making bows."

"A new way?" The king was instantly fascinated. He obvi-ously loved weapons, and he stood there while Stuart showed him how the woods had been glued together.

"It makes the bow very strong but flexible."

The king studied the young man and said, "You're coming to court with me, young fellow. You're clearly not still wet behind the ears, as your father fears. You are a man on the verge of greatness. You can help with my birds, and you can teach my armorer how to make these bows."

Stuart stared at him in surprise, then bowed low. "Your Majesty, nothing would please me better."

"You will leave with us when we resume our progress."

"Yes, Your Majesty, I'll be ready!"

"A young fellow moving into the life at court needs a few things." Henry dug into the purse he kept at his side and produced several coins. "Get yourself some proper clothes."

Stuart stared at the three gold sovereigns that the king placed in his hand and gasped. "Thank you, sire!"

Henry laughed and winked at a handsome man standing close by. He was not tall and was somewhat overweight, but he had a pleasing expression. "Take this young man under your wing, Clayton. See to it that he doesn't go wrong."

"I will guard him from all temptations, my lord." The man came to stand beside Stuart, saying, "Well, it seems I'm the keeper of your morals, Winslow. My name is Simon Clayton. Come along, and we'll begin your education. Let's fill our bellies, and then I'll introduce you to your new companions."

Stuart was too stunned by the attention of the king to say much, and in truth there was little need for him to speak. Simon took him to the tables where food was laid out, and as they ate, he got Stuart's family history. He was a charming fellow.

After they had eaten, he said, "Come on, Stuart. My purse is getting somewhat flat. I must fatten it a little." He rose and as they left the great hall, asked, "Do you like gaming?"

"Gaming? You mean playing games?"

Simon grinned at this. "I don't mean children's games. Do you like to make wagers?"

"I don't know, sir. I've never gambled—for money, at least."

"Well, lucky for you, you have a great teacher." Simon clapped Stuart on the shoulder; his smile was broad. "Now, those three sovereigns the king gave you. How would you like to turn them into six sovereigns?"

"Why, that would be magic!"

"Come along, and I'll show you that I am a magician!" Simon laughed at the stunned expression on Stuart's face. "Keep your eye on me, Stuart. We'll get into a game, and when you see me squeeze my right earlobe, bet those three coins."

"But I might lose them."

"No, for I'm a magician! Trust me, and you'll see my magic."

They made their way to a room from which came the sound of loud laughter. Simon pulled Stuart in and cried out, "Now, I've come to win all your money!"

The room was packed with men, most of them young, and a chorus of hoots followed Simon's challenge. A tall, lean man with a hawklike visage dominated the group. He had a pair of gimlet eyes, a trim brown breard, and glittering rings on eight of his fingers. "More ale!" he cried, fixing his eyes on Simon Clayton. "Who's your friend?"

"Stuart, this is Sir Leon Case, who loses money to me regularly. Gentlemen, this is Master Stuart Winslow, a new favorite of the Crown. The king has put me in charge of keeping him pure."

Case laughed with the others. "I doubt you'll be able to manage that. But come, now, I need your money, Simon." He picked up a pair of dice from the table and grinned wolfishly. "Put your money down, Clayton. I've got my eye on Ives's fine mare, and when I take your cash and buy her, I'll let you watch as I ride her."

Stuart's gaze moved to Edith's son, who glared at him from across the table. The man didn't want him here, didn't want him anywhere near the court. *It must infuriate him, this newfound favor.* Stuart could not help the grin that edged his lips. When Ives found out that he was to leave with the king . . .

The game began. Stuart did not say a word. He had played a few games of dice with young friends, but never for money. As the game progessed, he studied the players and kept careful watch on Simon Clayton. Money changed hands rapidly, and Clayton was obviously the best player. Many of the players dropped out, and finally only Simon Clayton and Leon Case were locked in a fierce battle. The cash seemed to be evenly divided between them. Then Clayton rattled the dice in his left hand. "I feel lucky, Sir Leon." He shoved all his money to the center of the table, saying, "I would advise you not to bet."

Case stared at the money, then lifted his eyes to meet Clayton's gaze. "Your luck has just run out, Simon." He counted out enough to meet the bet, then looked around the room with a thin smile. "You'd better get your money down. Clayton's going to lose!"

"No, I'm going to win." He reached up and squeezed his right earlobe.

Stuart stared at Clayton but could not move. But Clayton gave him an urgent nod, and he reached into his purse and pulled out the three coins. He laid them down and heard Case say, "Better keep your money in your purse, youngster!"

"No, no, let him wager his coins," said Ives, setting three gold sovereigns next to Stuart's on the table. His eyes glittered and he smiled, clearly thinking that he was about to take all Stuart had. Stuart's heart pounded. "I'll see his bet."

Clayton ignored him. "Here's my little bit of magic!" He tossed the dice almost carelessly, it seemed, and when they came to rest, a silence fell over the group. Clayton laughed, "I warned you. Sorry to take your money, Sir Leon." He scooped up the cash and fished out six sovereigns. "Here you are, young Winslow."

Stuart stared at the six coins. He could not speak. He stared at Simon Clayton's face and when they had left the room, he whispered, "How did you do that?"

"I cheated."

Stuart could only say, "But—that's wrong!"

"No, it's gambling. All good gamblers cheat, but I'm the best." He laughed at the stunned expression on Stuart's face and said, "I'll show you how it's done later. If you're clever, you won't ever have to work. Just fleece the poor devils who don't have the secret of gambling down as I do!"

Grace, Claiborn, and Leah were staring at Stuart, all of them displeased.

"It's not a fit place for a young man to be," Leah said.

"But I'll be serving the king."

"He's not a man you wish to emulate," Leah said, "and the court, as I have told you, is a terrible place. It's a place of temptation. Morals are almost nonexistent. I'm ashamed to tell you what goes on."

Claiborn said, "I heard about your gambling, Son."

Stuart blinked with surprise. *Ives.* "It's just a game, Father. There's no harm in it."

"Yes, there is. I've seen many men lose everything because of cards and dice. Promise me you'll not gamble again."

Stuart saw that his mother and his grandmother agreed with his father. "I don't see any real harm in it."

"I beg you not to go, Stuart," Lady Leah said. "You'll be putting yourself into an evil world."

Grace and Claiborn added their voices but could not budge him. Stuart finally said, "The king has commanded me to go. I give you my word that I will avoid temptation. I promise it. I simply want to serve him. Prepare yourselves, for I shall depart with them."

⚜

Stuart rode over the next day to say good-bye to Heather and to William Tyndale. His visit was not a success, for Heather was grieved.

"I wish you wouldn't go, Stuart. The court is a wicked place."

"That's what my parents and grandmother said too."

"You should listen to them."

"I only want to be a king's man. Don't you see? This is my opportunity—my opportunity to go where life and change occurs. I'll be in the thick of it."

The two argued until William Tyndale came in. He had been giving the boys a lesson in history, and when he heard what had happened he said, "I don't think you know what you're letting yourself in for, Stuart."

"But the king is a religious man."

Tyndale shook his head. "He's religious on his own terms. He will do as he pleases, our King Henry, in religious matters, no matter what the pope or anyone else says."

Stuart shifted uncomfortably, for those he loved best were all opposed to the new life that lay before him. But he was excited by the prospects of life at court. And he could not shake the desire to answer Simon's offer to teach him all he knew about gambling. It was so easy! Think of what he could do with that kind of wealth!

In misery, he made his way back to Stoneybrook, muttering, "They all mean well, but they don't understand. There are bad things at court, but I won't give in to them. I'll simply make the most of the good and avoid what I should."

12

A group of Queen Catherine's maids-in-waiting at the palace looked up as Stuart passed along the corridor. "Well, there's that handsome young master of the hawks," one said, loud enough for him to hear. He glanced shyly in their direction, but his eyes skimmed over her and rested on another.

She was by far the most attractive of the queen's ladies-in-waiting. She had dark eyes and dark hair, and her figure was set off admirably by the expensive gown that she wore. She fixed her eyes on Stuart and asked, "What's your name, man? You *are* a handsome thing."

"A little young for you," the first one said, pouting now that the second speaker had clearly caught his eye.

Stuart, who had been headed back to the mews, stopped, uncertain whether they were sincerely interested in speaking with him or if they were merely toying with him. Amidst their finery he felt awkward in his plain work clothes. Deciding at last, he stepped forward, took off his hat, and bowed stiffly. "Yes, ladies, do you want me?"

"I'll have your name," said the beauty.

"Stuart Winslow, my lady. And yours?"

"I'm Nell Fenton. Let me introduce you to the other members of the queen's service." She named them one by one, and all of them smiled at Stuart with their eyes.

"Why don't you show me your birds?" Nell asked. "That's what brought you here, isn't it?"

"Yes, my lady, it is. I'd be glad to show you the new falcon."

"We'll all go," said another, winking at the other two.

"No, I want Stuart all to myself," Nell said. She moved forward and smiled at him. "Come. I must see the king's birds."

Stuart was dazzled by the beauty of the young woman. He had been at court for only a week, and most of his time had been spent either in the mews or working with Ben Styles, the chief armorer. He had spent some time with Simon Clayton, learning the fine points of gambling, but he had not seen anything like this young woman. She was, he assumed, a year or two older than himself, but there was a certain knowledge in her dark eyes that could come only from some sort of wisdom, experience. She exuded a charm that he had never encountered before. She questioned him closely, and by the time they got to the mews, she knew more about him than he did about her.

He stepped back and waved her inside. She looked at the falcons and cried out, "Oh, aren't they beautiful!"

"I think so. Let me introduce them to you, Miss Fenton." He showed her each of the birds, told her their names and what they were capable of doing. He did not notice that she was paying more attention to him than she was to the falcons and hawks.

Finally she said, "I'm a little warm. Perhaps you would go to the kitchen and get us something cool to drink."

"Why, certainly, if you wish it."

Afterward, Nell dismissed him saying, "You must show me some more. I'd love to see you fly some of the birds."

"Well, that's the king's pleasure."

"I'm certain he would allow it if you properly inquire."

"I would never ask him," Stuart said. "After all, I'm just the keeper of the birds."

"You're much more than a mere keeper. You draw people, as bees to the hive. I bet you left a sweetheart to come here."

He paused. "No, not really, Mistress Nell." For so she had told him to call her.

"Come, now. Don't be bashful. A fine-looking young man like you. You saw how those other maids were giggling and ogling you."

"Ogling? Uh—no, I didn't notice."

Nell Fenton shook her head in wonder. Here was as good-looking a man as existed in England and he didn't seem to know it. This amused her, and she made a vow to herself that she would help him discover the power he could wield simply by trading on his looks. Not that there would ever be anything serious between the two of them, of course, but it would be amusing.

⚝

The next day Stuart was carrying a message from the king to the queen. Ordinarily there would be a page to do this, but they had been flying the hawks, and King Henry had scribbled a few words on a scrap of paper, blown on it, and handed it to Stuart, saying, "Take this to the queen."

"To the queen?"

"Yes, you can find her. Ask anyone."

Stuart took the slip of paper, bowed to the king, then walked away at a rapid pace. He was going to meet the queen of England! He had heard much about Catherine of Aragon and was curious.

He asked one of the servants at the palace to tell the queen that he had a message from the king, and after a brief wait, she returned, saying, "Her Majesty will see you." Stuart followed her, hoping that he might catch a glimpse of Nell Fenton, but did not.

He found the queen in the garden without any of her ladies around her. Stuart was surprised to see how plain she was. She looked ill and unhappy. "I beg your pardon, Your Majesty. I bring you a note from the king."

Catherine was sitting in the shade of a large oak tree with a small child in the grass at her feet. She read the note but slipped it into her pocket without comment. "You're new, aren't you?"

"Yes, Your Majesty. I'm Stuart Winslow. The king brought me here to help with the birds."

Catherine gave him a close look, then said, "I hope you will like it here."

Stuart was surprised that the queen of England would be interested in him. Before he could speak, the child said, "Play with me!"

Catherine laughed. "This is my daughter, Princess Mary. She wants you to play with her."

"She's a beautiful child, Your Majesty. How old is she?"

"Nearing three years. I have to get something for the king. Could you entertain Mary here?"

"Wouldn't she be afraid to be left with a stranger?"

"She never meets a stranger," Catherine said, and there was pride in her tone. "I'll return in ten minutes." The queen left without another word. Stuart thought it strange that she would trust a stranger such as himself.

He sat down on the grass beside Mary. She was playing with three dolls, and she handed him one of them. "What a fine baby!" he said. "Just as pretty as you are."

Mary did not speak like a typical child of her age. She launched into a long story concerning the dolls, and Stuart was amazed at how quick she was and how well she spoke.

They were engaged in playing a game that Stuart had made up when the queen returned. She smiled quickly and said, "Are you having a good time, Mary?"

"Yes! We're playing with my dolls."

Stuart sat on the ground, his legs crossed in tailor's position. The queen sat down and watched the two play. She was amused by young Winslow's ability to entertain a child he had just met with such ease. *A fine-looking young man. I'll have to keep him away from my maids. I fear one of them will corrupt him.* There was an innocence about the young man that was lacking in most of the men at court. She was the daughter of royal parents and had seen that corruption firsthand.

Finally Stuart said, "I'm taking up too much of your time, Your Majesty."

"Oh, no, there is no call upon my time at the moment, and Mary's having such fun. Could you stay a little longer?"

"Oh, as long as you'd like, Your Majesty!"

So the morning went quickly. The queen sent for refreshments, and Stuart ate and tried to make it a party for himself and Mary—and the queen, of course.

"Do you like it here at court?" Queen Catherine asked at one point.

"Oh, yes, I do very much." His eyes were bright. Catherine thought she had never seen such blue eyes in another. They almost seemed to sparkle. His hair was beautiful, full of intriguing colors, rich and thick. She soon knew much about him and his family, liking him more and more. At last, she rose and said, "I hope you'll come back sometime and see Mary again."

"Yes, we will play," Mary said, smiling at Stuart.

"I will certainly do that with your permission, Majesty. I'd best get back to my work."

Later that day, Stuart told Simon about his encounter with the queen. "I wonder why she looks so sad."

"She has things to be sad about." Simon shrugged. "The king wants a male heir, and the queen hasn't given him one. "

"That's not her fault."

"It is if the king says it is." Simon shook his head and added,

"Henry never sees anything as his fault. If there is no son in his marriage, it's the fault of the queen."

"I'll go back and see her—Mary, that is. The queen seemed glad enough to have me play with her. Mary's such a pretty little thing, and she's smart as a whip."

Stuart did go back twice over the next week, and each time Queen Catherine was receptive and glad to see him. He got on fine with Mary, and he found out that she had a vivid imagination. The two of them made up games and played with dolls. Mary once told him, "I like you!" and gave him hug.

Catherine, watching, was amused. "You've made a conquest, Stuart. Just don't turn your charm on any of my ladies. They're not as innocent as Princess Mary."

❧

The trouble started when Stuart heard Charles Vining speaking of the king. Vining was an aristocratic man of twenty-five or so, and he spoke loudly to another man who Stuart did not know. "Well, the king doesn't have to go to Catherine's bedroom. He can go to his mistress any time he pleases."

Stuart was a great admirer of King Henry. He went up to Vining at once and said, "You, sir, are a liar! How dare you spread such foul stories about our lord!"

Charles Vining stepped back in surprise. "What do you want, fellow?"

"You will not speak of the king in a disrespectful way."

Vining's companion took in Stuart's working clothes and sneered, "This stable hand's going to teach you a lesson in morality, Charles. He may be a monk in disguise."

Vining's face flushed. "How dare you challenge me! Get back to your stable, boy!"

"I hold you accountable for speaking ill of our king! And I back it with my sword."

"I don't fight duels with stable boys."

"You're a coward as well as a liar!"

Vining reached out suddenly and struck Stuart with his open hand. "Now, get away from here!"

Stuart glared at him. "I'll go to the king. You'll be thrown out of court."

"Why, you stupid clodhopper!" Vining drew his sword, but his companion quickly grabbed his arm. "Cease, Charles. This young fellow is the new keeper of the birds. The king is quite taken with him."

"Oh, you foolish, foolish boy," said Vining, still trembling with rage.

Stuart stood still. He had no weapon, but he was not afraid.

Vining was drawn off by his friend, and they went to the king, with Stuart right behind them. Vining told the king that the stable hand, as he referred to Stuart, had challenged him to a duel. "I should have run him through!"

"Why did he challenge you?"

Vining was uncomfortable. "He was listening to a private conversation, and he got angry at something I said."

"What did you say?"

Vining was on the horns of a dilemma. He knew he could not tell the king the truth. It was true, as everyone in the court knew, that Henry had more than one mistress, but young Winslow had obviously not been at court long enough to know it.

Henry glanced over at Stuart, then back to Vining, and said, "You shall not hurt young Winslow. I'm fond of him. And he's going to be a fine master of the hawks."

"Yes, Your Majesty, but he needs to be cut down to size."

"I'll do all the cutting, Vining," Henry said. He stared at the courtly man for a moment. His eyes narrowed. "Were you talking about me?"

"Well, sire, I'm afraid I was."

At once understanding filled Henry's eyes. "We shall speak of this further."

"Yes, Your Majesty."

He watched the two men depart and then gestured to Stuart. "Come, son, let us walk together out to the mews."

"Yes, Majesty," Stuart said, rising from his bow. The two walked down the center of the court, ignoring the people bowing about them. Outside, the king leaned closer to him. "Now, Stuart, I'll have the truth. What caused the trouble with Sir Charles Vining?"

"He spoke slightingly of Your Majesty."

Henry smiled. "That's a tactful way to put it. He spoke slightingly of me. What exactly did he say?"

"I do not care to repeat his words. They're unbecoming."

"Did he refer to my morals?"

"If you'll pardon me, Your Majesty, I would rather not say."

Henry stared at the young man. "I haven't seen such innocence in a long time," he said, then he shook his head and said, "Don't you know that you could be soundly whipped or put in the stocks or even sent to prison for challenging a gentleman?"

"I didn't think about that."

"Well, you must stop and think, Stuart, and I want you to stay away from the court gossips and certainly away from any brawling."

"Yes, Your Majesty."

"You'll hear all sorts of tales floating around. Pay no attention to them. Especially the young ladies. The queen's attendants and others."

Stuart was surprised. "Careful, sire?"

"Yes! Yes, boy! You're innocent, but they may not be."

"Yes, Your Majesty, I'll do as you say."

"You're a good young fellow, and I want to see you prosper. Not only are you doing fine work with my birds but my armorer says he's never seen such a stout bow as flexible as yours. So he'll be asking for your help to work out a way to make more of them."

Stuart felt the warmth of pleasure. He had the king's own approval! "I'll do all I can to serve you, Majesty. That's all I want to do. To be a king's man."

"I wish I had a thousand like you, Stuart, but I don't," Henry said. "Well, mind what I've said."

"Yes, Majesty."

The king stopped. "You know life isn't usually as it is in the fairy tales or in the songs."

"It isn't?"

"No. Here you are, a poor boy who suddenly finds himself with the king who can do all things, or so it seems. It's not impossible that one day you might do something that will please me so much that I'll knight you." He laughed suddenly. "How does that sound? Sir Stuart Winslow. You like the ring of it, boy?"

"I doubt I could ever do anything that would merit an honor like that."

"Don't be foolish. I made a man a knight the other day who's a drunk and a fornicator and everything else. You know why I did it?"

"No, sire."

"Because he contributes a lot of money to the Treasury. He's a fool and an imbecile and not worth the powder to blow him up, but I knighted him. So not all knights are like the ones you read about in Malory. I'll bet you listened to those tales of the knights of the Round Table over and over."

"I have read them, sire."

"Yourself? How did you learn to read? Surely you didn't go to school."

"My father taught me. He taught me Latin too."

"You read Latin? What do you read?"

"We only have one book in Latin back at Stoneybrook. The Bible."

The king shook his head.

"I keep finding out strange things about you. You're an inventor. You're an expert with the sword, if your father was not boasting. And now I find that you're a Latin scholar. I have a book in Latin you might like to peruse."

"Oh, yes, Your Majesty."

"Sir Stuart Winslow." He laughed when he saw Stuart's face. "It sounds good to you, doesn't it?"

"Yes, sir. But it's more than I could hope for."

"You keep your humility, son. It's especially becoming in court." He turned away, but then wheeled and fastened his eyes on Stuart. "I hear you're getting a reputation as a gambler. Better be cautious. Many a man is ruined by that vice!" With that, he turned again and walked away. Stuart watched him go. He was filled with admiration for the king. He said the words over again. "Sir Stuart Winslow."

13

Stuart had haunted the palace for a week, but Nell was always busy with someone else. Finally he lay in wait for her, hiding himself behind a tall pillar, and when she had crossed to the pavilion he came up quickly, before she could escape into the queen's quarters. "For weeks, now, we've kept company, but now you avoid me. Don't you love me at all, Nell?"

"You're such a sweet boy," Nell cooed, taking his arm and pulling him away to a quiet corner. She patted his cheek, "You're so very young."

"You're only one year older than I. Does that make you an aged woman?"

Nell smiled and paused, as if conflicted.

"Come with me tonight, Nell. We'll go down to the lake. You love it there."

"I cannot. Queen Catherine wants us with her tonight."

"You can sneak away."

"And if I got caught, what then? They'd send me back home again for disobeying the queen. I couldn't bear that!"

Stuart pleaded, but nothing would change her mind. But she looked left and right, pulled his head down, and kissed him. So sweet, she tasted! At first he was surprised, but then he pulled her close, hungry for more.

She turned her head aside and shoved at his chest. "Now, that's enough for now. Maybe tomorrow we'll be able to meet for a little while."

"Come to the old oak tree at the beginning of the forest."

"The last time I went there with you, you were very impudent." She saw his face redden, and she laughed with delight. "You are the most innocent young man I've ever seen! You're just a baby really."

"I'm not a baby!"

"Well, you're young and pure and innocent, probably the only man that fits that description in all Henry's court."

"Meet me there. Say you will."

"All right. I'll meet you there at seven o'clock."

He reached for her, but she laughed and pulled herself away. "That's enough for now. Go on now. Take care of your birds."

"Until then," he said, lingering beside her, wishing he could grab her and kiss her again. But she was already turning away. He hated the hold she had on him and loved it. Never before had he been so taken with a woman, not even when he had first fallen for Heather Evans. That was a boy's love. This was a man's passion.

He knew Nell was here to land a nobleman for a husband, and misery seized his heart as he walked to the mews. There was only one way in which he could make her his own—by persuading the king to knight him and adding to his gaming winnings. Perhaps with those two things in hand—a title and some wealth—Nell would cease toying with him and allow herself to fall in love.

⚕

A horseman covered in dust met Stuart at the mews.

"Whom do you seek?"

"I need to find Stuart Winslow."

"You've found him. Who are you?"

"Just a messenger. Here, this be for you."

"Do I pay for it?"

"You can give me a coin if you'd like. I wouldn't say no." The rider was a small man, thin and emaciated but with lively dark eyes. He took the coin that Stuart offered him, tossed it in the air, caught it, and put it in his pocket. "God be with you, Stuart Winslow."

"And with you."

As soon as the rider was gone, Stuart examined the slip of paper. It had been sealed with a tallow candle, but there was no personal seal in the wax.

"It has to be from Father," he murmured, and opened it.

> *Stuart,*
>
> *You must come home at once. Your mother is having great difficulty. The doctor thinks there is danger for her and for the baby. Come as quickly as you can. And pray, Son, pray with me. I fear we're about to lose them both.*
>
> *Your loving father,*
> *Claiborn Winslow*

Instantly Stuart folded the paper up and stuck it in his pocket. He ran quickly to the master of horse, a tall individual with gray eyes and a thick neck.

"Felin, I must borrow a horse. My mother's very ill. The king is gone, but he said I could use that gelding, Tyrone, at my leisure."

"Aye, he gave me that word as well. But it's poor weather for a run. Can it wait until the morrow?"

"Afraid not. I must get home immediately."

Felin stared at him for a moment. "Want me to saddle 'im for you?"

"No, I can do it." Tyrone was the horse that Stuart used when he went on the hunt with the king. "I don't know when I'll be back," he said, "but I'll take care of Tyrone. See that someone takes care of the mews, will you?"

"All right. But see that you return before the king. I do not care to be here if he discovers that both his mews keeper and his horse are gone."

Stuart urged the gelding into a lope, one that would cover ground without tiring the horse out. He wanted to run him at full speed but knew that would break the horse's wind. And with the winter weather upon them, he dared not risk the horse's health. He held to the same lope for four hours, praying all the way, and finally pulled up in front of his home. His father came out to greet him and help him unsaddle Tyrone and put the horse out in the pasture.

"You made good time, Son."

"How's Mother?"

"She's having a very hard time. Much harder than she did with you."

"But she's going to be all right, isn't she?"

"God knows. Come. Let me make you something to eat."

"I'm not hungry."

"You must eat, Son. I'm not hungry either, but we must keep up our strength."

Claiborn prepared a simple meal, and the two sat down to eat. But it was as tasteless as weeds to Stuart, and he saw that his father was staring out the window rather than eating.

"I wish I could help, Father. I want to do something."

"The good Lord can help. If you want to do something, pray. That's what I've been doing day and night."

"I'm not sure my prayers are worth a lot."

His father glanced at him in surprise. "We've spoken of this before. I thought you understood just how worthy your prayers truly are."

"I'm not like you and Mother. You're so close to God."

"You're younger. It will come."

The two men alternately sat in the parlor and walked to and fro outside. Once Father Simon, a local priest, came by and inquired to how Grace was doing, but there was no word from the midwife.

It was almost midnight when the midwife came out to them. "You have a fine son, Master Winslow. Look, he's got red hair just like you." She glanced up at Stuart. "And you."

"And my wife? How is Grace?"

"She's had a rough go of it, but she's strong. I have hope."

"God be praised! Here, now, let me see him." Claiborn took the small morsel of humanity from her and looked down into his face. "Another Winslow."

"What will you call him, Father?"

"Your mother was favoring Quentin, after her uncle. I've always liked that name myself." He looked down at his new son, cradled in his arms. "Quentin Winslow," he said softly, "born in 1519. I wonder what the world will be like when he's your age—or mine."

"You can go in and see your lady now, Master Winslow," called the midwife.

"Yes. Let me see her first, Stuart, and then you can go in."

Claiborn's heart sank when he saw how pale and wan Grace looked. She looked dead for a moment, and his heart almost stopped, but then her eyes opened, and she smiled. "That's a fine boy, we have."

"Yes, he is. You did fine, Grace—just fine."

"Quentin." She reached out and touched the baby's hair. "Let me hold him. Put him here." He put the baby into the crook of her arm, and for a while the two were silent. Then she said, "I heard you talking to someone."

"Yes, Stuart came home. It's a wonder he didn't kill that horse."

"Tell him to come in."

Stuart looked shaken by his mother's pale appearance and evident weakness.

"You've given me a beautiful baby brother." He knelt down and took her hand. He held it in both of his, and Claiborn remembered how once, Stuart's hand was as small as Quentin's. His boy, now a grown man—and a new son, just beginning!

"I'm glad you came home," Grace said.

"So am I, Mother."

"Will you stay a few days?"

"One or two." He reached out to touch her face. "I am so relieved you are well. I feared . . ."

"The worst," she said.

He nodded.

"Forgive me," Claiborn said, "but I wanted him home if you were . . ."

"Going to die," she said.

"Yes." What would he have done had he lost her? He couldn't imagine life without Grace.

"Well, cease your morbid thoughts, you two," Grace chided them with a smile. "I have plenty of life to live yet and three men who are depending on me."

꩜

Stuart's two days at home passed quickly. During much of that time Grace, who was growing stronger, talked to him about his walk with God. She said once, "I don't see how anyone can grow in the grace of God, living in the middle of Satan's court."

"It's not all bad."

"That means there's a little good and more bad. Are the people there very immoral? The women, I mean."

Stuart could not find a way to answer that and finally said, "Some of them are rather wild."

"That's what the court does to a person. They were probably innocent young girls when they went, and now they have fallen."

"That won't happen to me, Mother. I'm on my guard."

Grace looked at Stuart directly. "Have you kept your word about gambling?"

Stuart had been expecting such a question, and he had told himself that he would stop—when he had gotten enough money. "I don't need to gamble," he said, and managed to keep guilt from showing on his face. "Don't fret over me, Mother."

Grace reached her hand out for his, and he took it. "I'm going to pray for you, Stuart."

"I'd like that, Mother."

Grace prayed simply, as she always did. To Stuart it was no different from her conversation with him or his father, and he wondered if he would ever be able to approach God as she did. "Father, be with this son of ours. Build a wall of fire about him so that the evil one cannot come into his heart. Give him wisdom so that he will not make unholy alliances of any kind. Let him grow to love you more each day."

Stuart said, "Thank you, Mother." He leaned over and kissed her. "I must get back to court now."

"Come back if you can. And if God moves you to do so, leave that place, Stuart."

Stuart could not think of a proper answer. "Thank you for my beautiful baby brother." He kissed the baby's auburn hair, the same hue as his own, and then he kissed his mother's cheek.

Stuart rode Tyrone at an easy gait, but he did not go straight back to court. He went to Sir John Walsh's house.

As soon as he crested the hill, he saw Heather in front of the house. She was working in a garden of flowers and did not see him at first. He gave a shrill whistle. Heather looked up, she came to her feet, and he saw a glad smile on her face. He kicked Tyrone into a run then pulled him up short in the yard and came off in one smooth motion.

Heather came to him, her eyes shining. "It's so good to see you, Stuart. How is your mother?"

"On the mend. And you should see my baby brother, Quentin. He's as good-looking as me."

"Well, you haven't found your humility."

As they went into the house, Stuart remarked, "I remember the first time I came here. You gave me cider."

"Yes, you thought it was what they would drink in heaven."

"I still think so. I would like—"

There was a knock at the door. Heather opened the door, and a compact young man with direct brown eyes and crisp brown hair stood facing Stuart.

"This is Miles Howard. Miles, I'd like you to meet my good friend Stuart Winslow."

"I'm happy to know you," Howard said. His grip was firm.

"We're just having a cup of cider. Will you have some?"

The two men sat down and talked about what made the Evans cider special.

Stuart was puzzled. He did not know why the young man had come. Perhaps to see Sir John, but he did not appear to be eager to leave. Stubborn as Stuart, he kept his seat. Finally, after an hour, Howard rose and said, "I'll see you tomorrow night then, Heather."

"Tomorrow night. Yes."

"Good to have met you, Master Winslow."

"And you, Master Howard."

As soon as the man was gone, Stuart asked, "Who was that? Did he come to see your uncle?"

A smile appeared on Heather's lips, and she said, "No, he came to see me."

"To see you? About what?"

Heather was disgusted. "Is it impossible for you to believe that a young man would come calling on me?"

"Well, no—"

"Well, that's what he's doing, and for your information two other young men are calling from time to time."

"Do you like this fellow, Howard?"

"I like him very much."

Stuart thoughtfully chewed on his lower lip and tried to think of a way to ask what he wanted to know. "Does he come from a good family?"

"Very good family. They have money and considerable property."

They were interrupted when William Tyndale walked into the room.

He and Stuart talked mostly about the work Tyndale was doing. He had started translating the Latin Bible into English, and he spoke of it eagerly. "Of course, I haven't got far, Stuart, but by the grace of God I will."

"I wish you success, Master Tyndale. It will be a great achievement."

Shortly after this, Tyndale began to question Stuart about his spiritual life. Stuart knew it was coming, because it always did.

"Have you ever considered pledging your life to God?"

"Why, I thought I had done that when I was baptized."

"Nonsense! You didn't do anything when you were baptized except get a little water sprinkled on you. That doesn't give a man a new heart. I'm surprised at you. You need to offer your life to Christ and ask God to bless it. Can you ask God every day to bless your activities now?"

Stuart thought of some of the things that he had seen and even done, especially the gambling and the drinking that went with it. He also thought of Nell Fenton and his lustful thoughts of her. "No, sir, I really cannot."

"You know the Bible tells us that whatever we do, whether we're eating or drinking, we should do everything to God's glory."

"That would be difficult. How could peeling a potato be for God's glory?"

"All work is sacred if it's done with the Savior and the good God Almighty in mind. I think Jesus probably worshipped when he was making furniture at Joseph's carpenter shop."

Stuart felt highly uncomfortable. Tyndale always had that effect on him. It was as if the older man was asking him for something, and Stuart wasn't quite sure what it was. He believed in God. He went to church. He read the Bible. He tried to do the right thing. But he knew that his dedication to God himself was nothing compared to William Tyndale's. Tyndale, Stuart was sure, would gladly go to his death if it would please God. He was not so sure that he would do the same.

Stuart stayed for nearly another hour and then took his leave of them both. Heather walked with him to his horse. "I'm glad you came, Stuart."

"So am I." He hesitated. "This fellow, Howard. I'd like to know more about him."

"He's not courting you, Stuart. He's courting me."

"I know, but I have to look out for you. You're my sister, aren't you?"

"No, I'm not your sister!"

"Well, I mean you're somewhat like a sister. I always pictured you as such."

"You can picture me as that, but it doesn't give you any right to know more about my suitors."

"Are you serious about this man?"

"Good-bye, Stuart."

He saw that she did not mean to answer concerning Howard, so he mounted his horse and tried to summon a smile. "I'll come again as soon as I can." He hesitated and then said, "Don't marry this man until you talk to me first."

"Shall I have him come and ask your permission to marry?"

"Don't be silly. I'm not your father."

"No, you're *not* my father *nor* my brother! Good-bye, Stuart."

Somehow he had offended her; he did not know how. But as he rode back to the court, his thoughts were mostly on Tyndale and his question. *"You need to offer your life to Christ and ask God to bless it."* He thought he had found blessings in King Henry's court, but now he wasn't so sure. He was quiet all the way back, thinking of the life that lay behind him and wondering what was ahead.

჻

Henry found Catherine and Mary reading together. "Well, well, what are we reading? Come here, Princess." He put out his arms, and Mary ran to him. He took her, held her up high, and then sat down and held her on his lap. He knew this pleased Catherine, for she longed to have Henry accept her daughter as a possible heir to the throne of England.

They talked for some time, and she said, "I heard that young Winslow almost had a duel."

"He could have killed Vining, and I would have had to hang him. He's a firebrand and yet as innocent as a new-born kitten. Probably the last innocent twenty-year-old in England."

"I wish he would stay that way."

Henry ran his hand down Mary's shiny hair, and then, after a time, he put her down and rose to his feet. "I need to speak to you alone, Catherine."

"Of course. Mary, go to your room and look at your books. I'll be there soon."

"Yes, Mother."

As soon as she was gone, Henry said, "Catherine, I need a son."

"You have a daughter."

"That's not good enough, and you know it."

"England could be ruled by a queen."

"It's unnatural."

"Well, what more can I do? I didn't kill those babies. God took them, and we'll never know why."

Henry tried to think of a reply. He could speak to Bible scholars, politicians, even the court jester, but this woman baffled him. He was sure she loved him, and he had loved her at one time, but this matter of a son and heir rose between them like a dividing wall.

He left shortly after that and went right to Wolsey, who handled all his affairs. Cardinal Wolsey was the most powerful man in the kingdom other than Henry himself.

He rose to greet the king, but his greeting was still in his mouth when Henry said, "Wolsey, I'll have to divorce Catherine."

Wolsey seemed to gasp for air. He knew his politics. A divorce would break all relationship with Rome, and that was where his connections were.

"Sire, you can't do that!"

"Then get the marriage annulled. I must have a son. England has to have one of my sons as an heir."

"But Mary—"

"Mary is a girl. She'll be a woman, but she won't be the queen." He glared at Wolsey, and there was a threat in his cold eyes. "I'll have an annulment, Wolsey. See to it."

PART THREE

The Convert

(1524–1527)

14

March 1524

S tuart leaned back against a wall, only vaguely aware of the music and many babbling voices that filled the great hall. He was looking for Nell Fenton and paid little heed to the crowd of guests who had come for the masque dressed in fantastic costumes. A wry thought came to him. *Before I came to the court six years ago, I didn't even know what a masque was. Now here I am taking part in one.* A sour smile touched his broad lips, as he thought of the education his years at court had given him. An education that shamed him every time he thought of how he had been seduced by money and lust.

He grieved over what he had lost—his innocence, his youth, and the solid trust in God that his parents and his grandmother had sought to instill in him.

He had attempted to tear himself away from the sensual life of the court with thoughts of returning home and assuming the life he'd given up for what he now had. But he could not, for the court was like the magnet that one of the scholars who came to court had demonstrated. What force could pull him away from the life he now led?

Theodore, the keeper of the king's hawks, had died before he arrived, and with years of service in the mews, there was clearly no one better at training the raptors than Stuart. The king had given him the office, which carried a handsome salary that he could never match back at Stoneybrook. Simon had made an expert gambler out of him, so he won large sums of money. With a large income and the ability to draw the women, Stuart fell prey to two temptations: sex and liquor.

His fondness for wine and ale began with a quest to avoid tainted water, but his weakness for drink startled him. He made determined efforts to curtail his drinking—and he never drank to excess on his visits to his family—but the freedom, the relief of drinking to drunkenness continually called to him.

As for lust, Stuart had armed himself at first with a firm determination to keep himself from this vice. But there were no barriers to sex at the court. He laughed at himself for once defending the king. Well he knew now of Henry's conquests. The king himself acknowledged his illegitimate child, Henry Fitzroy, born five years past.

The women of noble rank were immoral as a rule, but it was a voluptuous lady's maid named Betty who seduced Stuart. She caught him when he was half drunk, disgruntled over an early refusal from Nell, and laughed at his attempts to turn from her. She had drawn him to her bed and was experienced in love, as she liked to call it. Stuart knew that what they had was not love, but he found himself unable to resist her. She was a lusty woman, and within a few weeks, Stuart found himself as much captive to the pleasures of bedding a woman as he was to wine. And it was not only Betty who had assuaged his need over the years.

As Stuart stood at the edge of the great hall, he was approached by Simon, dressed for the masque in the costume of a court fool. He was half drunk. He pulled at Stuart's arm, saying, "Come, lad! Join the fun!"

But Stuart was deep into one of his guilty moods. "Simon, at what point did I lose my honor?"

Simon stared at him, then laughed. "Why, you lost your honor the same way I lost mine."

"And when was that?"

"A crumb at a time, lad! Do you think I woke up one morning a fine, innocent man and said, 'Well, now, enough of this good behavior! I'm going to become a drunk, a lecher, a cheater at cards, a liar, and a thief'?" He leaned closer, the wine on his breath wafting about them. "No, Stuart, I lost my honor a little bit at a time. Just a little sin, you know? And then another—and another." He stared at Stuart with bitterness in his eyes. "I was as good a man as you once—at least, as good as you were when I first met you. But a tiny mouse came and carried away a little of my goodness. Then another came and got a crumb. And little by little the mice carried away all that was good in me. That's how I lost my honor, and that's the way you lost yours too."

Simon's bitter words entered Stuart's breast like a hot sword. "My father read me a verse in the Bible once, from the Psalms. The verse spoke of men who lose their honor. Honor in the dust! That's where I've thrown it, Simon!"

Simon Clayton regarded him with regret. Finally he said, "The king ordered me to look out for you, Stuart, but I've failed his charge. Forgive me." He whirled and moved quickly through the crowd, leaving Stuart feeling alone and alienated from all that was good. Wine. Wine was what he needed.

He reached a table and poured a goblet full, then turned to view the masque. Masques, sometimes called *mummeries,* were entertainments loosely organized around an allegorical plot, performed on movable stages. Singers and musicians were employed, but the principal feature of the masque was dancing by disguised members of the court. The dances were intricate and demanding, taking many hours to learn.

Simon had once told him, grinning, "Actually they're just another excuse to get drunk and wind up in bed with a willing female." King Henry loved masques and almost always joined in the fanciful activities; the more elaborate they were, the better he liked it.

A castle of timber had been set up in the hall, and as Stuart watched, three knights came out of the door ready to do battle with challengers. The challengers soon appeared, and the six fought with blunted spears and then naked swords. After they left the scene, a queen and six of her ladies came out.

All the guests were dressed in extremely colorful and expensive gowns and dresses, and the men no less so. Some of them wore satin mantles trimmed with silk; others wore masking hats and Asian-influenced fashion of yellow and red sarcenet.

Stuart still searched for Nell while he watched the guests, still fascinated by their costumes. The room was full of Italian, Greek, German, and Turkish fashions, and the styles changed rapidly, with the cut of men's hose and doublets often more colorful and elaborate than that of the women's gowns. The room was aglow with an array of silks and brocades and metallic fabrics of gold and silver.

Indeed, guests—who were permitted occasionally at court masques—found Henry's courtiers magnificent. They wrote of the handsome gold chains the men wore, thick links of gold as much as a hand's breadth wide. There were also smaller chains around ankles, as if some of those who wore them were prisoners. So in a gorgeous array the courtiers formed a spangled, bejeweled backdrop—but always in front of this was King Henry VIII. He outdid all the others, of course. It would have been a fatal mistake for any of the guests to have outdressed the king.

Henry came by now, dancing. The king was a fine dancer indeed. For all his size he was light on his feet, very graceful, and the masque gave the king a chance to show off this particular expertise.

He was holding a young woman in his arms in a dance that was astonishingly sensual. His costume was luxuriant and brilliant. It dazzled with jewels. Gold ornaments hung from his doublet, cap, and sleeves. His goldsmith had wasted more of the precious metal in this one costume than most men would see in a lifetime.

"You're not dancing."

Stuart's attention had been on the spectacle in front of him. It quickly shifted at the sound of the voice. He saw a small but full-figured young woman who wore an ornate and fantastic mask that covered the upper part of her face but left the lower part bare. The costume she wore was pure silk, crimson and emerald green, and glittered with inset jewels and a mass of pearls. He had seen the woman dancing with a man and wondered who she was. Now he turned to face her and bowed slightly. "No, I am not."

"What a shame." The woman's mouth formed a Cupid's bow, and she shook her head and raised her hand in a mock blow. "It is un-English not to dance at one of the king's masques."

"I would not offend the king."

"Then come. You must dance with me. I can tell you are a fine dancer."

Stuart smiled. He was wearing a relatively simple costume, his mask leaving his eyes free. As they began to move across the floor amid the other masquers, he was aware of a strong incenselike perfume that rose from his partner. He was also aware that she moved in a sensuous fashion in his arms, leaving no question in his mind about her interest in him.

Finally the woman, who had obviously been drinking a great deal, stumbled a little. She fell against him and whispered, "Oh, my, you're so tall and so strong. I am quite impressed."

She ran a hand down his arm and then reached up to cup his cheek. "Who are you? You are a handsome man. Why is it that we have not yet met?"

"I suppose that's why masques are so enjoyable. You never know who you might meet."

"Or bed," she said quietly.

There, Stuart thought, *it's out in the open. Nothing subtle about this at all.* He did not respond. She took his arm, pulled him off the floor, and led him toward a convenient corridor. He hesitated. "Why, what is wrong with you?"

"Nothing, madam, at all."

"Come. We will enjoy ourselves." She reached up, put her arms around his neck, and pulled his head down. Her lips were hungry as she pulled him ever closer; he could smell the wine on her breath.

Suddenly Stuart straightened up and broke contact with her. He knew that he had accepted such offers before, but his reflections on what he had become disgusted him. "I am sorry, madam, you must find another partner."

"What is that you say?" The woman suddenly flew into a rage. "You are rejecting me?"

"It is nothing personal."

She attempted to slap Stuart's face. She was so drunk that only her fingertips came into contact with his chin. She whispered a curse at him and, staggering somewhat, moved back onto the dance floor.

"That's right, lovely," he whispered, "go find yourself a more willing partner." He moved back into the shadows.

"Well I know what my parents would think of this," Stuart muttered. And then another thought came, equally troublesome. *And what Heather would think.* They had all warned him often enough. They had been steadfastly and completely against his coming to court. His grandmother had been even more outspoken, saying more often than not, "They will corrupt you, Stuart. You will not be able to resist." He had insisted that he would, and lamented his failure.

Then he caught sight of Nell Fenton.

He had really come to the masque in order to see her. For years he had pursued her, and she had tantalized him and laughed at him, but he was so bewitched by her that it did not seem to matter. She seemed to welcome him, appreciate him, love him for weeks at a time, and then all at once, all this seemed to have been a dream.

He went to her at once, admiring her dress and the strand of Venetian glass and diamonds glittering at her throat. He wondered where she had obtained such finery, for he knew that Nell did not have the resources to pay for it. It was most likely one of the wealthy women of the court who had treated her to this costume. Or was it a suitor? Was this the reason for her coldness of late? She was moving across the floor, but he caught up with her.

"Good evening, Nell."

"Why, Stuart, I'm glad to see you." She had a way of looking at a man as if he were the only man who existed in the world, but he knew that it meant nothing; as soon as she left his side, she'd make the next man feel the same.

"I must have a word with you, Nell."

"Not now."

"Yes, now. Come along." Without apology he pulled her from the room and into an alcove filled with flowering plants. He turned and faced her. "Nell, you haven't allowed me to see you for weeks now. Are you angry with me again?"

"Well, of course not. Why would you think that? I've been occupied. And so have you."

Indeed, that was partially true. More and more the king relied upon Stuart for companionship on hunts and even in court, but he knew that the ladies of the court did nothing but primp and work on costumes and exchange gossip. He shook his head almost violently. "There's been time enough. Why are you treating me like this?"

Nell grew more serious. "Stuart, I've tried to tell you before that you need to find another object for your love."

"Do you think I can simply turn from you?"

"You must."

"Why? Don't you care for me at all, Nell?" Anger flooded him now at the thought of her leaving him. In desperation he said, "Why don't we marry?"

Nell laughed with pure amusement. "That would be impossible!"

"Why? Do you love me?"

"We both of us must marry for money."

"Some people are happy without money. My parents are."

"Come, now. You've told me what a terrible time they had."

"But they still love each other and always will."

Nell sighed heavily, put her hand on his chest, and gave him a slight shove. "That kind of love is like a rare exotic animal seen in a king's menagerie. Unattainable for most of us. I must go."

As Stuart watched her walk away, something seemed to grow cold inside him. *Have I lost my mind? Am I bewitched by this woman?* The thought pursued him. He could not stand the thought of any more of the masque.

He turned and left, as depressed as he had ever been in his life.

❦

The memory of Nell telling him to marry for money and that she would do the same plagued Stuart.

A week later he was at the lists to watch the jousting. The king liked to have him present at all courtly functions. Evidently Stuart was still finding favor with him, regardless of his somber mood.

Feigning interest, Stuart watched as the king mounted his horse and his opponent at the other end of the field prepared himself. Henry was an excellent jouster. He was bigger than most men, two inches over six feet, stronger and athletically inclined in every way. He bore a wooden lance—as did his opponent. Now, as he cried out, his black horse churned forward. The two came against each other, the horses' hooves on the turf thundered, and then came the tremendous clash of impact. Neville, the king's opponent, flew out of the saddle and hit the ground with a crash.

"Looks as if he has broken every bone in his body," Stuart said.

"No, I doubt that," Vining said. "He knows how to fall even if he doesn't know how to joust."

It still surprised Stuart that he now called Sir Charles Vining friend. After their first meeting, when he heard Vining speak ill of King Henry, he thought never to go near him again, but somehow, over the months and years, the two had drifted together. In time, Stuart decided Vining was a well enough intentioned fellow, even though he found it amusing that Stuart had been ready to die for the good name of King Henry.

"Really, Stuart," he said, "you are the only man in the court who would be upset by hearing Henry's mistresses mentioned." He then laughed and slapped Stuart on his shoulder. "It's not talked about elsewhere, but here at court it's like keeping score at a joust. Who is the king sleeping with now? Everybody knows it, the king knows that everybody knows it, and it's no trouble to anyone."

Stuart remembered his words again now. *It's like keeping score at a joust.* Then he looked down to the field where the king's opponent now lay. Two men ran out to help him rise. "I wonder why the king would risk his life."

"I don't."

"I wish you'd tell me. I can see that it would be important to fight in a battle, where you could win something, but nobody wins anything at these competitions."

"Why, man, don't you understand? These jousts, they're for Henry's childhood dreams of knighthood. He grew up reading all the stories. It got into his blood, and he's determined to be a noble knight."

"Do you think he'll survive?"

"It's very hard to be noble in this day and age."

The two men went over to the king when he dismounted, and Vining said, "Well done, Your Majesty. Well done indeed."

"I've done better. What about you? Would you like to try a little jousting, Vining?"

"If you please, Your Majesty."

"No, I think I've had enough." Henry was wearing enough armor to buy a small kingdom. He glittered in the sun, and when he removed his helmet, his red hair caught the glow. "Now, what about a go at the birds, Winslow?"

"Yes, sire. I think you'll be pleased." Next to jousting and perhaps dancing, the king loved to fly his falcons best. It was for this reason that Stuart had become such a favorite. Now the king pulled Stuart after him. "Come along. I'll get rid of this armor, and we'll see what mood our birds are in."

"Yes, sire, it will be a pleasure."

An hour later the two men were examining the raptors. The king selected a falcon named Hook and asked, "What do you think of him, Winslow?"

"A fine bird, Your Majesty. Worthy of a king."

Henry reached up and ruffled the hawk's feathers and laughed when the bird uttered a harsh cry. "Well, let's try him out." He leaned toward Stuart. "I saw you conversing with Mistress Fenton last week at the masque."

Stuart felt his face flush. "Yes, sire, I was there."

"Did she deny you?"

"Indeed, sire, she did."

"You take these things too seriously, Stuart. I know you think you're in love with Nell, but you're at court! It will happen to you a dozen times. She's your first. Let her go, and you'll see I'm right."

Indeed, it has happened to you a dozen times! The king laughed, as if he could read Stuart's thoughts. "Come along, then. And by the way, you've worked very hard lately. Take a holiday. Go see your parents. It may help your spirits."

"You mean it, sire?"

"Of course. Go tomorrow. Tell the horsemaster I said you could take Tyrone."

"Thank you, Your Majesty. It would be good to see my family again."

"A man should honor his parents, my friend, always remember that."

⚭

Even as Stuart dismounted in front of his parents' house, his mother came out the door. She flew to him, and he caught her up and swung her around.

She cried, "Well, don't crush me, Son!" But she was laughing.

Putting her down, he said, "You're looking very fine. Far too lovely to be my mother. But where's that little brother of mine? That's who I really came to see."

"He's somewhere near," his mother returned. "Somewhere very near," she added, cocking a playful eyebrow.

Stuart looked down. There Quentin was, peeking around her skirts. He dodged back behind her as soon as they made eye contact.

"Come here, little brother. Let's see what you look like." Slowly the boy edged out, biting his finger. Stuart smiled. "You look pure Winslow."

"It's odd, isn't it," she asked, looping her arm through his, "that in some families, all the members look alike. In others, they look as though they were found under a bush. No resemblance at all."

"Well, it's a good thing the Winslow men are fine-looking, isn't it, Mother?" He kissed her on the cheek and repeated, "You're looking very well indeed."

"And so are you, Son."

"Where's Father?"

"Oh, he's out on some errand for Lord Edmund. I'm sure you're hungry. Come along. I'll make you a meal."

The meal turned out to be full scale with hot mutton and fresh bread.

Stuart plied his mother with questions about the life at Stoneybrook and finally he asked, "What about Father and Lord Edmund?"

Grace dropped her head for a moment. "Lord Edmund will never forgive either of us. We keep praying, but it never changes."

"I'm sorry to hear that. Does he still overwork Father?"

"Well, not so much as he once did. Your grandmother sees to that." She laughed suddenly, and her eyes danced. "Every time Edmund tries to do something unthinkable to your father, she just mentions that perhaps she had better leave the land and this house to him. That quiets Edmund down very quickly. He's actually a very selfish man, but then he always has been."

"What about Lady Edith?"

"She still spends money as if it were dirt. Wears a dress once and then gives it away. She drives Edmund almost crazy, and I can see why."

Half an hour later Claiborn came in. "Well, you're here, my boy."

Stuart rose at once, moving Quentin to his hip. "Hello, Father," he said. "You're looking well."

"Well enough for an old man."

The two men sat down to catch up. From time to time Grace would leave to take care of some household chore.

Stuart said, "Mother is really happy, isn't she?"

"Yes, she is, and so am I. That brother of yours has brought joy into our life. It's just like when you came to us. We were so happy then."

"What do you think he'll be when he grows up, Father?"

"He'll be a good man. That's what he'll be. A man of God."

As always, Stuart felt awkward when his father or mother mentioned God to him. He knew they were disappointed that he had not found the Lord and that he was living what they considered an immoral life at court. He changed the subject by saying, "Well, I don't know what kind of a world he will face."

"It'll be the same world as this one." Claiborn smiled gently, "Full of sin but also full of God. That's the way it has always been, and that's the way it always will be."

꒰꒱

Heather's eyes opened wide. "Stuart!" There was welcome in her voice and in her expression. "Come in. I didn't know you were home."

"A surprise visit. Are you busy?"

"Never too busy for you."

"You're looking absolutely fetching, Heather Evans." He took in her blond hair and her deep-blue eyes and noticed with surprise that she was a young woman now. He had always thought of her as somewhere between childhood and womanhood. Now he said, "You're growing up."

"That happens, Stuart. Are you disappointed?"

"Oh, no."

"What's wrong?"

"You sound like one of the ladies at court. They go around trying to get men to tell them how beautiful they are and how wonderful."

"And do you tell them?"

"Not very often."

The two sat there talking for a time, and he finally said, "One of these days you're going to be sought by young men."

"Why, I already am."

"Oh? Is that Howard still coming around?"

"No. He wasn't right for me."

Stuart had always enjoyed teasing Heather. "Well, I'll tell you what," he said, putting on a sober expression. "I'm going to insist on meeting these other young suitors."

"Why would you want to do that?"

"I want to be sure their intentions are honorable and that they show my dear sister the proper respect."

"Stuart, we've discussed this. I'm not your sister, and I don't need your protection."

"Well, you know how young men are with young girls."

"No, why don't you tell me?" She leaned forward, resting her pert chin in her womanly hands.

Stuart laughed. "So you've already learned some of the ways of a maid with a man. Look at you!"

She leaned back and blushed, as if embarrassed that he'd caught her out.

"Heather, you'll soon be the most beautiful woman in England. You need not cultivate any womanly wiles to draw men to you."

"Now, Stuart, let's have none of that court talk."

"You're right. That's all I hear. Nobody ever means anything they say. So I might sound as if I'm lying, but I'm not. You are beautiful."

She looked at him with a pained expression. "I wish you'd leave there."

"I can't."

"Why? You're not in love with one of those women, are you?"

"No, of course not."

Heather stared at him. "You spoke much too quickly, and I suspect you are not telling the entire truth."

"Well, there's nothing that is ultimately truthful about anything at court."

The two sat on, debating whether Stuart should leave the court or not, until an hour later when William Tyndale came in. He was delighted to see Stuart.

"Tell me about the court."

"You don't want to hear about that, not really."

"No, I don't. I was just being polite."

"What about your translations?"

"It's going to get him into trouble. That's what's going to happen," Heather said.

"Why, the king would never permit that."

"You don't know the king if you think that, Stuart," Tyndale said. "If he decides that there will be no Bibles in English, he'll burn people at the stake in order to stop it."

"No, he would never do that."

Tyndale shook his head sadly. "I can tell you've changed, my boy, but I'm praying that one day God will use you in a mighty way."

His words made Stuart uncomfortable, for he loved Tyndale. As he left the next day to go back to the court, he thought about what the man had said. "I don't know how God could use a fellow like me," he muttered. Because never had he felt more distant from God than he did now.

15

*V*ining sat beside Stuart on a bench outside the court kitchens. They had scrounged up a baked chicken and were now picking the carcass clean. Vining smacked his lips. "Delicious," he said. But his eyes were no longer on the chicken bones, but rather on a courtier passing by. He had loved women, many women, although he was married and had two children.

"I have never met your wife and children," Stuart said, setting down his chicken bone. "Where do you keep them?"

"Oh, I never let them come to court."

"Why not?"

"Because my wife is too plain. The king doesn't like plain people. He likes good-looking chaps like us and even bonnier women."

"You shouldn't speak of your wife that way."

"What way?" Vining's eyebrows shot up in surprise. "What did I say?"

"You said she was plain."

"Well, she is plain. She's always been plain. But she had a lot of money. From her first marriage. Her husband had the good grace to die and leave all his wealth to Millie. So she was glad enough to get a handsome fellow like me with a title. It works

well for both of us. I share her money, and she has something
good to look at now."

"You are a scoundrel, Charles!"

"Well, of course I am. Always have been. But the king under-
stands that."

"So where do you keep your family?"

"Oh, we have a country house not far from London. I go
there on occasion to give her a little cheer and comfort. She
gives me a pocketful of money. Otherwise how would I possibly
afford to stay here?"

"I thought the king supplied you with money."

"Well, he does. He's very generous, but it's not nearly
enough. Not when one dresses as I do. You'd be wise to spend
some of your winnings on a new wardrobe, Stuart. Some day
soon we'll be meeting the king's new bride."

"New bride? Please tell me he is not serious—that he will
not really divorce Catherine."

Vining gave him a wry look. "Ah, prepare for more disillu-
sionment, my young friend. The king wants a son more than
anything else. And haven't you discovered yet that whatever
Henry wants, Henry is going to get? He can do that, you know."

"But he couldn't make a harlot the queen!"

"Oh yes he could. Some of the mistresses have been rather
nice, actually. Anne Stafford was a pretty girl, soft and pleasant.
I think I might have made headway with her myself, but of
course that wouldn't have been a politic choice, would it now?"

"How many have there been?"

"Oh, I've lost count. There was one called Jane Popyngcort.
A horrible name, isn't it? Well, anyway, she was his mistress.
She was maid of honor to Queen Catherine." He suddenly
laughed again. "Honor. A maid of honor. Isn't that a laugh?
Henry got tired of her and sent her off with a reward of a hun-
dred pounds."

"And the others?"

"Oh, the others, the others. Elizabeth Blount, or Bessie, as she was called, was a court beauty. She sang and danced beautifully and was rather loose in her morals. Back in the year eighteen she became the king's mistress. A rather ironic thing it was, Stuart. Henry was guarding Catherine's health, hoping that the child she was carrying would be a boy, while Bessie birthed a child that was a boy—and lived."

"What happened to him?"

"His name is Henry Fitzroy, and he's been assigned a princely household like that of the king's legitimate daughter."

"He's still alive?"

"Oh, yes. He may be king some day. Who knows? Henry could do that. Then after Bessie there was Mary Boleyn—well, actually, Mary Boleyn Carey. Henry kept her for quite a while. And so it goes. It's all become rather boring, actually."

It was not boring in the least to Stuart. His own fall into immorality had brought shame to him, but he was still capable of being shocked. Now knowing this history in full, he felt that the world was a lesser place. He had admired King Henry and seen in him a strong man full of courage and knightly virtues. To find that he was no more than a mere serial adulterer sickened him. He'd known enough of the story, of course. It was impossible to dodge the gossips, impossible not to see it with his own eyes over the years. But the idea that it was all common knowledge was truly outrageous.

He thought of Queen Catherine and her daughter, Mary. Catherine had few friends who were not seeking some favor from the king or from her, but Stuart sought nothing but to be a companion to both mother and child. Stuart wiped his mouth on a cloth and rose.

"Where are you off to?" Vining asked.

"To see the queen, I believe."

"You won't mention—"

"Of course not. Give me a little credit, Vining. I've learned a bit about how the court moves over the years. I know what is a safe topic for our lady—and what is not."

"Mind that you don't let anything slip," Vining said doubtfully. "She can be fearsome in her wrath. And Henry's current, mad ideas about religion frustrate her and make her fearful. One doesn't want to be caught between them."

He would play any game that Mary wanted for hours at a time, and today was no different. So hard did they play, running about the corridors and gardens in a game of hide and seek, that he finally persuaded her to sit beside him to read a book, only to have her fall asleep, her face against his shoulder. Stuart looked up to see Catherine leaning against the doorframe, watching them.

"She's such a beautiful girl, Your Majesty."

"More than some," Catherine said with a smile. "She dotes on you. She talks about you all the time. You're her favorite playmate."

"She must give you a great deal of pleasure."

A slight cloud crossed Catherine's face. "She does. If only she had been a boy. That disappointed the king."

"Does he love her?" Stuart asked cautiously.

"He doesn't think about her." There was sadness in Catherine's tone, and she said quietly, "It was my task to bring a son to Henry, and I haven't done it."

"You may yet."

"If God wills." She turned suddenly and said, "Are you a Catholic? You never talk about your faith."

"I'm a very poor example when it comes to faith. I was baptized, of course, when I was a baby. But my religion has become . . . unimportant. Other things occupy my mind."

"You should do something about that."

"I'm sure I will in time. For a while I spent a great deal of every day reading a Bible."

"It's difficult to be a good Catholic."

"Why do you say so?"

"Because in England it's different from Spain, my country. In Spain there was no question. Everybody was religious. They had to be."

"Was that good, in your opinion? A forced religion?"

"It's the right thing, the right way," Catherine said firmly.

He looked into her dark eyes, saw her furrowed brow. "But something is troubling you, Majesty, about the church?"

Catherine's eyes almost glittered with her passion. "God made the church, the Catholic Church, beginning with Saint Peter. There are not two churches. Only one. Men want to change that." She hesitated, then said, "My husband may be one of them."

"But the pope has bestowed on him the title Defender of the Faith."

"He wrote a paper defending the church. That was why he was given that title, but he feels little allegiance to her."

"I'm sorry to hear it."

"As am I. It grieves my heart."

"How do you think people want to change the church?"

"They're never satisfied," she said with disgust, pacing now. "It's mostly this man Martin Luther stirring up trouble among the people. Some even wish to take the Bible out of Latin and translate it into English."

Stuart asked as mildly as he could, "Please, I don't understand your fear. What harm might be found in an English Bible?"

"It could be very bad."

"How so?"

She stilled and faced him, incredulous. "Because only priests are trained to understand the Scripture. It's kept in Latin so that the common people will not take the Scripture and twist it. They do that, you know. They've already tried through the ages."

And so can the pope, Stuart almost said, but luckily caught himself. "I know a man whose whole purpose in life is to do exactly that, translate the Bible into English."

"Who is he?" Catherine demanded, leaning forward, and then at once she closed her eyes and leaned back. "No, don't tell me. I would have his life in my hands, and I don't want that."

"You don't mean that he could be harmed for translating the Bible!"

"Under certain conditions he could be burned at the stake."

At once Stuart saw the work of William Tyndale in an entirely different light. He knew that there was a movement to stop the translation. The king, so far, had taken no active part, so he asked tentatively, "Is the king opposed to an English translation?"

"Not at present, but I think he will be."

"I didn't know that."

"Perhaps you'd like to meet with my chaplain. I'm sure he could help you answer some of your questions—the questions that obviously keep you from investing in your faith."

"That would be most kind, but your husband keeps me very busy."

"I can see to that. Perhaps the three of us could pursue this matter together."

Stuart paused. Vining's parting words—"*One doesn't want to be caught between them*"—echoed in his mind. But what was he to do? Queen Catherine awaited his answer. And he had never refused her. "I would be most honored, Your Majesty."

※

Three days later, when Stuart was walking along one of the broad pathways in the garden next to the castle, deep in thoughts of Queen Catherine, he heard his name called and turned to see Charles Vining with an attractive young lady.

"Come, Winslow," Vining called out. "Come and walk with us a while."

At once Stuart joined them. "Mistress Anne," he said with a nod.

"Master Winslow."

"Welcome back to court."

"I confess I missed it," she said, with a smile that was impossible not to return. "The country is terribly boring. This is where I belong." She looped one hand through Stuart's arm and the other through Charles's, and they resumed their walk around the gardens. Stuart's face burned, and he scanned the windows, hoping the queen did not spy them together.

Anne Boleyn was not what one would call a beautiful woman, but she was an intensely attractive one. She had a heavy cascade of glossy black hair that freely fell down her back. Her best features were her large dark eyes. They were lively and curious and gave an impression of intimacy even upon this first, casual meeting. "So, do tell, Master Winslow," she said, with a graceful inclination of her head, "How fare your birds?"

"Do you speak of the king's hunting birds," Charles put in, "or Nell Fenton?"

Anne had a deep, pleasant laugh. "Nell mentions you often, sir."

"I'm surprised," Vining said. "Winslow here claims she hasn't thought about him in months."

"Oh, a lady's attention can always be recaptured. Just as a man's can." She cocked an eyebrow at Stuart.

"I wish it could," Stuart said regretfully. "But I fear I've tried everything with Nell over the years. It appears hopeless."

"Leave us now, Sir Charles. I'm going to instruct Master Winslow on how to secure the affections of the young lady he so desires."

"If anyone could teach such a thing, it would be you, my dear." Charles grinned and moved away, laughing softly.

"Shall we continue our walk, Master Winslow?"

"My pleasure, Mistress Boleyn."

She spoke freely of her life in France, but hardly mentioned her family. She was the most vivacious woman Stuart had ever seen, and in spite of his devotion to the queen, he was completely taken by her.

"Well, now, tell me about your prospects."

"Well, to be truthful, I don't have many, madam. I have no title and no property and little money. I am merely keeper of the mews."

"Come, now. I happen to know the king is very proud of his birds. But about Nell?"

"I fear it's hopeless."

"Oh, you must never say that! There never was a woman born who couldn't be taken by spirit and determination. Now, let me tell you how to catch her interest. . . ."

❧

"She'll be the next queen," Charles said quietly in Stuart's ear as they watched Anne with the king. "Mark what I tell you."

"I don't believe it. The king has a wife."

"Nearly nine years at court, and still you remain naive! Just watch how the king hangs over Anne, and watch her when she speaks to this fellow Wyatt. There! Are you watching? He's head over heels in love with Anne."

Stuart watched as Anne moved through the crowd, stopping to speak to a lady, then greeting a lord. All the while both Wyatt and the king had a difficult time looking anywhere but in her direction.

"Heavens, Vining, you just may be right." He looked to the queen, who was managing to watch the court festivities as if nothing at all was wrong. "He's a poet, you say? The man who seeks Anne's attentions?"

"A dead poet, if he doesn't end his pursuit and the king finds out about it."

Three days later, Stuart had the opportunity to put Charles Vining's assertion to the test. He had followed the crowd that was
watching the king playing at bowls. Also in the crowd was the
poet Wyatt, and Stuart heard an interchange between the two.
During the game, Wyatt had displayed a trinket belonging to
Anne, and King Henry produced a ring that she had given him.
The atmosphere grew tense.

It had never occurred to Henry, Stuart saw, that Anne might
give one of her favors to another man. Henry could not conceal
his anger. He fixed his eyes on Wyatt and said gruffly, "You have
been deceived, sir."

Charles, standing next to Stuart, whispered, "Well, that's the
end of whatever romance there was between Wyatt and Anne
Boleyn."

"What do you mean by that?"

"Why, the Boleyns and the Wyatts depend on royal good will,
and you won't find either Anne or Thomas doing anything to
endanger that. No, I wager we'll see Wyatt melt sadly and wisely
into the background."

"I'll take that wager. A sovereign?"

"Make it two, you fool. I'm happy to take your money. You
must have noticed the king's infatuation with Anne Boleyn,"
Charles insisted. "Why should you be surprised?"

"I just don't believe she's that kind of young woman."

Charles stared at his friend in disbelief. He started to argue
and then changed his mind. "Well, time will tell. And when it
does, I'll have two new coins in my pocket."

"Isn't there anything that can be done for this gossip,
Charles? It is most damaging to Mistress Anne."

"No, there isn't. Henry doesn't burden himself with the
morals of ordinary men. He thinks he's above such things. It's
merely a part of courtly life. You know that by now."

"But Henry is married to Catherine. Such idle stories will hurt her."

"But if Henry pays no attention to God or man, why should he pay attention to his wife? And if he decides that Anne Boleyn will be his mistress, then it's as good as done."

❧

"There's a man to see you at the gate, Master Winslow."

"Who is it?"

"Don't know, sir."

Stuart went to the gate and found Orrick, one of the Stoney-brook servants. One look at his face told him that bad news was his errand. "What is it, Orrick?"

"It's your grandmother, sir, Lady Leah. She's very sick. Your father said to bring you at once."

Fear filled him. His whole family depended upon Lady Leah. *What will happen to Mother and Father and Quentin if she dies?*

"I'll come at once. Let me get a few things, and I'll fetch a horse from the stable."

❧

Stuart tumbled off his horse and threw his reins to a Stoney-brook stableboy who said, "I'll take care of the animal, sir."

As soon as Stuart came into the hall, he saw his father sitting at the oak table, his hands clasped and misery on his face.

"How is she, Father?"

"She's dying, Son."

"Surely not! There must be something that can be done. Is the doctor here?"

"Come and gone. There's nothing he can do. It's the sweating sickness."

The words brought a cold chill to Stuart. The sweating sickness was much like the plague, a lurking danger every spring and summer. Stuart had seen the disease even among the court.

It struck without warning. Its victims broke out in a heavy sweat and emitted a horrible odor. They turned red all over and developed a high fever. In the last stage a rash appeared, and death soon followed.

And now his beloved grandmother had it.

"Are you certain?"

"The doctor is. Just pray God it doesn't affect the rest of the family."

"Where are Mother and Quentin?"

"At a neighbor's. I don't want them anywhere near. But I knew you'd want to see her, regardless of the danger."

"You were right. Thank you."

Stuart went to the bedroom his grandmother favored. He saw there was no hope. She looked like a shrunken mummy, and she was covered with red blotches. Going to her bed, he knelt down and whispered, "Grandmother, can you hear me?"

There was a long silence, and then Lady Leah's eyes opened. Her voice was so faint that he had to lean forward. "I'm glad you came, Stuart. I have a final message for you."

"What is it, Grandmother? "

"You must learn to love God." The words were broken; speaking took all of her strength. "And you must leave the court."

There was no answer for that except "God bless you, Grandmother. You've been such a blessing to us."

"Get your father."

Instantly he jumped up and ran to open the door. "Father, come at once!"

Claiborn came in and went to the other side of Leah's bed. Neither of them seemed to fear death.

She reached up her hands, and each man took one. "You have been my treasure. Claiborn, you are a true man of God." She said a few more words to him, and then her voice faded as she said, "Follow Jesus, Stuart. Always follow Jesus." There was a long silence, and after a time she whispered something that Claiborn could not hear. "What did she say, Stuart?"

Stuart's throat was tight, and his lips were dry. "She said, 'I'm going to be with my Savior.'"

That was the last word spoken by Leah Winslow, and shortly afterward the two men rose to their feet. "She was a woman of God, and she loved you dearly," Claiborn said. "Never forget what she said."

Stuart's throat was so tight that he could not answer. He just nodded. "Yes," he finally managed to say. As he left the room, he knew that something had changed that could never be brought back again—at least not in this world.

⚭

"Well, the old woman is finally gone," Edith said almost carelessly.

Lord Edmund was stricken, for he had cared, in his fashion, after his mother. He was shocked by his wife's callousness. "She was a good woman," he said.

"Of course, I know that. I didn't mean to be cruel."

"You never cared for her."

"I did! I just didn't show it the way others do," Edith said.

"The lawyer was here this afternoon," Edmund said. There was something furtive in his manner of speaking, and Edith gave him a sharp glance.

"Why are you looking so odd? She left you all the land, didn't she?"

Edmund cleared his throat. "No, she didn't. She left that tract of land to Claiborn—and the house too."

"She couldn't have!" Edith's face flushed, and anger poured out of her. "It's yours by right!" Ives moved behind her and placed a hand on her shoulder.

"No, that acreage was hers all along, I'm afraid. That's what the lawyer says. She could leave it to anyone she wanted to. We'll have to persuade Claiborn to put the land in his will in order to unite Stoneybrook at some point, make her stronger."

"He'll never do that," Edith snapped.

They argued and tried to find a plan, but Edmund finally said heavily, "There's nothing we can do. The land is theirs." He was upset, but he had halfway expected it. "She loved Claiborn the best. She always did."

❦

Claiborn looked out the window but saw nothing, for his thoughts were of his mother. Grace came to stand beside him, and said gently, "She saved us, didn't she?"

"Yes, she did. I don't know what would have happened to us if she hadn't brought us here."

"What will happen to the land now?"

"This land? Why, it's ours, Grace. Mother's tract of land, this house. She showed me her will."

"You mean we don't have to live under Edmund's rule?"

"No, not in the least. We're freer then ever. We can elect to separate the land from Stoneybrook, till this soil as our own."

"Thank God! I could never tell you how hard it was for me seeing Edmund mistrust you as he did."

"Well, I still have hopes of Edmund's changing. I'm hoping that this final act of mother's will encourage him to take another look at me, at us."

"Edith won't be pleased."

"No, but we can live with that." He took her in his arms. "We've followed where God has led us, and see what it's brought us."

"Our own home. Ours, Claiborn. Only ours." She shook her head. "I never really thought I'd see the day again, short of returning to Ireland. It almost makes me hopeful enough to join you in your hope that you and your brother can someday be reconciled."

He pulled her closer. "God will see to it in time. I'm confident in him."

⚶

The funeral was performed at once. It was a simple family affair. No one wanted to be exposed to the sweating sickness. Stuart went through it almost as if he were asleep, but actually he was stunned. He was glad when the ceremony was over and stole away to walk with Heather. She had been one of the few who had attended the services for his grandmother, and she took his arm with sadness still on her face. "Stuart. I'm so sorry for your loss. How are your father and your mother faring?"

"We're all stunned, Heather. Somehow we thought Grandmother would always be with us."

"I've heard many speak of how wonderful she was. I wish I had known her. She sounds like a fine lady."

"Thank you for coming. I didn't expect it."

"I had to come. You're important to me."

He gave her a small smile. Would anyone at court do the same for him? He couldn't imagine it. They walked and talked for a while, as comfortable together as if they saw each other every week. She said, "I have a message for you from Mr. Tyndale."

"For me? What did he say?"

Heather brought him to a stop and stared up into his eyes. "He said to tell you, Stuart, that God has a plan for you."

"God has a plan for me, eh? I must say, I'm not convinced."

"He said he knows God will use you. He's going into hiding, you know."

"Hiding!"

"Yes, his work has made him the target of many a hunter."

"That's terrible!"

"Yes, but nothing Master Tyndale seems to truly fear. Stuart, he thinks that dangerous times are coming for all of

God's people and that you're going to have to make a choice one day."

"I can't believe that the king would ever be cruel."

Heather did not answer; she knew that Stuart still had confidence in the king. She was watching him carefully. He took her hand. "You've been so kind to me always, Heather. I appreciate that more than you know."

"I could never be anything but kind to you, Stuart."

A little unnerved by the intensity of her tone, Stuart gave a half-laugh and hugged her.

He had a sudden knowledge that there was something in him that desired her, and he was shocked and appalled at his desire. He stepped back quickly and saw her smile.

"What's the matter, Stuart? You've hugged a woman before, haven't you?"

"I—I'm sorry. I'm not myself." He shook his head. What did her peculiar smile mean?

"You must return soon," she said.

"I shall. Thank you again for coming."

He could not get away quickly enough. He rode away at a full gallop.

16

Catherine was not surprised when Henry arrived. There was no secret of his intentions of late. But she would not make it easy for him.

He marched into her bedroom and after making a few false starts said, "My dear, I think you can guess what I'm going to say."

"Not at all, sir."

"I have been studying the Scripture, and it becomes more evident to me and to the priesthood of the church that we have not had a marriage. Therefore we are going to end something that never really existed."

"I do not understand you."

"You must be aware that it is stated in the book of Leviticus chapter 20, verse 21, 'If a man shall take his brother's wife, it is an impurity. He hath covered his brother's nakedness: they shall be childless.' Obviously, when I married my brother Arthur's widow, I committed a terrible sin. You, perhaps, were not aware of it, and neither was I. But there it is."

"I do not believe this is the truth," Catherine said. When Henry just stared at her, she began to weep.

"We have never been married, Catherine. We are not married now, and we never shall be." He turned on his heel and walked away, leaving Catherine to give in to her grief fully.

It was Anne Boleyn whom he wanted, Anne who he believed would bear him the coveted male heir.

Catherine watched when Henry left the castle and strode away, walking as if free of a burden. Herself. Mary. She pounded the stone wall as she watched him stride, almost floating. On the far side were three ladies-in-waiting. One was Anne Boleyn.

The woman turned to greet the king. He drew her away and tucked her hand in the crook of his arm. He leaned his head down to hers, talking. Anne stopped, then looked over his shoulder at the queen's apartments. Catherine lifted her chin and squared her shoulders, boldly meeting the temptress's gaze.

But Anne just gave a small smile, then turned and led King Henry away.

※

The king stared at Wolsey and said bluntly, "Wolsey, I have never been married to Catherine. I've explained this to you. God has chastised me and punished me by not giving me a son. And you're going to help me rectify that."

Wolsey saw what was coming and dreaded it. "But, sire, there's no way—"

"Say no more, Wolsey! You will go to the pope and you will explain to him that I have no wife and never had a wife. All he has to do is pronounce that my previous connection to Catherine was null and void and not of God. The Scripture plainly says so." The king did not need to observe formalities in private.

"Please, Your Majesty, do not do this!"

Henry's voice was tinged with the threat of something dark and deadly. "This is your task. The one thing I ask of you. Do not fail me, sir." He turned and walked out.

Wolsey began to tremble. He knew that if he failed in this,

he was in danger of dismissal—if not death. But however he viewed it, he had no hope of success.

☼

The king loved to write letters, and he sent a series of love letters to Anne Boleyn. One of the first said:

> *My mistress and friend,*
> *I and my heart commit themselves into your hands be-seeching you to hold us recommended to your good favor, and that your affections to us may not be by absence diminished.*

Henry had discovered that he could not live without Anne Boleyn. It was that simple. He sought to keep himself constantly before her and in her thoughts when he was not present. He sent her his picture, bracelets, fine jewelry. In every way he could, he tried to draw the dark beauty.

Not long after this letter the king received a gift in reply. It was a piece of jewelry, a beautiful diamond, and a miniature ship with a tiny passenger. The passenger was a solitary damsel. Henry was thrilled and completely charmed by the gift. It told him that Anne felt affection for him. As soon as he received it, he began to write more urgent love letters stating plainly that he could dedicate his body to Anne and desired her as his own.

Yet Anne did not respond, which surprised Henry a great deal, for women always did. Anne confessed at the start that she had never in her heart wanted to love the king. Her letters sent him into despair. He had loved her for more than a year now and wanted never to stop.

And so the king's "great matter," which was what the divorce with Catherine came to be called, became a matter of international news, and the characters in the drama, Henry, Catherine, and Anne Boleyn, were watched constantly to see how the drama would end.

❧

Stuart, of course, was aware of the king's insistence on a divorce. One afternoon he visited Mary; as usual, Catherine was there. He played with the girl for some time, and Catherine sat to one side. From time to time she would smile, but there was a cloud over her, and when Mary went off to gather some flowers, she said in a wan voice, "It was kind of you to come by, Master Winslow."

"It's always a pleasure, Your Majesty."

Catherine seemed to be debating whether to speak her mind. Finally she did. "I suppose you know that the king is determined to divorce me."

"Well, Your Majesty, I have heard talk."

"Of course you have. Everyone in the kingdom has heard it! It's foolishness! We are man and wife, and I have borne him many children. Unfortunately God saw fit to take them from us except for Mary. He says we were never married." And then for the first time she broke down and began to cry.

Stuart watched her helplessly. If she had been anyone except the queen, he might have gone to her, taken her hand, and shown his concern. But she was the queen.

He bowed his head and waited until the fit of crying was passed. Then he heard her say, "Thank you for bearing with a weeping woman."

"I'm so sorry, Your Majesty. I'm certain that it will turn out better than you fear."

"No, it will not. Thank you for coming by." She rose and walked away, her head bowed and her shoulders stooped. For the first time Stuart thought of King Henry with bitterness. *He's a beast! To treat a woman like that is inhuman!*

❧

In the afternoon of that same day, Peter Morton, a young buck who led a group of equally wild young men of the court, stopped by to visit Stuart at the mews. They talked about the birds for a while, and Morton surprised him with his knowledge about them. He was a smallish young man with sharp features and compelling gray eyes.

"A group of us are going out tonight to have an adventure. We'd like to have you come along, Stuart."

Stuart was aware that Morton's set often went out to seek adventures. He had never been invited, and he had been envious, for they told high tales of their deeds. They did such noble things—at least, so they claimed.

"There's a poor young girl who's being persecuted by a villain. He's threatened to harm her if she doesn't give in to him. We're going to give him a little lesson in chivalry." He smiled and said, "Not going to stab him through the heart. Just, you might call it, an encouragement to leave the poor young woman alone."

"Sounds like it might be interesting, Peter."

"It's like something Arthur's knights would do."

Stuart hesitated. He wanted to join them, but something told him not to. "Unfortunately, I have other plans this eve."

"Oh, well. If you change your mind, let us know."

"I shall." Later, when he saw Charles, he told him of the offer.

"Better stay away from fellows like that. They're going to get into trouble and bad trouble at that."

"I didn't plan to go."

"Best thing all around."

⚬

Stuart never did understand at what point he changed his mind. Perhaps because he was half-drunk, or perhaps he was angry with the king and wanted some action. Perhaps he wanted to belong to this group of young men, who seemed to have such a fine time. He had a horse, weapons. They were friendly fellows.

For whatever reason, he found Morton in the great hall and said, "Peter, I've changed my mind. I'll go with you tonight."

Morton's face lit up. "Good! Be ready at about dusk. We'll all meet by the eastern gate."

"I'll be there."

"Remember. Bring a fast horse and come armed. The fellow isn't likely to cause any trouble, but you never can tell. There are lots of brigands roaming these hills at night."

"I'll bring my sword."

Excitement grew within him, and by the time dusk came and he had drawn his horse, he was ready for an adventure. He rode to the eastern gate, where he found Morton and four other young men. They all greeted him by name, for everyone knew the king's bird master. They were all in their early twenties and all well dressed.

"Have you brought a mask?" Morton said.

"No, I haven't."

"Well, we'll find one for you."

"Why do we have to wear masks? Let the villain see who we are!"

"You never know what you might run into," said Clive Beason, a muscular young man with a broad grin. "We're going to have a good time tonight. Just like the knights of old."

Morton rode out, and the rest followed him. They went to an inn outside London. "What are we stopping here for, Peter?"

"Well, this is thirsty work. We're going to have a bit to drink, and we'll see what action we can get here."

The action that they got there proved to be getting half-drunk and some dalliance with the local harlot. This went on until rather late, and finally Stuart said, "Peter, I didn't come out here to get drunk and to chase around after harlots."

"You're right. Let's go, men." He got up, swaying a bit. All of them were drunk except for Stuart.

They mounted up and rode for half an hour, but only managed to get themselves lost. The moon shed its silver beams on the landscape and as they found the road again one of the men said, "Look, here comes a courier."

"That's Samuel Marshall. He comes along this road every night about this time, and he always has money."

"He isn't alone this time."

"Let's take them. We'll see what Marshall's got in his pouch. Maybe some juicy love letters from the king himself."

Stuart was alarmed. "We don't need to be doing that. Let's get about our business."

"Right after we stop these fellows and shake them down," Morton said. "Come on, men."

The four rode forward. Stuart followed reluctantly. He watched as they stopped the two riders and then was alarmed when he saw a brawl break out. Morton drew his sword and pierced the courier. The other man immediately turned and fled.

Hurrying forward, Stuart bent over the wounded man and said, "This fellow is dying."

"We have to get out of here," Peter said. "Come on."

"You can't just leave him here."

Even as he spoke, they heard horses coming. "It's the night guard," Morton shouted. "Come on! Get away!"

They all fled except Stuart. He remained, trying to staunch the blood that poured from the man's chest.

"Whoa! What are you doing here?" boomed a large man. "What's wrong with that man?"

"He's been hurt. We must get him to a doctor."

The leader came forward and said, "That's Marshall. He's carrying the gold for the king's purpose."

"Well, it's gone now," another said in disgust. "This fellow's dying."

Stuart rose, shaking. "He's dead already."

The leader said sternly, "You are under arrest for robbery and murder of the king's man. That makes it treason."

His words seemed to ring in Stuart's ear like a funeral dirge. He tried to explain. "But I wasn't even part—"

"You'll have your day in court, but I'll tell you one thing," the leader said harshly. "You've killed a popular man here and robbed the king's treasury. You're apt to be hanged, drawn, and quartered! Tie him up and put him on his horse. "

A numbness came over Stuart Winslow. He thought, *What a blasted fool I've been! I should have had better sense. But surely it will come out all right.*

He would explain how it all happened. Instantly he recognized that none of Peter Morton's men were likely to stand by him. They would not want to bear the punishment of this terrible crime. He alone would bear it.

17

*S*tuart was dreaming of emerald-green fields and flowers the color of Heather's eyes. He was lying in a field, and overhead he saw a beautiful sky across which fleecy clean clouds moved with infinite grace . . . but something brushed against his face. It disturbed the beauty of the dream, and he reached up with one hand to brush it away.

Something clamped down on his hand. He uttered a shrill cry, opened his eyes, and there by the feeble light of the single candle was a huge rat! Stuart's entire body froze. The rat looked up at him and bared yellow teeth and twitched a scaly tail.

Stuart yelled and knocked the ugly creature away, but the rats had learned boldness in the prison. It came charging back at him. Stuart kicked at it, missed, and the rat bit into his ankle.

Stuart picked up a bucket, the only thing he had for a weapon. It was full of waste. He brought it down on the rat. The bucket hit it on the neck, and it squealed but continued its attack. Again and again Stuart raised the bucket, using the edge of it as a weapon. The waste matter sloshed all over him, but he struck the rat until the filthy creature was dead.

With a shudder of revulsion, Stuart picked up the rat by the scaly tail and dropped it into the bucket. He put it as far away as he could from the sleeping mat, which was not far from him in the eight-foot cell.

The stench was overwhelming.

For two weeks Stuart had been in the cell, and he still was not used to the horrible odors of confinement. And now his own waste covered his hair and clothes. He dropped his head into trembling hands.

"Oh, God," he cried out, "why am I in this awful place? Have you forgotten me, God?"

This was typical of Stuart's prayers during his incarceration. He called out to God, sometimes bitter, other times pleading for help, but the result was the same. None of the prayers, no matter what their tone, were at all effective.

He rose and paced the floor, a a short distance in the narrow cell. *Back and forth, take three steps, the last shorter than the others, turn, and repeat until you reach the other wall.* It made no difference whether he had his eyes open or shut, so well did he know this cell.

He had been in prison now for only two weeks, but it seemed like a millennium to him. The stone blocks that made up the cell were damp, and it seemed to Stuart that into their porous fiber had soaked the misery of the poor wretches who had been confined within their stony walls. The stones were clammy and the floors were damp, and he had not been warm in the two weeks he had been there. He had one thin blanket, which he wore constantly draped around his neck, but it did little to cut the awful chill that seemed to emanate from the stones and seep all the way down into his bones.

As he walked back and forth, it occurred to Stuart that worse than the terrible odors, worse even than the rats or the fleas, was the boredom of the cell, from which there was absolutely no break. No books, no paper, no ink to write with, nothing to see. There were no windows in the cell. He thought at times that he would lose his mind just sitting there hour after hour after hour with no one to talk to, no one to listen to him.

The guards came twice a day and brought his food, such as it was. Most of them were hardened to the plight of the prisoners. There was one, however, Alfred Jennings, who had been, for some reason, kind to him. When Stuart had mentioned how awful it was to sit there in the dark, Jennings had said nothing, but the next time he came he brought a small sack. "I thought you might like these, Winslow."

"What is it, Master Jennings?"

"It's the stubs of candles. When they burn pretty low, we replace them. Might be a little bit of cheer for you."

Stuart's throat had grown thick at the unexpected kindness. "Thank you, Master Jennings. It will make a difference."

Indeed, the small candles, most of them less than an inch long, were a godsend. Stuart lit a dying light with another stub. They cast a feeble yellow glow over the cell, and even though there was nothing to read except the scratched dates and names of prisoners, at least it wasn't total darkness. He wondered how many prisoners had sat in this cell, how many had gone into eternity swinging from a noose or kneeling to place their head on the block for the headsman to finish the job.

Such thoughts were not unusual for him, and finally he walked until he was tired. He sat down on what was really nothing but a length of sackcloth sewn up on one side and stuffed with straw years before. Every time Stuart sat on it, tiny fragments would rise like dust, getting into his eyes and nose.

For a long time he sat there, counting the stones of his prison. There was no plan, no regular size for the stones. He knew well that there were a hundred and twelve stones in the inner wall, a hundred and twenty-three in the outer wall, and one of the short walls had one hundred and four and the other ninety-five.

There was little sound, for the stone soaked up anything that came from the outside. Stuart would have given anything to have heard the song of a bird or the barking of an excited dog, but nothing like that seemed likely to happen in here. Finally he leaned his head back against the wall and engaged himself in his favorite game. He went over his life as far back in his memory as he could reach. He had done this before and had thought over every moment of his past—or so he thought—but he had been shocked by how much had come out of some deep place in his soul where memories lingered as guests of his spirit.

Some of the memories were good, some were bad—and some were shameful. He thought of people he hadn't seen for years, and suddenly he thought of an incident that had taken place when he had been no more than eleven or twelve years old, just emerging from childhood. There had been a girl named Cassie. He couldn't remember her last name, but he could conjure up her face. She had red hair and green eyes with small flecks in them. They had been friends, for her family had lived nearby. He remembered that they had taken a shortcut through the woods beside Stoneybrook and finally come upon a stream that curved into a pool, where you could see the silver flashes of minnows as they scooted along the sandy bottom.

Cassie had said, "Let's go swimming."

"Are you daft, girl? It's getting onto autumn now."

"Don't be such a baby." She had started taking off her dress, and he remembered staring at her in consternation.

"What are you doing?"

"Going swimming. Get your clothes off, boy."

He saw the carnal knowledge in the girl's eyes and knew that this was nothing new for her. He had mumbled, "No, I'm not going to do it" and had turned and run away. She had laughed and called him some name that he did not even recognize at the time. So long ago . . . So innocent he had been. He wondered whether the girl had married, if she had had children, if she had died of the plague.

He went back and forth in his mind, like walking by a row of pictures. He would stop at one memory and think of it and savor the colors. Then he would go to another picture.

There was a rattling sound as the steel door of his cell opened, a cup of ale and another for food were shoved inside, and the door was quickly shut again. The cup held some kind of fish stew, which smelled foul, but Stuart had learned to eat whatever was given to him to keep up his strength. He stirred the soup slowly with a wooden spoon and found an eyeball in it along with some bones. A shiver went over him, but he was changed now. He had determined to survive, to live, so he ate the eyeball as if it were a delicious piece of candy. He ate slowly, holding the morsel of food in his mouth as long as possible, chewing it. Then he sipped the ale. Sometimes he was given ale, sometimes beer, sometimes tepid water. This time it was ale. He would take a little of it in his mouth, then he would run it over his tongue, and finally he had finished it all.

For a time he was almost in a trance, not asleep, not awake. He began to think of scriptures, mostly those he had heard his father read. One of his father's favorites, in particular, kept coming back; "It is glory of God to conceal a thing, but the honor of kings is to search out a matter."

Stuart thought it unfair of God to conceal things and make men look for them.

Sleep edged in, pulled him under.

18

S tuart had been in his cell now for three weeks, and except for several visits from his parents, the only faces he ever saw were those of the guards. There was no word from the king's court, nor from the king himself. Hope drained from him. He was filled with fear. A certain amount of terror came from recognizing the immensity of eternity. To be cut off from all that was good, all that was lovely, and all that was worthy forever! More than once he fought the desire to run at the wall and beat his head against it until the morbid thoughts left him. But something kept him from doing it.

He felt a great, barren sadness in him as he recognized what he would lose when the headsman chopped his head off or the hangman dropped the trap from beneath his feet. All the things he had planned—to prove his love to his parents, the excitement of new things, the face of a woman who loved him.

He spent hours thinking of what he would lose if he died. Foremost, of course, he dreaded to lose the company of his parents. The shame he had always felt because he had turned away from their simple faith burned in him, and he wept over the loss. He thought often of losing Heather and spent hours thinking of the pleasure he had always taken in her company.

And the simple things, such as the dew on the grass in the morning or pulling a fish out of a stream gleaming silver in the morning sunlight, feeling the weight on the line. He thought of the birds, the falcons and hawks that delighted him with their sweeps through the air and their plummeting drop onto the prey below. All this would be taken from him in a breath.

Then, his musings were broken off and he was surprised to see a priest come in. He got to his feet. The priest, a large man with a swollen belly and fleshy cheeks, stared at him with pale eyes. "Shut the door, guard," he said in a French accent. "I'll call you when I want out."

"Yes, Father."

The priest studied Stuart for a time. "I am Father Lafavor," he said. "I have come to give you instructions on what you must do as you face death."

"You're a little early, aren't you? I haven't even had a trial yet."

Lafavor smiled, but the smile never reached his eyes. His lips were thin though his face was fleshy; his neck was so fat that it rolled over his collar. "You certainly don't entertain any hope of being found innocent, do you, my son?"

His use of the words *my son* irritated Stuart. He almost said, *I'm not your son,* but didn't want to send away his only companion in days. "Thank you for coming," he said stiffly.

"Very well. Now, then, we must talk. I am glad to promise you that although it is not usual for prisoners to be executed to receive extreme unction, I am going to offer it to you."

"Why bother? What does it mean? Extreme unction?"

Lafavor glared at Stuart. "You do not know the elements of your faith?"

"Please. Indulge me."

"It is a ceremony, of course, and if it is performed a few moments before death, your soul will be safe although the body will be dead."

This seemed like foolishness to him. He could not believe that a man's character could be changed, saved, by another man mumbling a few words.

Lafavor went on with his explanation, his tone very dispassionate and learned. The explanation was studded with Latin phrases, and there was no comfort in him. He was a cold man. *Obviously he doesn't care about me,* Stuart thought.

Finally Stuart said, "I am sorry. I don't care whether I have this ceremony or not."

The priest's little eyes narrowed. "You will go to hell if you do not have it. A man who has done what you have done."

"You don't know what I've done."

"I certainly do. I read the charges."

A hot reply rose to Stuart's lips, but he shook off the temptation. There would be nothing gained by engaging in a debate with Lafavor. "I would like you to tell me where in the Bible we have this matter of extreme unction."

For the first time Lafavor looked uncomfortable. He cleared his throat and spat on the floor. "This is not a matter for laymen. It is a matter for men of the church. The pope. The cardinals. The bishops. They all have decided that this is true."

"Suppose they decided that it would save a man's soul if you poured tar all over his head just before he died. Would that make it so?"

"You are a heretic, sir, a heretic!"

"Just give me a scripture, and I will gladly do what you say. Just where in the Bible does it say that?"

"It does not say that, but it is a matter of doctrine. The church adopted it years ago, and it will stand forever."

"So you say, Father, that a man must receive this ceremony just before he dies or he will perish forever in the flames of hell."

"That is exactly what will happen."

"Did you never read the story of the crucifixion of Jesus?"

Lafavor's eyes widened. "Of course I have—many times."

"So have I."

"You lie! It's in Latin."

Stuart made his reply in Latin. *"Religentem esse oporet: Relegio sum nefas."* This quotation, taught to Stuart by William Tyndale, in English would be "It is reasonable to be religious, abominable to be superstitious."

Stuart's use of Latin brought Lafavor to a halt. He started to speak, changed his mind, and then said, "Where did you learn Latin?"

"My father taught it to me."

"Well, he undoubtedly instilled false doctrine in your mind as well."

"As I recall," Stuart said, and he smiled at the priest, "Jesus was crucified between two thieves. One of them was unrepentant, but the other told him to shut his mouth. He said, if I remember correctly, 'We're guilty. We deserve what we're getting. But this man had done nothing.' Then he said to Jesus, 'Remember me when you come into your kingdom.' Do you remember what Jesus said?"

"I—it matters not."

"It does. He said, 'This day you shall be with me in paradise.' We have the history of that thief dying, and we have no record of any priest or bishop or pope administering any ceremony."

Lafavor's face grew red. "Heresy! Undoubtedly the result of a Bible in the hands of laymen, who misinterpret it."

"Thank you for coming. I will forego the ceremony if you don't mind."

Lafavor glared at Stuart and then banged on the door. "Guard! Guard, let me out of here!" He said, "You will perish in the flames of hell forever."

"Good day to you, Father Lafavor."

The priest passed through, his back stiff, the door clanged shut, and for the first time since he had been in the place, Stuart laughed. It was not a healthy or a hearty laugh, but at least it was a laugh, and he said to the walls, "Come back any time, Father, for another lesson in doctrine!"

The keeper of the Tower guards straightened, and his jaw dropped in amazement. Not once before had the queen visited the prison, and her appearance struck the guard dumb for a moment. "Your Majesty," he whispered. "I didn't expect to see you here!"

Queen Catherine held Mary's hand. She said, "Put me in a private room, then bring the prisoner Stuart Winslow to me."

"But that would take an order from the king!"

"No, it would take an order from your queen. If you want to debate this further, sir, I will see to it that others come with more direct methods than mine."

"N-no, Your Majesty, not necessary! Please come this way." His face had turned pale. Opening the door to an adequate room, he said, "If you will wait here, Majesty, I will have the prisoner brought, but perhaps it would be best if we—if we gave him a brief bath."

"No, bring him just as he is, Guard."

"Yes, Your Majesty."

The guard shut the door quietly and hurried to the others. "Let Winslow out."

"Is it time for him to hang?" the corridor guard asked.

"Shut your mouth, fool! Just do what I tell you."

The guard shrugged and opened the door.

The chief guard, whose name was Gatlin, said, "Winslow, you have a visitor."

Stuart was on the cot with his back against the wall. He looked past the guard. "Where is he?"

"You're to meet this visitor in a private room. Follow me. Make no attempt to escape. It would be futile."

Stuart rose and followed the guard, wondering if he could manage to get to this private room, being so weak. But he was curious, and so he kept moving. He stared in wonder at the flickering torches; they were so much brighter than his feeble candles that it took a moment for his eyes to get used to the light. Finally the guard opened a door and stepped back, saying, "Your Majesty, when you are finished, please call me."

"I will do so."

Majesty!

Stuart stepped into the room, astonished to see Queen Catherine and Princess Mary. He bowed to them and said, "I'm grateful for your visit, Your Majesty. Hello, Princess."

"They've treated you badly, Master Winslow."

"Prisoners usually get bad treatment."

Mary had come closer. "You smell foul, and you're dirty! Why don't you take a bath?"

"I would love to, but they don't furnish such luxuries here in the Tower."

"What did you do to get put here?"

Stuart raised his eyes at the girl's question and met Catherine's. She was waiting expectantly for him to answer.

"I'm accused of having killed a man."

Mary's eyes flew open. "Did you do it?"

"No, I didn't."

"Then don't stay in this place."

Stuart laughed. "There is nothing I would like better, Princess, but I'm not permitted to leave."

"I am sorry you have had such ill treatment," Catherine said. "I will see to it that it improves. What would you like?"

"A bath, Your Majesty. I didn't realize how important bathing was until it was taken away from me."

"That will be easy enough. Your cell is uncomfortable?"

"There's no light except for little bits of candles. Nothing to read. Nothing to do. A man finds out who he is when he's locked up in a cage like that, and I don't like most of the things I've found."

"Tell me the truth, Master Winslow. It will never go past us. Just the three of us. Mary would never tell, would you, Mary?"

"No, madam."

"Are you innocent of this crime you are accused of?"

"With God as my witness, I am."

Catherine studied him. "I believe you," she whispered. "Have you obtained paid counsel?"

"No. I doubt if my family could afford it."

"I will go to the king. It has been some time since he has received me. This is as good a reason as any to approach him. Do not fret, my friend. I have a plan."

"Well, that's more than I have," Stuart said wryly, "but for any help you can give me, I will be most deeply grateful."

"You have been a good man. I've seen good men and bad men all my life, and now I want to help you, so I will go to my husband. Something will be done."

"I didn't bring you anything to eat, but I will next time," Mary said.

"Oh, Princess, that's so kind of you."

"But please take a bath. You smell so bad."

"Come, Mary. Don't give up hope, Master Winslow. I've never given up hope that God will do something in my life. You must hope for the same."

The queen had lost her early beauty, but at that moment, Stuart didn't think he'd ever seen a more beautiful person. "Thank you, Your Majesty. I am so grateful to you."

Catherine left, but she stopped outside, where Stuart could

hear her. "I want Stuart Winslow to be given water to bathe in, and soap, then put in a dry cell. I want it to have a window. I want him to have good bedding. I want him to have something to read and some paper to write on. I want him to get better food than the average prisoner."

The chief guard hesitated. Stuart held his breath. If he had Queen Catherine's command, surely that was all he needed.

"I will see to it, Your Majesty," the guard said at last. "You may depend on it."

⚸

The change came immediately. The chief guard took Stuart to a room that seemed to him like a palace. It was much larger than his cell. Yellow sunlight streamed through a barred window. It contained a bed, and a table and chair occupied one corner. There were several books on a shelf, and as he looked through them, two guards brought in a tub and filled it with eight pails of steaming water. One of them tossed some fresh clothing to Stuart, grinning.

"Last fellow wore these clothes was hanged, but they beat what you're wearing."

Stuart laughed, and stripping off his filthy clothes, soaked and soaked and washed his hair and reveled in the warm, soapy water. He finally got out, dried off, then put on the clothing the guard had left.

One of the two guards who came to remove the tub said, "That feels better, does it?"

"A thousand times."

"Well, I don't know how you did it, Mr. Winslow, but the queen's never come to talk about any other prisoner."

"Maybe I've just led a good life."

The guard grinned broadly. "Not likely. I'll bring your food. I've got some special supper for you."

The special supper was a delicious stew, some fried fish, and fresh bread. When Stuart had eaten the last crumb, he sat back and remembered every bite. Even considering all the marvelous banquets he had enjoyed as part of the court, no meal, ever, could top that one.

"Heather, I'm so glad to see you."

"I've tried to get in many times, but they would never let me. Something has changed."

"I expect Queen Catherine had something to do with that."

"How is that, Stuart?" She came closer and looked up into his face.

"She's always liked me, Heather. I paid a lot of attention to Princess Mary, played with her often. That won her heart."

"It's fortunate you're good with children. You'll be a good father some day."

An awkward silence followed, and Stuart almost said something about not living long enough to have children, but he saw that she was looking up at him with innocence and eagerness, and he smiled. "I'll be terribly indulgent, treating my children as if they were princes or princesses. Now tell me of news of home. How are your brothers? And Mr. Tyndale—have you heard from him?"

"He's still in hiding."

Stuart nodded. "That's a good idea. It is said that the king is growing more and more against the idea of an English Bible."

"Yes, it's bad news for Mr. Tyndale indeed! It won't stop him, though. He hides and translates a little bit of the Bible from Greek to English, and then he finds a printing press and persuades a printer to print some copies. He has it in bits and pieces, but one day, Stuart, it'll all come out the whole Bible."

"That'll be a good day for England. Now tell me about yourself."

"There's nothing new to tell. We're all praying every day for God to do a work and get you free from this place."

"That's what it will take," Stuart said quietly. "I've thought about that a lot since I've been here."

"All things are possible with God. The Bible says that. That's the way Mr. Tyndale has translated one of the verses."

"It's a good translation. I wish I—" *believed it*, he finished silently.

Heather's eyes fell, as if he had spoken aloud. She said quietly, "Aren't you afraid that if you die you'll suffer the pangs of hell?"

"Yes."

"Then why don't you do something about it?"

Stuart ran his hands through his hair and closed his eyes. "I don't know," he whispered finally. "Something in me is stubborn and willful. I don't know what it is. I don't know why I'm like I am."

"I'm going to pray for you, and I'm going to ask God to tell you what he wants with you."

Stuart held his hands out, and she took them, and she prayed a sweet but brief prayer. It was a prayer of innocence and hope. Stuart held her hands tightly until finally she ended her prayer. "Thank you, Heather. You're a good woman."

"Don't forget that God is going to use you in a mighty way. Mr. Tyndale always said that."

"He'll have to do something about this rotten heart of mine."

"We all have rotten hearts, but God can change us."

⚭

"Well, I can tell you want something, Catherine. What is it?"

Catherine had come into the room where Henry played billiards. He played usually with men who knew very well to lose, but there was no one with him now, and he was simply pushing the balls around aimlessly.

"What is it you want? I know it's something. Everybody wants something."

"That's the penalty of being king. You are the one who can give them something."

He stared at her and saw for an instant the beautiful girl she had been when he had first met her. It was at her marriage to his brother, and he remembered it as clearly as if it were yesterday. Her hair had been shining, and her face had a luster and a glow, and her eyes were alive. That was all gone now, he saw, and he remembered his lack of interest in her as a woman.

"I have a favor to ask. I'm concerned about Stuart Winslow."

"Now, Catherine, you know I can't interfere in legal matters."

Catherine stifled a laugh. "You interfere constantly in legal matters, Henry. You always liked the young man, and I do too. He's been very kind to Mary. His father's a good man. The whole family is."

"But he killed one of our royal messengers."

"He says he didn't."

Henry laughed and threw the cue down on the table. "What murderer doesn't say that?"

"I believe him, Henry. He doesn't have guilt written in his face. Just go look into his eyes. You'll see honesty there and truth."

"Honesty and truth," he said, pondering the words. "Honesty and truth," he repeated slowly. "We need more of both in England. But I can't interfere."

"Well, you can do one thing."

"What is that?"

"You can ask Sir Thomas More to defend him."

Henry's eyes opened and he stroked his chin. "Why, I hadn't thought of that. I can certainly do that. More will do it for me. He's the best lawyer in England and anywhere else for that matter. But tell me, Catherine. Why are you really interested in this young man?"

She ignored his tone of innuendo. "He has a kind spirit, Henry. I think there's something good in him that needs to be saved."

Henry lifted his chin. "I'll have it done. Now, you see I'm gracious to you when I can be."

"Thank you, Henry," she said, and exited gracefully.

⚭

"Why, Your Majesty!"

"No ceremony, Thomas! No ceremony!" The king had sent for Thomas More, and now stood before him with a slight smile. "You're wondering why I sent for you."

More, probably the most able man in England in the courtroom or out, smiled. "Yes, Your Majesty, I certainly am. I hope it's not to get me to write another book."

"No, write all the books you want or as few. I want you to defend a man for me."

Surprise washed across More's face. "What man is that?"

"Oh, you heard about it. A royal messenger was murdered. A young man named Stuart Winslow has been accused. He's been a member of the court here, keeper of the birds. The queen believes him innocent."

"And you believe . . ."

"It's neither here nor there. Get him off, if you can, Thomas. Make Catherine happy. As a matter of fact, it'd make me happy too to have him back. He's awfully good with the birds. We can't afford to lose a man that can fly a hawk as he can."

"That seems like a trivial reason to save a man's life," More said.

"Thomas, Thomas! You never cease to amuse me. I would think if you ask Winslow, he would tell you he will grab at any excuse to escape the noose."

"I didn't know you had such compassion. I'm glad to see it in you."

For a moment Henry was offended. He never liked any criticism of any kind. But his admiration for Sir Thomas More was boundless. He laughed and slapped him on the shoulder. "Go on, now. See that you get the boy off."

Stuart leaped to his feet. He knew Sir Thomas More, of course. Everybody did. He was the best lawyer in England, a man of culture, and his book *Utopia* had captivated every learned person in the country. "Sir Thomas," he said almost breathlessly, "you honor me."

"As the king says, no ceremony." He saw the shock on Stuart's face. "I make a little fun of the king from time to time—when he's not around, of course. Sit down."

"Yes, sir."

More drew up the other chair and put his hands on his knees. "Now, you tell me everything about this crime that you can. Start as far back as you want. Don't leave out anything."

"Yes, Sir Thomas. I was with a group of young men who liked to go out and play tricks and pranks, and sometimes their tricks would get out of hand. They kept asking me to go with them, and I would refuse them. But this time for some reason I agreed."

When he finished his tale, More had listened to Stuart for over forty-five minutes. He had asked a few questions, and finally, when Stuart fell silent, he said, "Is that all?"

"Yes, Sir Thomas."

"You did not draw a weapon on the man?"

"No, sir, I did not."

"Very well. I will represent you in court."

"Oh, thank you, Sir Thomas."

"Thank our gracious Majesty, King Henry."

Stuart smiled. "I think he was persuaded by our gracious Queen Catherine."

"Whatever or whoever brought the change, I'm always happy to see a good instinct in Henry."

More left without another word.

Hope began to grow in Stuart. "Maybe I won't die," he said.

19

*T*he door opened, and a tall man was shoved in by a guard.

"You got company, Winslow," the guard called out loudly. "He's going to hang, so be nice to him." He stepped back and slammed the door with a loud clang.

Stuart studied the newcomer. He had an aesthetic face and a pair of deep-set brown eyes, which were now fixed on him.

"My name is Jan Dekker."

"I'm Stuart Winslow."

"Stuart Winslow. I've heard of you."

Dekker stretched his arms out, arched his back, and said, "This is really a very pleasant cell compared to some I've been in."

"Yes, the one I was in before was rotten, but this isn't bad as cells go. What are you charged with, Dekker?"

"Preaching the Gospel."

"Why, I wasn't aware that was against the law."

"It will always be against some man's law. The Lord Jesus said that if the world hated him, it would hate his disciples." Dekker walked over to the window and looked out. He was very still. Finally he turned around, and with a smile said, "I have enemies, and I've been charged with heresy and treason."

"Are you a heretic?"

"According to some. I preach that there is no salvation in any other than Jesus the Christ."

Stuart stared at him. "I don't see anything heretical about that."

"The world will always find something heretical when the name of Jesus is mentioned. Have you ever noticed, Master Winslow, that you can mention the name of any religious leader in any company, and there will be very little reaction. You can mention the name of Buddha. No one would get excited about that or charge you with heresy because you have not followed the tenets of Buddha down to the letter. But you mention the name of Jesus, and that name has a strange power. It arouses the fury of hell, and if a man has hell within him, the Devil will use it to destroy the truth of salvation."

"Have you been tried?"

"Oh, yes. I'll be executed in three days. I don't know why they delay. Mind if I sit?"

"Of course."

Dekker sat down loosely in the chair, apparently as calm and collected as any man Stuart had ever seen. Stuart studied Dekker. *In three days his heart will not be beating anymore. Perhaps his hair and fingernails will still grow, if the old women are right. But he won't be here. He will be in eternity. He will be with God.*

"Ah, Mr. Winslow, you have a Bible, I see."

"Yes, the queen was kind enough to send me one."

"Oh, you know the queen?"

"Yes, I have been an admirer of hers for some time."

"Poor woman! She's married to a man who has no moral code. He is like a ship without a compass. Henry goes left, goes right. He would go up and down if he could. His only key to life itself is 'What can I get out of it for me?'"

Stuart looked nervously at the door. Even in the privacy of

his cell, such talk was not safe. "How do you know I won't repeat what you've said, Mr. Dekker?"

"Just call me Jan. It would make little difference. But what do you fear? Do you not think I speak the truth? Or do you doubt the truth of the Lord Jesus?"

"I don't know what the truth is. My father and my mother are Christians, and I've known others, but I'm not a man of faith myself."

"I hope that you will become so."

Dekker's calm spirit surprised Stuart, and he sat listening as Dekker read passages from a Latin Bible and spoke eagerly of the truth of the Scripture. After he went to bed that night, Dekker began to sing hymns. "I'm not a great singer," he said. "I trust my singing won't bother you."

"Of course not."

"I love to sing of praise to my Savior. There was a time when I couldn't do that, but now I can't wait to get before the presence of the King."

"Maybe you won't die. Maybe God will set you free."

"No, I must die for Jesus. Many others have done so before, and he has told me I am to do the same."

Stuart shifted uncomfortably. Dekker was amiable enough, but the shadow of death was on him. And yet it did not show in his smile or in his eyes. It seemed that the more Stuart tried to give him hope of finding freedom in this world the more Dekker insisted that he was looking forward to meeting Jesus.

Why, he's really happy! Stuart thought. *You can feel his happiness and joy.*

Seeing this in Dekker had the reverse effect on Stuart. While Dekker was totally convinced that the moment life left his body he would be standing in the presence of God and of the holy angels, Stuart knew that in the same condition, he would have nothing with which to plead to God for his excuses for not serving him.

For the next three days, he heard Dekker singing the hymns of faith. He heard him speaking of the glories of Jesus and of heaven and how he yearned to be there, and the more he heard, the more fear grew in him. He became almost consumed with fear. He kept this concealed from the jailers and from Dekker himself.

Jan spoke often of what life in Jesus was like. "God is life," he said. He was lying flat on his back, his hands locked beneath his head, and speaking easily. "God is life. All else is a funeral."

"But what of love? Isn't that life? Isn't that a taste of the eternal?"

"Well, we love others, but if we are saved and they are lost, why, my friend, they are lost to us forever. Only in Jesus do we find true eternity. The truest of loves."

It was this truth that Dekker managed to get across to Stuart in the three days before he was to die. On the last night, they talked for a while, and Stuart could not find a way to say what was in his heart. The fear that had grown in him had become an agony, and he watched with envy as Jan knelt beside his bed, prayed a cheerful prayer, committed his soul to Jesus, then lay down. To Stuart's consternation, he fell asleep almost at once.

How can he do that? The hangman arrives at sunup! The thought pounded at Stuart's mind, and the more he thought of it, the worse he felt. The night wore on. Time was running out, but Dekker slept better than the fattest babe. Stuart fell into a restless sleep and saw himself standing before a throne, but he was not able to see clearly who was upon it. He heard a voice saying, "Depart from me, ye cursed into everlasting fire prepared for the devil and his angels."

Stuart awakened with a start and sat up. He'd always considered himself a man of courage, had more courage than most, perhaps, but his courage had abandoned him. He got up and tried to pace the floor, but his legs seemed to have turned to water. They would not hold him up. He barely made it to his cot, sat down, and saw that his hands were trembling. He covered his face with them and tried to drown out the voice that kept saying, "Depart from me ye cursed into everlasting fire."

Without realizing it, Stuart had been drawing deep breaths as if he were drowning, gasping like a swimmer too far from shore, now sinking beneath the waves.

"My friend, you need God."

Stuart straightened. He had almost forgotten Dekker, and now he saw that his cellmate had swung his feet over the side of his cot and was staring at him. The candle guttered and cast its yellow beams across Dekker's face, which was filled with so much compassion and love that Stuart crumbled. "I'm lost, Jan! I'm lost!"

"Yes, you're lost, but Jesus knows exactly where you are. Jesus said that when a man has a hundred sheep, if one of them is lost, he will leave the ninety-nine and go find that one. And he'll put it on his shoulders, and he'll bring it back to safety, and he will cry out with joy, 'I have found my sheep that was lost.' That's what the Lord Jesus is longing to do for you, my friend."

The words flowed from Jan's lips, words of encouragement. The gospel that Stuart had heard for many years from his father and his mother and from others, from William Tyndale himself, now seemed to be written on his heart with a white-hot iron. He was unworthy. Never had his parents, Tyndale, even Dekker done the things he'd done.

"There's no hope for me, Jan!"

Jan came over and sat down. He put his arm around Stuart and held him tight. "Yes, there is hope for you. Christ Jesus died to save sinners, and the apostle Paul said he was the chiefest of sinners. It is by his blood that we are saved. He is the Lamb of God, slain on our behalf, and when his blood washes us, we are clean as Christ himself. He becomes our righteousness."

On and on Jan spoke with scriptures pouring from his lips,

and the more he spoke, the worse Stuart felt. But finally he cried out, "I'm just a sinner, Jan!"

"That is good!"

Stuart stared at him. It took him a moment to speak. "How can that be good?"

"Because Jesus said that he was the friend of sinners, so you have a friend that has died, lain in the grave for three days, and come forth resurrected and now is at the right hand of God. He pleads for his friends, the sinners, you and me, Stuart, anyone who comes with broken hearts."

As the two of them sat together, Stuart felt the fear coming in great waves, and then Jan would give him a scripture and encourage him with the promises of God, and the fear would slip away. It always came back, however.

Finally Jan said, "It's time. Look, the sun is coming up. I shall be gone soon. But I cannot go to my Father's world without seeing you become the man of God that you should be."

"I don't know what to do, Jan."

"It is not what you *do*. Haven't you been listening? It is what Jesus *has done*. He came to this earth and lived a perfect life. He became the Lamb of God, and on Calvary he died, and his blood washes away every sin of every guilty human being who looks to him as that thief did."

Stuart began to tremble, and Jan quickly said, "Let's kneel, brother, and we will find our way to the throne of God."

Forever after Stuart remembered how he began to cry out, at first in a muffled voice, and then as Jan continued to pray in a strident tone, more loudly, "Oh, God, I'm a sinner! Forgive all my sins and wash me in the blood of Jesus!"

They were still on their knees when the guards came in. Two of them, burly men. "Well, come along, Dekker."

Dekker got to his feet and smiled. "Is it time?"

"Time for you to meet the hangman."

"I will see you one day," Dekker said. "My dear friend, Stuart,

God has entered your heart this morn. See to it that you serve him forever, and when you get to heaven"—he smiled then—"I'll be there to greet you. Good-bye, dear brother."

"Good-bye, Jan." Stuart's throat was thick. He could not say another word, and when the door closed, he found he could hardly stand. He leaned against the wall and tried to think of Jan Dekker leaving this world. Then once again he fell on his knees. "Oh, God," he said, "I have not been a faithful man or a true man or a good man, and I still do not feel worthy. But whatever it is that you want me to do, I will do it. May thy will be done in Stuart Winslow as it is done in heaven!"

The day of the trial had come, and Stuart was allowed to dress himself in fresh clothes. "You can't go before the judge looking like a scarecrow," the chief guard, Gatlin, said. He studied Winslow carefully. "Are you afraid?"

"Not anymore."

"How can you not be afraid? Every man fears death."

"Jan Dekker wasn't afraid."

"No, he wasn't. I'll give you that. He went to his death with a smile on his lips, and the last words he said were, 'Glory to Jesus.' I'll never forget it."

"I hope you'll let that be your cry, Mr. Gatlin. Glory to Jesus. That's going to be mine."

The two guards took him into a large room. There were three judges and a handful of spectators. His eyes swept the courtroom, and he saw Sir Thomas More sitting at a table. More motioned him over, and he went and sat down beside him.

More smiled. "Are you afraid, my boy?"

"No, not now."

"How is it you're not afraid?"

"I called upon the Lord, and I'm putting my faith and my trust in him. Live or die, I'm God's man."

"Good man! Good man!"

Almost immediately the trial began. The prosecutor, tall and gaunt, with the strange name of Friday, was a savage man. At the judge's instruction he marshaled the evidence. He stood before the judge and said, "This man was part of the gang that held up a royal messenger. There's no question about that." Then he called witnesses, all of them men that had come upon Winslow as he stood over the bleeding body. "They'll all testify to that."

The lawyer sat down, and the judge said, "What do you have to say, Sir Thomas?"

Sir Thomas rose. He was calm, the calmest man in the room, perhaps. He looked at the judge and smiled benevolently. "I have only one witness, sir."

"Only one?"

"Yes. Bring in Peter Morton."

Peter Morton was brought in and, after Morton took the oath, More asked, "Did Stuart Winslow murder the king's messenger?"

"No, sir. I did."

"You confess to the crime of murder? You know you can be executed for such a crime."

"I've already confessed to another murder, for which I am sentenced to die. What possible use would it be for me to lie about this? Stuart Winslow was the one innocent man among us. He had no idea at all, sir, that there would be even a robbery."

"And that is the final fact I wish to note," Sir Thomas said. "Stuart Winslow is charged with armed robbery and murder, and yet not one of the king's gold sovereigns was found upon him. Am I right?"

No one answered him. He looked to the leader of the palace guard, sitting in the front row of the gallery. The man shifted, uncomfortable under his intense gaze.

"Of course, I'm right," Sir Thomas said at last. "Because the messenger's parcel and the king's gold was where, Morton?"

"With me," he said. "I took it and split it with the others."

"And left this man to take your punishment."

Morton eyed Stuart. "I'm sorry, Winslow." He looked at the judge. "It is the truth of it. I am the one you seek, not him."

Sir Thomas More turned to the three judges and spoke to the chief justice. "Sir, I move that the prisoner be dismissed and the charges against him dropped. You heard the witness."

The judge leaned forward and whispered to the man on his left, then to the judge on his right. They both nodded, and the judge said, "Your request is granted, Sir Thomas. The court finds Stuart Winslow innocent of any wrongdoing."

At that, the crowd cried out, some in outrage, some in relief. Stuart's parents came forward, crying out his name. The three embraced.

Heather was there, and after his parents had embraced him, she came and held out her hands. He took them. Her eyes were filled with tears. "You're free, Stuart."

"Yes, I'm free, but I'm not free at the same time."

"What do you mean?"

"I want to find William Tyndale. God has told me I'm to serve him. I am going to help him in his task of getting the Bible to every plowboy in England!"

PART FOUR

The Fugitive

(1528–1536)

20

After Stuart's release, he went at once to Stoneybrook, for going to live at court was not what he wanted. He was making plans to find Tyndale.

He spent much time with his parents but made frequent trips to Richmond Palace to visit the queen and Princess Mary. The pope had refused to allow Henry to divorce Catherine; Henry was still determined to divorce her. But only his queen's heavy heart bothered Stuart.

On one of his visits to the queen and Princess Mary, the queen opened her heart as she never had before. They were walking along one of the paths in the garden, the queen showing Stuart the beautiful roses, when suddenly she said, "You never mention my situation to me, Master Winslow."

"Why—why, no, Your Majesty. It's not my place."

"Everyone in England knows about it. I have no secrets." Bitterness scored the lines of her mouth. She stared down at the ground, and when she lifted her eyes, Stuart saw the pain and grief that marked her face. "I was a foreign princess brought here to produce sons. It's clear now to all that I will never succeed in bearing a son. After that is out in the open, what else is left to hide?"

The two continued their walk. Stuart was extremely uncomfortable. He had never seen Catherine in this mood before. He wanted to comfort her but did not know how. After a long pause, he said, "I am sorry for your situation, Your Majesty, but how can Henry do this? The church clearly forbids divorce."

"He's already informed me of how it will be," she said. "He says that we have never been married at all."

"Whatever does that mean?"

"I was first married to his brother Arthur, and Henry claims the Bible says that my second marriage to him is incest. The priest gave him a text found in the book of Leviticus to prove this. What foolishness! Even if it were so, it would not apply, because my marriage to Arthur was never consummated." Tears came to her eyes then. "Think of it, Stuart. Almost twenty years of being a faithful wife, and he says we are not married at all! I must go now. Forgive me—" She turned and walked away, and Stuart's heart went with her as she disappeared into the palace. But Henry was determined, and Stuart was struck by the same feeling, watching the queen disappear, as he was when Jan Dekker left his sight for the last time.

⚘

On one of his rare visits home to Stoneybrook, Stuart spoke with his father about Tyndale and his fierce determination to follow God's call. "I don't see why there's a problem, Father. I mean, after all, Henry has authorized the use of Bibles in English in the churches even though there are none in print."

"That was last year. This is now. His mind has been changed, and who knows why Henry does anything?"

"But it's foolishness! Doesn't he realize that there's a need in the churches to hear the Bible read in English? Hasn't he seen the people's enthusiasm?"

Claiborn shook his head sadly and ran his hand through his hair. "You're far closer to the king than I. If you do not know the cause of his reversal, I am that much more befuddled."

"Where is Mr. Tyndale now, sir?"

"Oh, he's in Marburg, a hundred miles north of Frankfurt and well off the beaten path of government agents."

"The king has sent agents looking for him?"

"Oh, yes. He has even offered him amnesty and a place in the government."

"That's hard to believe."

"Well, Tyndale doesn't believe it. He's found a printer there and he's turning out Bibles as fast as he can."

"He's selling them?"

"He doesn't make a penny from any of his work. He could probably have been a rich man if he had sold them, because there's a hunger in the hearts of many for the Word of God, but he refuses to make any profit from serving God."

The two men sat talking about Tyndale for some time. Claiborn smiled. "Do you know what part of the scripture he's working on now? The Old Testament."

"I wasn't aware that he knew Hebrew."

"He doesn't, and that's the miracle, Son. He doesn't have any opportunity to learn it here in his homeland." Jews had been banished from England since the reign of Edward I, and those who remained often hid their heritage for fear of being banished—or worse. "So he found an old Hebrew grammar and began the study of the language on his own. But it's hard, Stuart. He's in exile, living from hand to mouth, with the constant threat of arrest, and there he is learning Hebrew, translating and revising the New Testament, completing the first of the five books of the Old Testament. I don't understand how one head can hold so much."

"Neither do I, nor how one man can bear to defy the king. You well know that the king will take his head if he can find him."

"He knows that, I'm sure, but he just doesn't think about things like that the way most men do."

Stuart said in a voice of wonder, "He is a man to admire."

"Indeed he is. There's not another like him in all England. He will have the Bible to put before the peasants and potentates of England or he will die in the attempt."

Stuart had made up his mind to go to William Tyndale. He knew he had made a vow to God when God had delivered him from death, and part of that vow, at least, was to serve under William Tyndale's direction. He had no idea what he would do or even if he could find the man, for the secret agents of King Henry had not been able to find him.

He had prepared himself to go in search, but he wanted to make one more visit to court. He asked for an audience with Catherine and as usual she was glad to see him. When he told her of his plan to be gone for some time, her face fell. "Why are you leaving us, Master Winslow?"

"I must see to some private business, Your Majesty." He saw that the queen was depressed. "Try to keep your spirits up."

"I will never have a life. It's all over. My hopes are for Mary."

"She's a fine girl. Bright, smart, pretty. You can well be proud of her."

"I wish her father were as proud." The words were bitter, but at once she passed her hand in front of her face as if brushing away a thought. "Hurry back to us, Master Winslow."

"I will try, Your Majesty. Good-bye now."

"Thank you for your many kindnesses to me and to Mary. Be a friend to her if you can. When I am gone, she will need all the friends she can get."

"You may count on it. I will do my best to help her in every way I can."

Stuart ignored the giggling ladies-in-waiting, who stared at him with seductive eyes and boldly looked him over. Their attention sickened him, reminding him of Anne Boleyn and all that was wrong with the court. Nell was long since gone, off to marry an ancient French nobleman with plenty of money. But as one woman disappeared, another took her place, always with the same intentions, always on the same downward spiral. His grandmother was right. The court was an evil and dangerous place. He went down a flight of stairs in the gardens, eager to have the maids out of his sight. He thought of his new life, serving under William Tyndale. He would go and find Tyndale, and he would serve God by serving him.

❧

Edmund rolled over in his bed and opened his eyes. Sleep eluded him, as it had for weeks now. He stared at the pillow beside him, thinking of the last time Edith shared his bed; he really didn't miss her. He sighed and got out of bed. He pulled aside the heavy draperies, noting the beautiful morning. His eyes swept over his mother's house, now Claiborn's, and the lush land that extended from it, now heavy with ripening hay.

It was a relief to be past the bitterness and on to acceptance. If only Edith would let it alone! How long had he acted in the same manner, though, held onto the anger he'd felt over Claiborn and Grace? No love replaced it; he merely felt that he no longer cared. And even that was a relief.

Dressed now, he went for a brisk walk, exiting the castle gates with a nod to the guard, out into his own fields. He returned by way of Claiborn's tract of land and ran across his brother sitting on a bench, playing with a litter of puppies.

"Those are nice-looking dogs," he said, stopping in front of Claiborn.

"They'll be exceptional hunting dogs, Brother." Claiborn smiled. He lifted one in his direction. "This is the pick of the litter. I know you lost yours last year. Please, I want you to have him."

"Why, I thank you, Claiborn." Taking the puppy, Edmund stroked the silky fur and pulled at the long ears. He was surprised and embarrassed by the offer, more so over the fact that Claiborn had noted his affection for his old lead hunting dog and seemed to be addressing his loss. He had never given Claiborn a gift since his return, even at Michaelmas. "I'll take good care of him."

"He'll be the best. I remember when you gave me Chieftain. I was only ten, but you knew how to please a boy. I never forgot that gift, Edmund. Best present you could have given me."

"You did love that dog," Edmund murmured.

"You gave me lots of gifts when I was a boy and you took me to many places. I've never forgotten any of those times."

Edmund shifted uneasily, remembering his fondness for Claiborn when he was young, those trips to London. "I've treated you badly," he blurted out. He was shocked to hear his own words but realized they were true. "I don't know what's happened to me. Why I couldn't get past . . . you and Grace. Why I couldn't simply get on with life."

"I wronged you, Edmund."

"Not any more than I've wronged you." The confession seemed to open a part of Edmund that had been long closed. He suddenly sat down next to Claiborn on the bench and found himself overwhelmed by regret. "Mother would have been so pleased to see us reconciled. I—I wish I had had this conversation with you before she died."

"I think she knew that we'd again learn to love each other as brothers."

Edmund found that his eyes were suddenly blurred with tears. His voice was thick as he said, "Do you think so, Brother?"

"I'm sure of it. And we don't have a big family. We need each other, Edmund."

"Yes, that's true!" Edmund hesitated, then said, "I'd like

that very much." And then he felt Claiborn's arm around his shoulders. He could not speak for a time, then he whispered, "I can't undo all the cruel things I've done to you. To Grace. To Stuart."

"No need to speak of that," Claiborn said at once. "We'll start again. What if we went hunting, just the two of us. It'll be like when we were children. You can speak to Grace and Stuart when you feel ready."

"That would be fine!" he said. He put the puppy down and could not find the words to express what he was feeling. He said, "I'll get ready."

"As will I," Claiborn said with a smile, rising to shake his brother's hand.

Edmund was sure that he saw joy in Claiborn's eyes that equalled what he himself felt in his heart.

※

"I've made a decision, Mother." Ives Hardcastle had entered his mother's chambers. She was sitting at her dressing table putting cream on her hands. She was inordinately proud of them because they were graceful and youthful.

"What's your decision, dear?"

"I'm leaving Stoneybrook."

"To go where?"

"I'm going to offer my services to Cardinal Wolsey."

His words caught his mother's attention, and she turned around and studied his face. "Why do you think Wolsey would be interested in you?"

"I've already written him. I explained that I need a place. I need to learn about how things work at court. And I'd serve him well."

"And he told you to come?"

"Yes. I've just received his answer."

Edith sat very still for a moment. Then she nodded slowly. "That might be a very good thing. It's good to have powerful friends, Ives."

"Well, there's no more powerful man in England than Cardinal Wolsey. He practically runs the kingdom."

"King Henry has put him in his place of late over the Boleyn girl. Forced a rift between him and Rome."

"But here in England, only the king exceeds his power."

"He's an ambitious man, and he can be cruel. You understand that?"

Ives smiled. "So can I."

Edith laughed. "You learned it from me, my dear. Well, what do you need?"

"I need some money to live on. He said nothing about money. He probably thinks I'm wealthy."

"I have some that I put aside. It would be a good thing if you became a trusted servant of Wolsey. That would open all kinds of doors for you."

"For us, Mother, for us."

"When will you leave?"

"Today."

"What will you tell Edmund?"

"You tell him anything you please. Say that I'm going to learn a trade." Ives suddenly smiled; there was a wolfish look about his face. He was essentially a greedy young man without morals, and his mother understood this well enough. But she removed a bag from her wardrobe; she took out some gold coins, added a few more for good measure, and handed them to him.

"You'll have to use this wisely. It's getting harder and harder to get money out of Edmund."

"What a mercy it would be for us if he died." He saw his mother staring at him and laughed. "Of course you've thought of it. So have I. That would solve all our problems, wouldn't it?"

"He hasn't named you his heir yet, but I'm working on it."

"Work hard, Mother." He kissed her lightly on the cheek. "I'll keep in touch with you."

"Good success, Son."

Ives considered going to talk to Edmund, but he shrugged. "Mother can do it better than I can."

He left an hour later in one of the carts that held his belongings. His hopes were high, for he knew that Wolsey could do anything he pleased—as long as it did not go counter to what King Henry wished.

⚘

As Ives walked along the richly decorated corridors of Hampton Court Palace, the home of Cardinal Thomas Wolsey, he was impressed by the wealth and the sumptuous trappings of the magnificent structure that Wolsey had built. Hampton was an architectural marvel, built entirely of brick, but in the manner of one of the older castles. It was surrounded by turrets, giving the palace an impression of strength.

Ives eyed the large paintings in gilt frames, the magnificent statuary imported from Italy. He took in the treasures that came from all over Europe. The floor itself was paved with marble that came straight from the finest Italian quarries.

He reached the room of the cardinal and knocked on the door. The cardinal's voice boomed out, "Come in, come in." He stepped inside, and Wolsey looked up from his desk, covered with documents. He was alone. "Sit down, Hardcastle."

"Thank you, Your Grace."

While Wolsey finished writing, the silence was thick in the room. Then he laid the document aside, leaned back, and folded his hands over his large stomach. "So you would like to be in my service."

"Very much, Eminence."

"Well, I've learned you're a bright man and shrewd enough

to be included among my assistants." The cardinal smiled at the shock registered on Ives's face. "Surely you knew I'd investigate you before bringing you here. Ives Hardcastle, son of Lady Edith Winslow, potential heir of Stoneybrook, and yet not quite named as such. Menaced by the potential of Stuart Winslow taking it all in time. Hedging your bets by coming to court." A smile suddenly came to his lips but not his eyes. "You are clever. I can see that. If you were not, I'd have nothing to do with you. The king is impetuous enough to keep the country intrigued. It takes thoughtful men like us to insure that our sovereign's passions do not lead him into disaster."

"I believe I see what you mean, Your Grace. He is a difficult man to handle, isn't he—if one can speak of handling a king."

"That is exactly the word I might have chosen. He may call me an adviser, but I am, in effect, the one who must convince the king to do that which is best—in his own interest, of course." Once again Wolsey's thin lips turned up in a cold smile. His eyes flicked to the window. "Only in one matter have I failed at this task. It will not happen again." His eyes returned to Ives, looking him over.

Ives felt himself sweating under the gaze of the cardinal. It was like a bird being watched by a cat about to pounce!

"Let me tell you about power, Hardcastle. That's what you're interested in. I saw that when I first met you at Stoneybrook. I recognized very quickly that you are intelligent enough to rise, though I had to watch for a while to see if you had the kind of mentality for rule. I was the same sort of young fellow as you are. My father was a butcher, you know. I had to rise above all that, and I could not have risen to my position without learning the use of power."

"You've come a long way, Your Grace."

Wolsey appeared not to hear him. "Power. What is power? Well, in this country, power is Henry VIII, the sovereign of England. It's in his thick hands; it's in that mind of his that hides behind those small, guarded eyes. He's not the absolute monarch that other kings of England were in the past. He can no longer say 'Off with his head!' Oh, no, he must go through forms and legal maneuvers when he wants a man to go to the block or the stake."

"I understand that, sir."

"Well, that's what you and I, men like us, are for. You see, Hardcastle, when Henry wants something done, we see that it gets done. So the power lies in the king, that is true, but the king is surrounded by a pretty court of royal household officials, serving in all areas of life. And in some sense, the people who control the power—well, these men are the real power even though they do not wear the crown."

"Why, that's true enough, isn't it, Your Grace? If a man controls the king, then he is the power."

"Ah, yes, but what would happen if Henry discovered that someone else had the power?" Wolsey's eyes burned into Ives. "You see, don't you? He's sent many to the headsman already for doing what he wanted done. Henry not only has to represent the power, he must think that it lies solely in his hands. That's why a man such as I, with humble beginnings, has been able to rise. Because I've understood when to comply and when to push. When to step forward and when to retreat. That, my potential new assistant, will be vital for you to learn as well."

The two men sat there talking, Ives covering his surprise at the casual way in which the cardinal spoke of the king—which he knew Wolsey would not dare to use if the king were present. He asked, "How much power do you wield over the king?"

The cardinal scoffed. "It depends upon the day. Our monarch currently strives for something that I can't give him. If I fail, my remaining days will be few indeed. And those who are allied with me"—he paused to narrow his eyes at Ives—"might also find their neck in a noose."

He smiled as Ives shifted in his seat. "So what say you, Hardcastle? Do you have the stomach for such political intrigue? There is potential for great gain here but great loss as well."

Ives rose and bent his head in deference. "Your Grace, if you will teach me what you will, I will gladly serve you with my very life."

"Hmph," returned the cardinal. "Or you will serve me, anyway, while it suits you." He pursed his lips and tapped them with his index finger. "Nevertheless, it suits me to have someone from outside the court to enter in now. Congratulations, Hardcastle. You have obtained what you seek. Welcome to Hampton."

❧

"I have to be at the coast by morning, Heather."

Heather looked up at Stuart. He had come to say his farewells, and she felt sadness. She knew that she loved this man and that he did not love her. "When will you come back, Stuart?"

"I have no idea. I'm giving myself fully into Mr. Tyndale's hands. Whatever he says, I'll do. That was the promise I made to God when he saved me."

"You could not find a better man from whom to learn the ways of God. Where will you be going?"

"I have no idea. I must find him first."

Heather smiled at him. "You're like Abraham, aren't you?"

"Me? No. He was a man of great faith."

"Well, the Bible says he went out after God spoke to him and he didn't know where he was going. Isn't that your situation? God will show you the way."

"You always have a way of encouraging me." He took her hands and held them. "We've been good friends, haven't we?"

"Always, Stuart."

"Don't forget me."

"Never. Will you write?"

"It will be dangerous, so what I write will be more or less in code. You'll have to read between the lines. But I'll be saying this—that I'm thinking of you and wishing the best for you." He leaned forward and then slowly, reverently, kissed her on the cheek.

"Good-bye, Stuart. God go with you."

21

*S*tuart sat down on a bench outside a cobbler's shop and bowed his head. He stared at the pavement. He was aware of the guttural German voices that came to him from those who passed by on the street and once again was impressed by how ugly the language sounded. He thought French a rather attractive-sounding language and Italian also, but German seemed to be coarse, rough, and without the grace that even English had.

He had come to Europe to find William Tyndale but couldn't find a sign of the man. In the last two years he had called in every favor, plied spies with money, begged for information, certain that God would soon open the very next door and Tyndale would be standing there with open arms, happy to see him. But instead, every door seemed solidly shut before him.

He looked up at the sky. "Did I misunderstand, Lord?" he muttered, angry. "Was this not what you wanted me to do? Why do you not come to my aid?"

"I'll come to your aid," said a woman who was standing in front of him. "You need to have some fun?" she whispered suggestively.

He shook his head and saw the hardness in her eyes grow more adamant. She spoke what he thought must be a curse, turned, and walked away down the street. He decided that there were as many harlots in Marburg as there were in London. He glanced down the other way and saw nothing to attract his attention. Marburg was not a beautiful city. He wondered if he had come to the right place after all. The only evidence that he had of Tyndale's existence was a hurried whisper from a man in Antwerp, who had then faded into the darkness of the night. In desperation Stuart had come to Marburg, where Claiborn had said he'd heard Tyndale had gone, a hundred miles north of Frankfurt. He spoke only a little German, and noted that as soon as his English accent was heard, he was regarded with suspicion.

Wearily he got to his feet and made his way through the crowded street, stopping only once to buy a meat pie. He had not yet figured out how to use German money, and he was relatively sure that the peddler, a rotund fat man with a greasy apron and sly eyes, had cheated him. He walked on down the street and for the rest of the day moved from one point to another. Late in the afternoon, he stopped at a printer's shop, one that he had missed. He had gone to all the larger printing shops, but this place was a bare eight feet wide with a small handmade sign, *"Drucken"* ("Printing"). Without a great deal of hope, he moved into the shop, which was long and narrow, dark, and cluttered with papers and all the various tools of the printing trade. He saw a small man with a pair of direct gray eyes and nodded. *"Gutten Abendt,"* he said. *"Ich habe—"* He could not think of the next word in German; to his relief the man smiled.

"You are English, I take it."

"Yes. You speak English! Good. My German is terrible."

"I spent ten years in Dover. What can I do for you, sir?"

Stuart studied the man carefully; there was an honest air about him. *There's no sense in trying to be clever,* he thought. *I'll just have to come right out with it.* Aloud he said, "I am looking for a man, sir."

"A particular man or will any man do?"

Stuart had to smile. "No, not just any man. This is a good friend of mine, and I need desperately to find him."

"And what is his name?"

"William Tyndale." Instantly he saw something change in the eyes of the printer. His heart leaped, but he had discovered that finding someone who knew Tyndale was one thing, getting them to speak was something else. Quickly he said, "I know that he is a man wanted by the king of England, but I am not an agent of the Crown. I am his friend. If I could simply get word to him, I'm sure he would send for me."

"I've heard of Mr. Tyndale. He is a scholar, I understand."

"Yes, he is. Some of the work he is doing is not pleasing to the king, and he has to remain hidden from sight. But if you know anything of him, I would very much appreciate it if you would pass my name along to him."

"And what is your name, sir?"

"I am Stuart Winslow."

"Stuart Winslow. It may be that I will find someone who has heard of your man. Are you staying long in town?"

"I'll stay as long as I need to. I've about lost hope."

"The good God gives us hope, and we must hang on to it as a treasure."

"Your name, sir?"

"Robert Marx is my name."

"Thank you very much, Mr. Marx. I will come back from time to time, with your permission. I am staying at the inn next to the church. If you would send for me there, I would appreciate it."

"We shall see. Thank you for stopping by, Mr. Winslow."

Stuart left the darkness of the shop. When he came out, the late-afternoon sun was casting its beam on the hills that surrounded the city. The light was faint, and already there was a cloud coming up from the west. It would rain soon. But for the first time Stuart had hope.

✺

Stuart remained in Marburg for two weeks but received no word from Marx. He had heard a rumor that Tyndale might be in Antwerp, but he had no place to start looking. He made the rounds of the printers, and none of them would admit that they knew anything about William Tyndale.

Stuart had eaten a rather badly prepared meal at the inn and thought again that German cooking failed in comparison with the English. A part of him longed for home. He went to bed early and could not sleep. He tossed and turned, thinking that he might never sleep that night.

But sleep overtook him, and he found himself dreaming of a woman. At first he could not see her clearly, and he thought it was Nell Fenton and remembered all the desire that he had felt for her. But then, as his sight seemed to grow clearer, he discovered that the woman was not Nell Fenton at all but Heather Evans. In the dream she was standing in the sunlight, and the golden sunbeams made a corona that touched her head like a coronet of jewels. He reached out and called her name, and the sound of his own voice woke him up. He sat straight up in the bed and shook his head. The bed was hard and had a lumpy mattress. He swung his feet over the side and put his face in his hands.

"Heather," he groaned, "how I wish I could see you! You always knew how to encourage me."

For a long time he sat in that position, and as he did, he felt something that had come to him several times since he had given his life to Christ. He longed to pray as he had with Dekker but never had the same desire, the same passion. Stuart was sometimes ashamed of his prayers. They seemed awkward and ill-phrased, and more than once he had cried out, "God, can't you give me a more eloquent prayer? You must despise the weak, foolish prayers that come from my lips!"

He began to pray softly aloud. He had discovered that praying aloud was better for him. When he did not pray aloud, wandering thoughts would interrupt and take his mind off his desire to seek God. Now he whispered, "Lord, you are almighty. There's nothing impossible with you, but you know me, Lord. I am helpless. I am not able to do this thing that I felt you wanted me to do. I ask you to either encourage me or let me go home."

That was the extent of his prayer, and almost in despair, he fell on his knees, buried his face in the rough covers, and waited. At first there was nothing, but then out of his helplessness and his need, a sudden peace seemed to come upon him. He desperately wished that he could hear a voice, for he had heard of men who did hear the voice of God—or what was almost a voice, so clear were their impressions. He himself had not experienced that, but now he did. It was only an impression, but his despair seemed to evaporate, and he felt a warmth in his spirit. He waited. Then he lifted his head and whispered, "God, I believe that you have encouraged me and have given me comfort. I know that you are going to do something to help me."

⚬⚬

The next day Stuart began his search again, hopeful that God had spoken to him. He searched diligently, not only among the printers but openly asking everyone who might have seen William Tyndale. His lack of good German was a handicap, and after three days, his doubts slowly edged in again.

It was just my desire to hear him, he thought, as he made his way back to the inn late one evening. *God does not want me here after all.* The sky was dark; he had wandered the streets all day.

He was passing by an alley when he heard an odd sound. Quickly his hand went to the dagger at his belt, for there were thieves in this country as well as in London. But it was a moan he had heard. His eyes were growing accustomed to the darkness, and as he stepped into the alley, he saw what seemed to be a lump of rags. Leaning forward, he saw that it was a man doubled up and clutching himself.

Stuart said, "Are you ill, sir?" Only a groan came to him, and at first he fought an impulse to walk away. He remembered suddenly the scripture that he had been reading in his Bible about a Samaritan who found a man wounded and dying. The Samaritan took the man to an inn and saw that his wounds were dressed and made arrangements for his care. *Maybe I'm the Samaritan in this case.* He knelt down. His eyes were now more accustomed to the dim light.

"What's wrong with you?" he asked quietly.

"Ill—I'm ill. . . ." The voice was faint, but it was English that the man was speaking.

In an instant Stuart made up his mind. "Come along, old fellow. We'll see you right." He picked the man up and was shocked by how light he was. He was a very small man with almost no flesh on his body. He could not walk, so Stuart simply carried him as he would carry a child. As he walked down the street, he noticed some staring in curiosity, but he paid them no attention. His landlord saw him as he entered the inn. "Who's that?"

"An old man. He's ill."

"You can't bring him in here."

"Yes, I can."

Stuart did not like the innkeeper. He was a bulky man with a perpetual scowl on his face. For a moment Stuart thought he meant to forbid his entrance, but then he grunted. "You'll have to pay extra."

"That's all right. Is there a doctor around here?"

"Yes. He's down the street. Ask for Doctor Heinrich."

Stuart mounted the stairs, scarcely feeling his burden. He shoved open the door to his room with his shoulder and put the man down on his bed. He lit a lamp and turned to get a better look at him. What he saw was an elderly man, his hair dirty but plainly silver. His face was lined, and he had lost his teeth, which made his cheeks sunken.

"What's your name?" he said.

"Nathan—Nathan Kent. And who are you, sir?" The voice was weak, but the eyes seemed to grow clearer.

"Stuart Winslow. I found you in the alley."

"A good thing. I believe I would have died there if you hadn't helped me."

"Lie still. I'm going to get a doctor and something for you to eat. Doctor first."

Twenty minutes later Stuart was back with the doctor named Heinrich.

Doctor Heinrich stood up from his examination. "He doesn't have the sweating sickness."

"Well, that's a relief. What does he have?"

"He's plainly starving as well as suffering a fever. No trouble in the lungs yet. If he did, as thin as he is, he wouldn't survive."

"How do we aid him?"

"Give him good food. Just broth at first. Give him some good ale. Maybe even a little brandy once in a while." Doctor Heinrich stared at him. "Is he kin to you?"

"No, not a bit of it."

"Why are you helping him?"

"Because he's a human being."

Heinrich laughed. He was a small man, well-dressed, with keen hazel eyes. "You're right about that, but not many believe it. I'll stop by and see how he's doing tomorrow. Get some good food down him."

"Thank you, Doctor. How much do I owe you?" The doctor named a small sum, took the coins that Stuart gave him, and left.

At once Stuart said, "Well, Nathan, I'm going down to get you something to eat. Don't go to sleep on me, now."

"No, sir, I won't do that."

The burly innkeeper was alone, and he had no objection to selling an extra bowl of broth and a stein of ale. "That old man— what is he to you?" he asked, as he gave the food tray to Stuart.

"Nothing, really. I found him in the alley and couldn't let him die."

"He's been hanging around for several days now. I didn't think he'd make it through this cold spell. You're paying for him, are you?"

"Put it on my bill." Stuart returned to his room and set the tray down. He pulled the single chair up, straightened Kent in bed, and said, "Now, let's get some food down you." Kent's hands were too unsteady to hold the spoon without spilling the broth, so Stuart fed him.

He managed to eat half and then shook his head. "That's all, sir, for now."

"You did well. Now, see how much of this you can put down." Stuart gave him the stein of ale and watched as he drank it slowly. When he had finished most of it, his eyes were closing.

"Why . . . are you doing this?"

"I don't know. I think it's because I read a story once about a Samaritan who—"

"The good Samaritan. I know that story."

"You know the Bible?"

"My father did. He read to us every night." Suddenly Nathan Kent simply closed his eyes and slumped. This alarmed Stuart, but he found, over the next few days, that it was not uncommon. Kent would be wide awake, and then weakness would strike him, and he would simply go to sleep sitting up or lying down.

Easing the man back in the bed, Stuart wondered, *What have I taken on here?* He looked down at Kent, shook his head, then went down and made arrangements for an extra room. His money was not all that plentiful, but he felt that God was telling him to do this. When he went to bed that night after checking on the sick man, he lay awake for a long time wondering about it.

⚕

"Well, you're going to live after all, Nathan."

"That I will, sir. All thanks to you and the good Lord."

"Mostly the good Lord, I think." Stuart studied Kent, who now sat across from him in the dining area of the inn. They had eaten a good meal, and Stuart was glad to see that over the last week, the old man had put on some flesh and there was color in his cheeks. "What are you doing in Germany, Nathan? You're English."

"Yes. I've been a rolling stone, Mr. Winslow. My father wanted me to be a scholar, and I should have been. But I had wild ideas. I took a hard road too."

"What did you do?"

"I became a strolling actor, a player, as they're called in our country. That's a precarious profession, sir."

"How did you wind up in Germany?"

"I came with a troupe, but I got sick, and they left me behind. I need to get back to England."

"Well, I can help you do that."

"Oh, are you heading home? That would be grand. What brought you here, Mr. Winslow?"

For a moment Stuart hesitated. There was no one else in the dining area, just the two of them. He leaned forward suddenly and began to tell the old man his story. He did not know why he did this, but it seemed to come naturally to him. He related the whole thing, including his immoral life at the court of King Henry and God touching him and giving him a commission to help William Tyndale bring the Bible in English to the people of England.

Nathan smiled. "That's a big job you've got there. I understand the king's not in favor of such things."

"No, and if I get caught, I'll probably get burned at Smith-field."

"Indeed you might, but it's a fine thing, for the Bible is a wonderful book. Maybe I can help you, sir."

"Well, I'd be glad of any help."

He did not see how this weak old man could help anybody, but during the next few days he was aware that Nathan Kent was studying him carefully. Finally Kent was well enough, and Stuart said, "I'm going to pay your passage to get you back to England, Nathan."

"Not yet, sir."

Stuart was surprised. "Why not? Don't you want to go home?"

"I have a debt, Mr. Winslow, and I intend to pay my debt." He leaned forward and said, "I told you that I was going to help you. I've been seeking the Lord and racking my brain, and I've found the way that I can help pay back some of the goodness you have shown me."

Without any idea of what the man meant, Stuart was touched. "Well, that's good of you, Nathan. I would appreciate any help I can get, but the best help would be to help me find William Tyndale."

"You're not going to find him through the way you're doing it now."

"What do you mean?"

"You're an Englishman. Obviously the friends of Tyndale would expect you to be an agent of the king. The enemies of Tyndale would suspect you of being his friend. You must look like something other than what you are."

"I'm what I am, Nathan. I can't become another man."

Suddenly Kent laughed. "Yes, you can. That's exactly what an actor does. He becomes another man. And that's what I'm going to teach you, Mr. Stuart Winslow. You're going to become an actor."

Stuart blinked in surprise. "I don't understand you."

"Suppose you didn't look like an Englishman or sound like an Englishman. Suppose you looked like a Dutchman or a Frenchman."

"Why, I can't do that!"

"You'll be able to do it well enough after I've trained you for a few days. We need to get away from this place. We need to study every day."

Stuart had never thought of such a thing, but he listened as Nathan began to explain his plan. "If you're going to help Mr. Tyndale, the help you'll get him will be getting Bibles into England. That's what you've told me. He's having them printed here in Germany and other places, and he must get them to England?"

"That's right."

"Well, suppose you were a merchant from Amsterdam with a load of silk. Those looking for Bibles wouldn't be likely to examine you too closely, would they, now?"

At that instant a part of Stuart seemed to come awake. He thought for a moment, and he said, "That would be wonderful, Nathan, but can you really teach me? You must be clever to be an actor."

"Not too clever or I wouldn't be one," Nathan said cynically. "Well, come along. We'll have our first lesson."

※

The days went by quickly. Stuart was amazed to find that a month had gone by. He had been studying hard under the tutelage of Nathan Kent. He had learned a great deal about false hair and cosmetics, makeup, how to pad the body to look like a hunchback, or whatever the role called for. He had thrown himself into learning the art that the old man had spent his life in. One day Nathan said, "That's all I can do for you, sir, but now you can become anything you want. You have a natural flair for it."

"It's been a revelation to me, Nathan. Now, I'm going to get you on a ship for England. You have family there? Someone who will take you in?"

"I have two brothers in business there, and they'll take me in. They think I'm a foolish man, which I am, but they're kind. I wish you would come and see me upon your return."

"Give me their names, and I shall." He waggled his eyebrows. "If God smiles, I'll bring you a Bible in English."

Two days later Stuart waved good-bye to Kent, who had boarded a freighter as it left the harbor. The old man waved at him and said, "God be with you, Brother."

"And with you, Nathan." Stuart waited until the ship disappeared, and then his mind began to work. *It wasn't an accident that I met him. I must put his instruction to work.*

☙

Hans Bruker looked across the table to where his friend William Tyndale was writing. He had not moved except to push the pen across the page for almost three hours. Bruker could never understand how a man could concentrate for so long. He said, "You must stop now, my friend."

Tyndale looked up quickly. His eyes were tired, and he flexed the fingers of his right hand. "Why must I stop, Hans?"

"You must rest."

"I can't rest until this work is done."

"You can do it tomorrow. Come, Martha has something prepared in the kitchen. You must be hungry."

Reluctantly Tyndale put his pen away, looked at the sheets before him, and sighed. "There's so much to do and so little time."

"It took God six days to make the world. You're not going to translate the whole Bible tonight. Come along."

Tyndale had fled from one place to another, always chased by the agents of King Henry. Wolsey and the king were more determined than ever to bring Tyndale to trial.

The two men moved into the kitchen.

"Sit and eat," Martha Bruker said. "You are too skinny."

"Thank you, Martha." Tyndale sat down, and while the woman piled his plate high with vegetables and mutton, the two men talked about England. Many in England were unhappy. The matter of the king's annulment dragged on, and Henry had declared a war—which nobody wanted—against the emperor, Charles V. The country was devastated by floods, and worst of all, the sweating sickness had returned.

"This sweating sickness, it'll be the death of us all," Bruker said.

"It's almost like the curse of God."

The two men were interrupted by a knock at the door. "Martha, see who's there," Bruker called.

"Are you expecting someone?"

"No, not at all."

The two men waited rather tensely, for, indeed, hostile agents were never far behind Tyndale. Martha came back in and said, "It's a French gentleman. He asked to see you, Herr Tyndale."

"What's his name?"

"Duroy, he said."

"Well, show him in."

"Is that safe?" Bruker said with alarm. "You go with Martha. Let me talk to the man."

"Don't tell him anything," Martha added. "He can't know who you are."

"Then how did he know I was here? How did he know my name? He may be a friend."

"He may be an agent of the king," Bruker protested, but as the man entered the room, he went out. Tyndale stood up. The newcomer was tall. Dressed in the latest of French fashion, he wore a neat beard with a mustache, and his hair was in the latest of French styles.

"William Tyndale."

"Tyndale was here not long ago, but I'm afraid he's moved on."

"Oh, I don't believe he's gone far. You don't remember me, do you, sir?"

Tyndale stared at the man. "No, I have no memory of you at all."

"I am desolated, my friend, that you would forget me."

Tyndale was suspicious. "I fear you've mistaken me for Tyndale. If I cross paths with him again, I shall let him know you were seeking him."

Suddenly Monsieur Duroy began to laugh, and his voice changed. "Oh, Mr. Tyndale, all the trouble you took to teach me, and you've forgotten me."

Tyndale said, "I know that voice."

"You should. You've heard it enough. It's me—Stuart Winslow."

"Stuart Winslow!" he gasped. "It can't be you."

"Under all this French disguise it is."

Tyndale came across the room and looked at him closely. Then life came into his eyes. "It is you! Stuart, what are you doing here?"

Stuart then said, "I've come to help you with your work, Mr. Tyndale. I'm an expert at disguise now. I can become a Dutchman, a Norwegian, even a Chinaman, I suppose, if I have to, but God has come into my life."

"Sit down, my friend. Tell me everything."

Bruker and his wife came back and were introduced, and they learned that the handsome Frenchman spoke perfect English.

"This is my good friend Stuart Winslow, though you must not use the name. He's come to help us get the Scriptures into England."

"An angel from heaven!" Bruker exclaimed.

"No, just a stubborn Englishman who wants to serve God." Stuart laughed and said, "I'm ready for my first assignment."

"God has surely sent you, my friend," Tyndale said. "We have copies, but we haven't been able to get them through."

"I have a plan. I'll take them whenever you say, Mr. Tyndale."

"Come," he said, "let us thank God." The four of them knelt down, joined hands, and gave thanks unto God. William Tyndale ended his prayer as he always did: "O, God, get your word in English into the hands of every plowboy in England."

22

*T*he sun was well below the low-lying hills, and shadows grew long. Shading her eyes, Heather saw a man coming down the road that wound around and eventually led to London, but even a brief glimpse showed her that he was bent over and making slow work of his journey. *He must be a beggar,* she thought.

There had been trouble with beggars in England for some time. The authorities had grown worried about beggars living the life of vagabonds. Some of them refused to work, roaming the countryside or congregating in the city streets, begging, stealing, defying all authority. While many strict laws were passed during the time of Henry VII, the church viewed kindness to beggars as one of its most important works and granted them considerable freedom. Henry VIII, however, had replaced his father's laws with more stringent regulations. Old or infirm beggars who could not work were to be allowed to beg, but only in their own parish. If they went outside those boundaries, they were to be punished as if they were able-bodied vagabonds.

Local justices of the peace were ordered to draw up lists of all aged or infirm beggars and issue a license to each. A man without a license who was fit to work was apt to be severely punished should he be caught begging. Heather had seen for herself the punishment of such men in her own village. They had been stripped of their clothing, beaten, tied to the end of a cart, and slowly paraded through the village.

These strict laws were hard on the beggars, for those who would have helped them before were afraid to do so. Heather and her family had been more generous than most, and sometimes she wondered if there was a secret code among those people, for many of them came directly to her house after passing by many others.

She watched as the man very slowly drew closer. When he was within a hundred feet of her, Heather saw with horror that he was not just a beggar. He was terribly disfigured by some ravaging disease. His face was covered with a rash, the skin seemed to be peeling off, and his eyes were hooded by lids that were being slowly eaten away. The word *leper* immediately seared Heather's mind. Leprosy was a serious problem in England at one time. Now the disease had for the most part disappeared, but there were still those who bore the marks of its terrible disfigurement.

Heather stood still, resisting the impulse to flee into the house. The bent figure stopped ten yards away from her, and she managed to say in a strained but courteous voice, "Good day. Have you traveled far?"

Her greeting seemed to surprise the beggar. He wore nothing but rags. His fingers seemed to be twisted and looked like the talons of a huge bird. His forearms were scabbed in places, and there were patches of ugly raw flesh. The beggar's head lifted a little at her words, then he bent in a grotesque parody of a bow.

"Thank 'ee, lady," he mumbled. "Yes, I have come a very long way today."

Heather waited for him to ask for something, but he simply stood in silence. Then she realized that he was probably as afraid to ask for aid as she was of his disease. Impulsively she said, "You must be very thirsty. Let me fetch you a drink. Come this way." She walked to the well, and when she looked over her shoulder, he followed her with a crablike motion. *His feet must be damaged like his hands,* she thought. *And he keeps that one arm clutched to his side as if he were holding himself together.*

When they reached the well, she got the bucket, then hesitated. There was only one cup. The beggar reached into the old bag slung across one shoulder, pulled out a battered pewter cup, and timidly held it out. Heather carefully filled it to the brim, noting that his hand shook terribly as he lifted it to his mouth, which resembled a gaping wound. He drank it down thirstily and then croaked, "Please—more?"

Heather filled the cup again. It took three refills before the man sighed and lowered the cup. He wiped his mouth with the rag that did duty as a sleeve and whispered, "That wor mighty good, lady. I thank 'ee."

Heather was repelled by him, yet she well knew the admonition of the Scriptures to be kind to those who had no help, and she asked gently, "Are you hungry?"

"Yes!" He stood there, simply waiting. There was a stillness about him that was almost stonelike, as if he would move no more than he had to. His poor decayed body seemed to tremble in the afternoon breeze. But he said no more.

"Here, sit in the shade of this tree. I'll go get you something to eat."

"Thank 'ee, lady." The words were given in a whisper, and then he made his slow way to the tree with the same painful, crablike gait. Once underneath the tree, he abruptly slumped to the ground as if his legs had failed him.

Heather hurried into the house, heading straight to the kitchen. Quickly she gathered leftovers from the noon meal: bacon, potatoes, bread baked that morning. She added one of the apples of which her father was so proud. Looking around the kitchen, she spotted a large mug of cider and reached out to carry it in her free hand. Balancing her load, she went back to where the man rested and placed the nourishment on the ground beside him.

Heather was relieved when he pulled a battered pan out of his bag and held it out to her. Feeling slightly ashamed of her fear of catching his disease should he use her dishes, she served him his food. He sat cross-legged. The legs that poked through the tatters seemed as misshapen and blotched as his forearms and hands. Wordlessly he held out the battered pewter cup. She poured it full of the fresh cider.

He ate slowly, as though even his teeth hurt him, and without looking up, clutching the food closely, much like a dog that expects a bone to be snatched from it. Heather stood there, watching, yet feeling terribly awkward. But as hostess, her place was here, by her guest, such as he was.

Soon he had finished all but the apple. He held it up before him, admiring it. His eyes were almost hidden under the floppy brim of the old hat that covered his head and neck, and the white tufts of hair that covered his forehead shadowed his eyes even more. "An apple. It's been a long, long while," he whispered. His hand trembled as he began to gnaw at it.

Heather heard a voice and turned to see George Stenton, who worked for her father, striding up. He was frowning, and he barked, "Get that beggar out of here, Mistress Heather! You know what the law says. I'll wager he has no license, do you, old man?"

The beggar shrank back and shook his head. "No license."

"There. You see." George nodded. "Now, off with you!"

Heather was angry. George sometimes overestimated his own importance. "Go on with your business, George. I'll take care of this." He glared at her, but she looked back at him steadily, and he wheeled and went off, muttering darkly.

Heather turned to the beggar and said, "It's almost night."

She bit her lip doubtfully but felt impelled to ask, "Do you have any place to stay?"

"No, lady, just under the sky," he answered. "I got a blanket." He patted the bag and pulled out the edge of a tattered, torn, and very dirty blanket. His voice was weak and shaky, and his eyelids were fluttering. Heather thought he might be on the verge of passing out.

"Go into the barn over there. I will see that you have a place." She ran into the house, found an old blanket, and returned to the barn.

The man was standing in front of the barn as if he were afraid to enter. Heather opened the door and said gently, "Come in." She went into the barn and lit a lantern and hung it high up on a nail. It was a good-sized barn filled with hay and corn and feed for the animals. Her eyes swept it, and then she moved over to a small platform that had been built some time ago for holding equipment. She pulled some hay over it and said, "There. You may sleep here tonight."

The beggar looked down at the bed and then turned to face her. "The blanket . . . It will na' be clean if I sleep on it," he whispered.

"It's all right. You take it with you when you leave tomorrow. I'll make you some breakfast early and a little food to take with you."

He stood just a few feet away, close enough for her to see the skin peeling off in flakes from his cheeks and around his mouth. The lips moved, and she thought she could see the gums exposed as they drew back. "Your people—they won't like it."

Heather knew he was right. Her family were good people, but they were very cautious about whom they helped. This man, she knew, would give them cause for alarm. Not only was he diseased, but also he was unlicensed. She determined that she would make them understand.

"It will be all right," she said. "Don't touch the lantern," she cautioned. "If you should drop it, the barn would most likely burn down. I'll bring you some water so that you won't be thirsty." She picked up the milking bucket and went to the well. Carefully she washed out the bucket, filled it with water, then returned to the barn, placing it on the floor close to his bed. He was still standing in the same place, looking down at the floor. Suddenly he lifted his head and said, "Lady—" and then he stopped.

Heather looked at him curiously. "Yes?"

"Can . . . can I kiss your hand?" The voice was grating, and Heather was at once repelled.

He should not ask such a thing! she thought. But then a feeling crept over her that this was somehow, in some obscure way that she could not understand, a test of grace. Unbidden the thought flitted through her mind: *What would Jesus have done?* Suddenly she thought of a passage of Scripture that Tyndale had translated for her. *A leper asked Jesus to heal him, and Jesus reached out and touched him—and the law of Moses forbade touching a leper.* Instantly she knew what she must do and faced it squarely. She held her hand out. The old beggar bent over, his hat still low over his face, his ravaged features hidden. She felt a light touch, almost like the brushing of a butterfly's wing, on the top of her hand.

"'Tis the sweetest hand in all England!"

The voice was young and strong. Heather's heart lurched with shock as the beggar straightened up to his full height, well over six feet. He swept the hat off his head, and blue eyes met her startled ones. A smile was on his lips.

"Stuart!" She gasped. "Is it you?"

"Heather, it is I. Stuart Winslow—fugitive."

The barn seemed to blur and fade in Heather's eyes, and for the first time in her life, she was afraid she was going to faint. She blindly reached out her hand, and he took it. She felt the strong pressure of his hands and forearms as she desperately held on to him. She said breathlessly, "Stuart, I don't—"

"Sit down," Stuart said. "I'm a fool for doing this to you." He led her over to the platform, eased her down, and sat down beside her. He kept her hands covered with his. After a few moments he asked, "Are you better now, Heather?"

Heather drew a deep breath and stared up into the brilliant blue eyes. *Small wonder that he had to hide them with the brim of a hat and with hair down over his face. They were the eyes of a young man that could not be disguised.*

"Stuart, I would never have known you!" she whispered faintly. "Are you all right?"

"Oh, yes," he said with a smile. He gestured eloquently at his face. "Not a bad bit of makeup, is it?" Holding one arm straight out, he pulled up the tattered sleeves. Whatever makeup he had on his forearms to make them appear white and scaly and raw ended abruptly just above the elbow. She saw his tanned bicep corded with muscle.

"We—all thought—" she stammered, "that you might have been caught or—" She broke off, unable to finish.

"Or dead?" Stuart nodded. "It almost came to that. I want to tell you about it, Heather, and about something else that's come into my life."

He told her about his search through Germany to find William Tyndale and how he had met up with an old man, a sick actor, who had conceived the idea of teaching him how to disguise himself. "And it works! You didn't recognize me."

"Of course not. You don't look anything like yourself."

Stuart laughed. He held her hand and squeezed it firmly. "You should see me when I'm disguised as a fat Dutchman or an arrogant French duke or a dumb, slow-speaking Norwegian."

"Have you done all those things?"

"Yes, and more. That's my job now. That's what God has

called me to do. To deliver the Scriptures that Mr. Tyndale gets into print."

"That's very dangerous, isn't it?"

"Yes, but God will be with me. I have faith that I'm as clearly called to do this as Mr. Tyndale is called to translate the Scripture. It's dangerous, but it's exciting, and I know it's what God wants me to do with my life."

The two lost track of the time while Stuart described his studies: how he had mastered the art of makeup and had learned not only how to change his appearance but also his voice and the way he moved. "Since God has come into my heart, life has been different. And he's there now, Heather. Just the way he's been in yours for a long time—and my grandmother and my parents. All my life I've seen people who had peace with God, and now God has shown me his heart and drawn me to his side, and I'm going to serve him all of my life."

"What will you do now?"

"I must see my parents and brother. As a Dutchman, I brought a load of texts hidden in cases that are marked *Shoes*. They are back in London. I must get them to several people who will distribute them."

He got to his feet, and she said, "Will I see you again?"

"Yes, but I don't know when. I'm not my own man now, Heather. I'm one of God's outlaws. At least, the king would see me like that."

"The king is getting worse. He's having many arrested just for owning one of Mr. Tyndale's Bibles."

"I know." His face clouded over, and he shook his head. "The king is not the man I thought he was, but he's not greater than God. He won't stop the Word of God from going out to the English people." He stared at her and said, "You're beautiful, Heather. Every time I see you, it surprises me just how beautiful you are." He leaned down, kissed her hand, and whispered, "I'll come back as soon as I can."

He left, adopting the crablike gait at the door, and became, once again a poor leprous beggar. Heather watched him. "I love him," she whispered. "But he doesn't love me." It seemed strange that Stuart could so clearly see God's hand in his life but remained blind to a woman who was ready to give him her heart. Sadly she turned and walked into the house without looking back at the crooked figure that painfully made its way down the road. Away from her. Again.

⚘

Stuart had abandoned disguise, for as far as he knew, there was no evidence to connect him with William Tyndale. He could not be certain until he got to the king's court, and he certainly could not go there as a leper. He dressed in the best clothing he could afford. As he moved toward Richmond Palace, he thought warmly of his parents. They were shocked and then overjoyed to see him. He had disappointed them for so many years, but now they were filled with pride. They had also been filled with apprehension when he had explained what he was doing, but he could not be dissuaded from his call.

His father and his mother had reluctantly let him go, obtaining his promise to come back as soon as he could. They had also promised to take some of the texts and give them out discreetly. He had warned them: "Don't let anybody know about it. The king has become a mad dog about things like this."

"He'll find out one day that God always rules in the end," Claiborn said, not with vindictiveness but with sorrow. "He's a pitiful creature, and I'd hate to be in his shoes when he faces God on Judgment Day."

Henry's court had changed little. Almost the first man Stuart ran into was Sir Charles Vining, who gave him a hug, his face alight with pleasure. "Here to stay for a while, I hope. It's been years, man."

"I'm afraid it's only a visit."

"Where have you been? After that nasty business of your false accusation, I thought you'd return to court."

Stuart chose to not address the fact that Vining had never come to see him while he was imprisoned, never tried to aid him. Vining was Vining. A simple, shallow man of the court. He'd come to terms with that. "I've entered into a new business, Charles. Nothing interesting to you, really. But I'm doing rather well at it. Traveling a good bit. It's led me far afield, but I'm glad to be home for a bit. What's happening here?"

"Well"—Vining's face sobered, and he bit his lower lip—"some men we know have been burned at the stake. Richard Bayfield last month."

"What was the charge?" Stuart asked, though he knew the answer and had already heard the news.

"He was tied in with that fellow Tyndale who's sending Bibles over here. Bayfield was a good man, but the king is like a madman. The movement to put a stop to the Bible in England is gathering momentum. I fear they'll catch him sooner or later. Well, come on. You want to meet some of your old friends."

※

Stuart met several old acquaintances. He was once again struck by the frivolity of the court and the vanity of it all. He was glad when Vining finally left his side, and he went at once to the queen's apartment. He had planned to do this all along, and did not know whether he would be received or not. He sent his name in. The guard disappeared and then returned and said, "Her Majesty will receive you, sir."

Stuart was met by the queen, and Mary was by her side. He knelt and kissed her hand. "It's been a long time, Your Majesty."

"Rise, Master Winslow. Yes, it has been a long time."

"Why have you stayed away so long?" Mary demanded.

"I am indeed sorry, but look at you, Princess. A grown-up

young woman! We'll not be able to play our games anymore."

Mary was an attractive young girl with alert eyes. She
laughed and said, "We can play chess."

"Oh, you would beat me at that, I'm sure."

"Come along," Princess Mary said. Queen Catherine sat over
to one side while the two of them played chess, and, indeed,
Mary won.

"You didn't let me beat you, did you, Master Winslow?"

"No, indeed. You're simply a better player than I am. I can't
get over how pretty you are. You had better watch out for those
young fellows. They're going to be coming around like bees
swarming into a flower garden."

Catherine sat watching all this with a slight smile. Then she
said, "Now, Mary, let me talk to Master Winslow for a while."

"All right, Mother." The young woman ran out lightly.

"I can't believe how grown-up she is."

"She's the pride of my life on this earth. I wish the king felt
the same about her."

"Has nothing changed, Majesty?"

A bitterness came to Catherine's lips. "You haven't heard."

"Heard what, my queen?"

"Anne is pregnant. The king, of course, is the father of her
child. They've gone through a secret marriage ceremony—
which everyone knows about. I think the coronation will take
place any day."

Stuart had heard rumors of this but no evidence. Now he sat
staring at the sad woman whose life had come to such a pass.
"I'm deeply sorry, Your Majesty."

"You are, aren't you? So few people consider me. Thank you,
Master Winslow."

The rest of the visit was taken up by Catherine trying to find
out about his new business and Stuart evading her, saying
merely that he had gone into an import business that required

much travel. He stayed long enough to have tea with the Princess Mary and the queen, and when he left, Mary came to him and took his hand. "Come again."

"I will do my best, Princess, but mind that I am no longer a man of the court." And remember what I said about those young fellows who will be coming around. Believe none of us!"

Mary laughed. "I believe you. Maybe you'll come courting me."

"Well, I'm an old man, and I'm afraid my heart belongs to another. But you watch out for the young bucks who come around. Listen to your mother. She'll guide you well." When he left, a great sadness came to him. He knew that the king would have his way. Anne Boleyn would have a child, and if it was a son, that child would be the next king of England. He had heard enough from others to know that the king was convinced that the child would be a boy.

☙

Heather had not slept well since Stuart had returned. She had seen him only the one time when he came disguised as a leper, but her thoughts were constantly with him. There was a sadness in her, and those close to her saw it, but she would not reveal the reason to anyone.

It was three weeks after his return. There was a knock at the door. It was early morning, and she was making breakfast. Opening the door, she gasped, "Stuart, you're here!"

"Yes, I am."

"Not in disguise?"

"No need for it. Not now, anyway. May I come in?"

"Why, of course. Can I make you something to eat?"

Ignoring her question, he seemed to be tongue-tied. "I—I must say something and you'll probably think I'm mad."

"What is it? Are you in trouble?"

"I've been in trouble for a long time." He hesitated and then blurted out, "For years I thought I was in love with Nell Fenton."

"You made it plain enough."

"I did, didn't I? Well, I was a fool, Heather."

"What's happened?"

"Oh, she married an old man for his money two years ago now."

"I'm so sorry, Stuart."

Suddenly Stuart straightened up, took her hand, and drew her to sit down on a small couch. "I've been delivering some Bibles, and I'm so pleased to be doing the Lord's work. But something else has come to me. It's about you, Heather."

Heather's heart beat faster. "What is it?"

Stuart got up, came around, and pulled her to her feet. "For three weeks I've been wandering around, and do you know what's been on my heart?"

"Figuring out how to distribute your texts?"

"Well, yes, but more oft than nought, it's been you, dear girl! I thought about the first time I ever came here and you gave me cider. You were just a little girl then. As I grew up, I always thought of you as a little girl. Oh, I knew better, for I have eyes, haven't I? But I've been praying that God would give me wisdom, and I'm going to ask you one thing. Tell me the truth. Have you ever thought of me as a man you might marry?"

Heather's heart seemed to stop, and she cried out, "Oh, Stuart, of course I have—for years!"

"You have? Why didn't you tell me?"

"Because a woman can't tell a man that. She has to wait until he comes to his senses, and I thought you never would."

He took her in his arms then, and she came to him. She was a woman in every respect, fully rounded, wise, sweet, and when his lips touched hers, he had a sense of coming into a harbor after a stormy voyage. When he lifted his head, he whispered, "You'll have me, then?"

"I would have had you years ago, Stuart. I've loved you since I was a child."

He saw that tears were in her eyes. "I'll have to spend a lot of years making it right with you, but I love you as I love life. You understand I can't give up my work with Mr. Tyndale."

"I know that. Perhaps I can help you."

"Why, yes! Together we'll serve God, and we'll listen to him as he blesses us. Won't it be fun being married and having children! I'd like to have about eight myself."

Heather laughed and blushed prettily. "Well, we're getting a bit of a late start, Master Winslow. I suppose that will be up to God."

⚭

"You haven't done your job, Ives," Wolsey said.

"I know. It's been difficult, Eminence, but I have an answer."

"You'd better," Wolsey said. "The king is in a mood to hang us all or chop our heads off. What's your scheme?"

"I have found out that Stuart Winslow's parents have been sending money to help Tyndale. I think they've been receiving Bibles too, though I haven't caught them at it."

"Edmund Winslow doesn't care about Bibles."

"No, he doesn't, but his brother does. I think we could smoke the Winslows out, and it won't be too hard to trace the books back to wherever Tyndale is hiding out."

"What's your scheme?" Wolsey listened as Ives outlined his plan and nodded with grim satisfaction. "That's just wicked enough to suit me. See to it, Ives."

Ives at once began to lay a trap. It was designed not just to catch William Tyndale. He was determined to incriminate Edmund Winslow. A smile came to his thin lips. "When he's out of the way, than I shall be the master of Stoneybrook!"

༄

Edmund Winslow looked up as Ives walked into the room, accompanied by a man he had not met.

"Ives, welcome home," he said, rising.

"There's your man, Snyder."

"What are you talking about?" Edmund said. "Who is this?"

"My name is Aaron Snyder. You may have heard of me." Snyder was a thin man with a hatchetlike face and a colorless smile. "I am chief investigator for the king."

Edmund stared, and a shiver went through him. "State your business."

"I've come to arrest you, sir."

"Arrest me!" Edmund exclaimed. "What are you talking about?"

"Do your duty, Snyder," Ives snapped. "Arrest him."

"You're charged with treason. You and your brother have been receiving Bibles at Stoneybrook and distributing them."

"That's—that's not so!"

"We have found them in your house." Snyder held up a Bible and said, "This was found in your very chamber. It's one of William Tyndale's Bibles. It's treason to assist that man."

Edmund moved his doleful gaze to his stepson. "Ives, tell him I could have nothing to do with this."

"I have nothing to say to you."

Edmund's head went back, and his mouth dropped open. "Why, you planned this!"

"Certainly not. I merely reported what I saw. You, Claiborn, and Stuart will pay for your crimes. Arrest your man, Snyder."

Snyder summoned two men. "Take him to the prisoners' wagon." He said, "Shall we get his brother?"

"Oh, yes, that would be next in order." Ives accompanied Snyder and was pleased to see that the same trap had been laid for Claiborn Winslow. Bibles had been hidden in two corners by one of the servants, happy to accept his bribe.

Claiborn stared at Ives, his eyes burning. "So you're determined to have Stoneybrook." Grace stood behind him, hand to her mouth. Her son Quentin stood beside her, his eyes watchful. Ives considered having her arrested as well but decided that she would be driven out of Stoneybrook easily when the time came. She could return to her aunt's land in Ireland. Or she could beg on the streets of London for all he cared. She was no threat.

"There'll be no accusations, Winslow. All will come to light at your trial. Come along," Snyder said. "Join your brother. I'm sure you'll enjoy it in the Tower."

The two men were led away in chains.

Ives went at once to his mother's apartment, where she was waiting.

"Is it over?"

"They'll be found guilty. The evidence is plain. All we need do now is catch Stuart in the act of smuggling and all three Winslows will be sacked." He lifted his hands and laughed. "How does it feel to be the lady of Stoneybrook with no lord to watch your every move?"

"How does it feel to be the master of Stoneybrook?"

The two smiled at each other, and he said, "Does it pain you that they'll both be executed?"

"Let us not dwell on the past but review our future. Let's look over this new kingdom of ours!"

23

"Well, how do you like your husband, hah?"

Heather suddenly giggled. Ever since she had joined Stuart in Germany, she had blossomed. Stuart was carefully disguised as a fat Dutch merchant. He wore heavily puffed-out hose and a doublet that was swollen with padding. "You look awful!" Heather cried. "I'm glad you don't look like that all the time."

"You don't understand my art," Stuart said. His face was stiff with makeup. He had glued paper onto his cheeks to swell them out. He had donned a wig, which covered his auburn hair, and his face seemed to be older. He paraded up and down the room now, practicing the proper waddling walk for his character.

Heather took his hands. "I'm not going to kiss you good-bye, not with that mess on your face." Suddenly a line of worry appeared over her eyebrows. "I wish you didn't have to go, Stuart."

"Well, it may be the last shipment for some time." Tyndale had had to flee to a nearby town and was in search of a new printer. "I'm taking all William has on hand here, clearing the decks. I promise you that when I return we'll have a lot of time together. I'll be the handsome fellow you married."

"The handsome fellow I married certainly does not run over with humility!"

Stuart grinned, reached out, and grabbed her. He held her tight against the padding and teased her, saying, "You wouldn't really turn away from me if I was this fat, would you?"

Heather suddenly smiled. "Nay. And you'd love me, even if I were fat or ugly."

"You're right, woman. We're stuck with each other." He held her for a time, enjoying their last moments. "I must be off," he whispered. He kissed her on the cheek.

Heather grasped his arm. "Return soon. There are two of us counting on it."

Stuart blinked with surprise. "Two of us?"

Heather suddenly smiled a beatific smile that seemed to start somewhere in the depth of her spirit and shine out through her eyes. "Well, one of us won't be exactly present for at least six more months."

Stuart blinked in confusion. "Six months—" He broke off and peered at her. "Does that mean what I think it means?"

"Yes. We're going to have a child. A boy, I trust, just like his father."

Stuart picked Heather up and swung her around the room in a wild dance. "A son! What a wonderful present!"

"Put me down!"

"Oh, I'm sorry. I'll have to be careful with you from now on."

"Yes, you will. You have to give me everything I want and stay with me constantly as soon as you return."

"Is that customary with new fathers?"

"It is for my baby's father." She touched his cheek and said, "I'm so glad you're pleased, Stuart."

"Well, of course I am. Let's just hope he's as happy and witty and charming as his father."

"Oh, you're impossible, but I hope so too."

"I'll have something to think about on my journey."

Tyndale was delighted to see Stuart. Several times as they talked the older man shook his head, saying, "I would never have known you, Stuart. It's astonishing that you can so disguise yourself."

"Well, all thanks to Nathan. He was a good teacher."

"Do you speak Dutch?"

"Not very well, but I'll make them think I'm a Dutchman learning to speak English."

Suddenly Tyndale leaned forward. "You must be very, very cautious, Stuart. The king is burning people at the stake for smuggling and distributing Bibles."

"I'll be all right, sir."

"How are you taking the Bibles this time?"

"My favorite way—in crates. The labels are in Dutch and say *Shoes*. The Bibles are under the shoes."

"But Bibles are heavier, aren't they?"

"Yes, but I had them put in small crates with no more than twenty Bibles to a crate. I think we're safe. Nobody's interested in shoes. They'll never look inside. If they do, the top two layers are nothing but shoes."

"Very well. Let's pray that God will give you safe journey."

The two men bowed their heads, Stuart contemplating what an extraordinary man William Tyndale was. He had never made one penny from the sale of the Bibles that he had translated so arduously and printed at the risk of his life. When the final amen was said, he saw that Tyndale had tears in his eyes.

"Why, you don't have to worry about me," he protested.

"I'm putting you in God's hands. He'll take care of you. I was just thinking about the people who will get these Bibles from you. They'll have to hide them, of course, but God will speak to them. Isn't that marvelous, Stuart, that we're getting the Word of God to people who have never had it?"

"It's a wonderful work, sir, and the Lord is going to bless it mightily."

"Well, go on, my boy, and again, take close care."

"I shall. One favor?"

"Anything."

"Look in on my Heather from time to time, will you?" He hesitated. "She frets. And loneliness only makes it worse."

"Consider it done, Brother."

※

Walking down the gangplank of the *Amazon,* Stuart looked out over London's busy harbor. There were ships from a dozen different nations, some of them unloading, some of them loading. The officials were so busy that they would not have time to look at some Dutch shoes—at least that was Stuart's hope. He waited for a time, and finally, not seeing his merchandise, he inquired of the master of the ship.

"Ven vill my cargo be unloaded?" he said, imitating a Dutch accent as well as possible.

"Not until the morrow. They're down at the bottom of the hold, and I'm shorthanded. Come back at daybreak."

"Danke." Stuart hoped that *danke* meant thank you in Dutch, as in German, for the two languages, he knew, were similar. But he knew he was on shaky ground.

He decided to go home to Stoneybrook, stopping at an inn to change out of his disguise.

He was making his way through the streets when he suddenly saw his old friend Charles Vining. Vining was buying an eel pie from a vendor. Stuart edged over to him at once. *A good test for my disguise.*

"Guten morgen, sir."

Vining turned and stared at the fat figure before him. "Good morning," he said, and started to turn back.

"You like them eel pies?"

"Very much." Vining took a bite of the pie and said, "You just off the ship?"

"*Ja*, from Holland."

"Welcome to England."

"I hear things are not so *gut* here in your country."

"Nothing unusual," Vining said. He was about to turn away again when Stuart said softly, "You don't know me, do you, Charles?"

Vining turned quickly, his eyes opening wide with surprise. He knew that voice! "Is that—is that you, Stuart?"

"Yes. Don't say anything."

"I won't. But you shouldn't be here."

"I had to come home."

"You heard about your father and uncle?"

"No. What about them?"

Vining took a quick look around. "Let's get out of this crowd," he said. He led the way out of the teeming streets. The two men went into an inn that was almost abandoned. There was only one other customer there, and his head was on the table. The two men took a seat, and Vining ordered two beers. When they came and the server had left, Vining leaned forward. "I'm sorry to be the bearer of bad news."

"Something about my father and uncle?"

"Yes. I thought that was why you came back. But it's a good thing you're in disguise."

"What's happened, Charles?"

"They were arrested. They're in the Tower, and you'll be arrested too, if you are discovered here."

Stuart felt something close around his heart. The Tower! He knew what that was like. "Why?"

"They were arrested for treason. Mostly for helping William Tyndale and having unlawful Bibles in their homes."

"Tell me all of it."

Stuart sat listening to every word. When he had got the whole story, Vining said, "You must leave England at once. You're disguised, but all you need is one slip and you'll be with your father and uncle."

"I can't do that. I must see them as well as see to Mother and Quentin."

Vining's eyes opened in alarm. "You mustn't attempt it! They're not allowed visitors. Certainly not you. The king is quite paranoid now. His people are attempting to separate the smugglers so as to stop the flow of Bibles. The minute you showed yourself you would be clapped in irons. I'm telling you the king is serious. There were four people burned yesterday in Smithfield for the very charge that's been brought against your family."

"I can't help that. I must see if I can aid them."

Vining shook his head in despair. "Stuart, you cannot be serious."

"Yes, I'm going to save my people somehow."

"I'm telling you, there is no way, man!"

Stuart said, "I'll be in touch with you."

"Where can I reach you?"

"You can't. I don't know where I'll be, but I'll be getting back to you. I'll probably need some help."

Vining shook his head. "Not me, Stuart. I—"

Stuart grabbed his arm and stared hard into his eyes. "I needed you once. When I was in the Tower. Did you come to my aid then? Or even come to visit me, give me succor? Nay!"

"Yes, well, I'm sorry about that. I had my position at court to consider—"

"I almost died in there, Charles. If it had not been for the queen, I think I might have. We were friends, and you did not come to my aid. You owe me."

Vining sighed heavily. "I shall do what I can." He stared at his friend. "I would never have known you. But some of these agents are clever people. Take my advice. Stay as hidden as you can."

Stuart patted him on the shoulder. "It's good to have you as a friend, Charles. I never thought it would come to this after the way we met."

Vining smiled. "No, you wanted to cut my heart out in defense of the king. Things certainly do change."

The two men separated.

Stuart walked the streets of London until he found a quiet place by the Thames and sat there praying. He well knew he was not leaving England until he had retrieved his cargo and set his father and his uncle free, but he had no idea how to go about it. For two hours he sat there, remembering some of the psalms that he called the make haste psalms, in which the psalmist pleads with the Lord to come to his aid at once.

"Father, please help me! You know I have no wisdom. I don't know what to do, but you do. You already know how things will end. Save my uncle and my father, for they are only doing your work."

He continued to pray like this for some time, and then he simply sat there, and scriptures continued to run through his mind. Most were promises that he had memorized, and now one came to him that he felt was an answer. He said it aloud, "Commit thy way unto the Lord, and he shall bring it to pass." At the moment he could not remember where it could be found in the Bible, but he knew it was in the psalms. He said it over and over again, "Commit thy way unto the Lord, and he shall bring it to pass." It was the kind of promise that he liked, and he got up and walked slowly back to the harbor, knowing that he would have to find a place to stay.

"I put this burden on you, Lord, for you have told us to cast our cares on you. Guide me, for you must help and direct, and I give you thanks now for what you're going to do."

As he walked, he passed a monastery. He stopped and stared at the monks working in the garden, and a little light seemed to go on in his spirit. And then he prayed, "Lord, I think I know what you want me to do. Thank you for your guidance!"

"Here's your food. It's a little better tonight."

Claiborn looked up at the guard, who had brought two bowls into the cell. He set them down on the table and said, "Now I'll bring you some ale."

"That's kind of you, Jennings."

"All I can do." The guard stopped at the door and turned around. He had been kind enough to the two prisoners, which was unusual in Tower guards, but he remembered Stuart fondly, calling him a good sort. He hesitated, then blurted out, "I hate to tell you this, but there was six burned at Smithfield yesterday."

"For what charge?"

"Same as against you. Caught with Bibles." Jennings hesitated, then said, "Best you two get ready to meet the good Lord."

"I am ready to meet God."

"What about Mr. Edmund there?"

"Well, I'm praying for him. You might do the same."

"My prayers don't amount to much."

"They might," Claiborn said. He had talked to the guard before, and knew that he was a Christian. "I'd appreciate it if you'd pray for us."

"Well, sir, I'll do just that."

The guard left, and Claiborn said, "Well, Jennings was right. This does look better."

"I'm not hungry." Edmund had lost weight and looked unwell. His clothes hung upon him, and his cheeks had sunk. He had not been well for some time before his arrest, and now he was not only physically ill but also sick at heart. The treachery of his wife and stepson had been a blow to him. Claiborn had tried to tell him that God was going to set them free one way or another, but Edmund had lost all hope.

"Look, there's some meat in this stew. You must eat to get strength." Claiborn handed the bowl to him, ate his own, and worried Edmund until his brother downed half of it. "You can have the rest later," he said.

There was little enough to do in the cell, so Claiborn tried to keep the conversation going, but Edmund was no help.

"God will get us out of this, you'll see."

"It was my own wife who did this to us," Edmund moaned for the hundredth time. "She and Ives arranged it."

"We don't know that," Claiborn returned with a sigh.

"Yes, we do. I know it anyway."

Claiborn had no answer, for he secretly concurred with Edmund that Edith and Ives were behind it all. He had had to pray much, for anger broke out in his spirit every time he thought of them. All it took was one look at poor Edmund to see that they had destroyed him.

Some two hours later, a new guard entered their cell. "Got a priest here that says he wants to help you," he said. A tall priest entered, then the guard shut the three men in. The priest wore a monk's robe with the cowl pulled over his head, concealing his face.

"Well, we thank you for coming, Father."

The monk threw back the cowl. Claiborn gasped. "It's you, Stuart!"

Even Edmund looked up, his eyes widening. "What are you doing here, boy?" he whispered.

"I've come to get your story."

"Don't you know that they'll arrest you if they catch you?" Claiborn said. "You're charged as we are."

"I know. But in order to fight an enemy, you must know who he is. An old soldier once told me that."

Claiborn embraced him. "I'm glad to see you, Son, but it's terrible, you being here."

"I had to come." Stuart put his hand on his uncle's shoulder. He saw the man looked bad and that he was ill, so he said, "We'll see you back to health, Uncle Edmund, once you're free from here."

Edmund stared at him. "You can't free us."

"God can."

Claiborn suddenly laughed softly. "Yes, he can, and he'll have to."

"I don't have much time. Tell me everything that happened. How did the Bibles get into your house? I know you were careful to keep them out in the barn."

For the next fifteen minutes Claiborn outlined the history. When he finished, Stuart said, "It has to be Ives. Edith found out about the Bibles—perhaps through a servant?—told Ives, and Ives told Wolsey."

"Yes, and that servant probably helped plant those Bibles in our houses. It wouldn't have been easy with us always about."

"They betrayed me," Edmund said dully.

Stuart exchanged glances with his father, and Stuart said quickly, "I'm going to go now, but don't give up. I'll find a way out of this."

"Be careful."

"Where's Mother?"

"They didn't arrest her. I don't know why. I imagine she's staying with the Murphys."

"I'll go and see her."

"Be careful, Son. The king has eyes everywhere."

"I will, Father."

Stuart banged on the door, and the guard let him out.

When he came out into the bright sunlight, he knew he could not wait. He had to do something. His father had told him that Orrick had been released, that he had gone to work for a family to the north of London. He had the family's name. When he got there, still disguised as a monk, he saw Orrick out exercising one of the horses. He went closer and said huskily, "Your name Orrick?"

"Yes, it is. What do you want with me?"

Stuart came closer. "It's me, Orrick—Stuart Winslow."

Orrick's eyes flew open and his jaw dropped. "Master Winslow, sir! What are you doing here? Don't you know what's happened?"

"I know all about it. I've been to see Father and Sir Edmund. I'm going to get them out of that place, Orrick."

"That would be a wonderful thing—but how?"

"Somebody betrayed them."

"It was that Ives, it was, and his mother too, I think. I looked a bit crossways in their direction, and suddenly I was out on my arse. Gave my life to Stoneybrook, and they sent me on my way! How do you like that?"

"Help me, Orrick, and I'll see you get your job back. They didn't act alone. Who do you think helped them?"

"Well, for my part, I think it was Jacob Fowler."

"Who's he?"

"He's new. Ives hired him some time ago. I never liked him, but he had the run of both houses. It would have been no trouble for him to plant them Bibles."

"Do you think he did it?"

"I can't prove it. Just a feeling I have. As soon as your father and your uncle were arrested, he quit his position. Suddenly had a thick purse. Bought a fine horse. Fine clothes. Went after lots of fancy women, he did."

"So you think he was paid to betray my people?"

"That's what I think, but he won't ever own up to it."

"He may. Where do I find him?"

"Why, he's staying at the Blue Parrot, last I heard."

"Not a very fancy place."

"No, he spent all his money. Lost it gambling."

"Then he may be ready to listen."

"You really think you can get your father and your uncle out of the Tower?"

"God can."

Orrick laughed. "You sound like your father! Well, God bless you, sir. I'll be looking for you, coming to offer me my old position back."

"I shall, Orrick. And I won't be dressed as a monk when I return."

꩜

The darkness was falling fast now, and Stuart had not found Jacob Fowler. Carrying a sword beneath a robe was awkward, but he had to have a weapon. He was on his way across London Bridge to see if he could locate him in an inn that he had heard the man frequented. It began raining in huge drops that splattered loudly on the road. He pulled his cowl over his head. The rain became visible sheets that swept across the road in front of him.

There was something frightening about the streets to Stuart. He was totally conscious of what would happen if he were caught, but he hoped that his disguise would keep him safe.

He was halfway across the bridge when he heard the clatter of hooves behind him.

He had always been fascinated by London Bridge, but now all he wanted was to pass over it. He glanced at the houses that were built on both sides of the roadway. Most of the houses joined those beside it, but narrow alleys gave access to the lip of the bridge, mostly for the purpose of allowing garbage to be tossed into the Thames. If they had not been there, the bridge would have been wide and easily passed. But the houses were jumbled together in no order whatsoever and rambled along the length of the bridge, some of them two and three stories high.

He glanced up and saw the heads of the traitors stuck on poles, but it was too dark to identify any of them. The rain beat on his face, so he pulled the cowl closer over his head and forged his way through the rain.

The horses were nearing him. He paused when a man called out, "You, there! Stop!"

There was no choice, so Stuart turned and waited.

Soldiers. Stuart muttered a quick prayer.

A sergeant approached. Rain had soaked him through, and he was in a bad humor. "What's your name?"

"Father Francis."

"Where are you going, out in this foul night?"

"One of our flock is sick. I'm going to visit him."

"What's his name?"

"That isn't a monk." One of the soldiers had come forward and was staring at Stuart.

"How do you know that, Simpkins?"

"He's too big and well fed. Look at him. Them monks are all scrawny."

"Let's see your face."

The sergeant jerked the hood from Stuart's head. "You don't look like a monk to me."

Stuart said, "Yes, I am a monk. All you have to do is ask at the monastery."

"Who's in charge of that monastery? What's his name?"

Stuart knew that he was trapped. Any monk would know the name of the head of the monastery. He had to improvise. "His name is Father Jerome."

"That's a lie, Sergeant! I know that bunch. Used to live over there. The head of it is a monk named Father Xavier."

"So why are you dressed like a monk if you are not truly a man of the cloth?"

Stuart whirled and ran down the street. He heard the sergeant yelling, "Catch him! Go get him!" Footsteps pounded behind him. He knew that he would have to outrun his pursuers, but one of the men was even more fleet than himself. He felt a hand grab him and jerk him backward. He fell to the ground. The soldier had drawn his sword. Stuart had no choice. He rolled, regained his feet, and pulled the sword from beneath his robe. He threw himself to the right, but his opponent was ahead of him. He was an expert swordsman. The blades clashed. Stuart knew he had no time, for the rest were nearly upon them. He dropped the tip of his sword, pretending to retreat, and just as the man lunged at him, uttering a wild cry, he lifted the sword, and the man ran into the blade. Awareness leaped into his eyes, and his mouth opened. He tried to speak, but only blood leaked from his lips as he fell down.

There was no time to hesitate. Stuart's father had told him that, over and over, when they sparred. *If one enemy has been slain, always assume another is behind him. Your life depends on you continuing to move.*

The other soldiers were upon him. There was one in front eager to fight. His eyes were bright with excitement, and he yelled, "I've got you now!"

There was only one door open, and Stuart took it. He knew that behind him there was only blackness. He could hear the rushing of the river, and he knew it was flood tide. The water of the Thames rushed between the arches of London Bridge at a frightening speed. Anyone caught in the turbulence of the river would in all probability be battered to death against the sides of the massive arches. But he ran to the down-river side of the bridge.

In the darkness and rain, Stuart had no idea exactly where on the bridge he was. He might be on one of the sections, built of rock and rubble, from which the arches stood. Even if he took his chance and jumped, he might land on one of those and break every bone in his body.

"Come along, man. You're caught!" The sergeant had arrived, his weapon drawn, and his men fanned out, making a semicircle. "Put down your sword."

It was hopeless. As they edged in, Stuart knew he had only one choice. Without a word, he launched himself out into the darkness.

As he turned in the air, he heard the cries of the men above.

"Now he's done it! Get to the bank!"

He heard the whistling of the wind, and spread his arms and half-bent his knees. Down he plunged through the darkness. His mind raced. *If I die, my father and my uncle will die. God, keep me alive so that I can help them!*

He had time only for those few words, and then the darkness and the water swallowed him.

24

*T*he dark water made a rushing sound, but it was silenced as Stuart struck the surface and was sucked under. He landed on his back, and the blow made him expel his breath, so that when he went under he nearly suffocated. The water seized him. He expected at any moment to be bashed against the pillars that held up the bridge.

Fighting his way to the surface, he gasped at the air and thrashed in the water, which rushed madly along. He was a good swimmer. When he got his breath back, he began pulling straight for the shore. The force of the water lessened, and he reached the rocks without any problem. He climbed out through the mud, the stench of the raw sewage that made up a great deal of the Thames making him gag. Now the monk's robe that he wore did nothing to keep the cold air from him. He had lost his sword.

He made a quick prayer of thanks. "Thank you, Lord, for not letting me die in that river. Now guide my steps." He huddled beneath some bushes, seeking to avoid some of the rain that pelted him and stay out of sight in case the guards chose to search for him. Apparently they considered him dead and gone, however, for the river remained silent. He shivered uncontrollably but persuaded himself to wait until most of London had gone to bed before he made his way to his lodging. A soaked monk roaming the streets of London at midnight might draw unwanted attention.

Hours later he reached the inn, crept inside, and climbed the stairs. When he got inside his room, he threw off the wet, heavy robe with a sigh of relief and toweled himself down with an extra blanket. He lay down on the bed and pulled the blanket over him, his mind working rapidly. *I must find Jacob Fowler!* he thought. *Right after I meet my contact and hand off the Bibles.*

He drifted off then into an unsettled sleep in which he dreamed of fast, dark rivers and men with swords.

Jacob Fowler opened his eyes painfully as a ray of bright sunshine struck him in the face. It was almost like a red-hot iron passing from temple to temple. He moaned softly, held his head, and thought of the previous night—or tried to think. All he could remember was that he had been enormously drunk and a harlot had appeared from nowhere. Not an unusual sort of evening.

Rolling out of his bed, he went across the room to where he kept his scanty store of cash behind a loose board in the wall. Moving the board, he found the small leather sack there and breathed a sigh of relief. He emptied the sack, fingered the coins for a moment, and then whispered, "I must do something soon." He'd be out of money within days.

He dressed quickly, trying to ignore his headache, then sneaked out the back way so that the innkeeper wouldn't see him. He was hungry, but he had no money to spare for food.

All morning he waited outside the office of the chancellor. At length he saw Ives Hardcastle come out. Ives was wearing a rich robe, and there was a satisfied look of prosperity about him.

Fowler went up to him quickly and said, "Mr. Hardcastle—"

"What do you want, Fowler?"

The brevity of the reply told Fowler much of Hardcastle's feelings. The man never had a kind word for anyone. But Fowler forced himself to be pleasant. "I tell you, sir, I'm in need of employment." He winked and went on, "Sure there must be something useful you can find for me to do."

Hardcastle stared at the man in disdain. "There's nothing now, Fowler. I'll send for you should I need you."

The words were like a dash of cold water, and anger welled up in Fowler. He wanted to shout, *You weren't so cold when you needed me!* But he knew it was useless. So he left the court and returned to his lodging.

He spent the day trying to borrow money, with no success. The money that he had received from Hardcastle on the last job had vanished; how it had all drained away quite mystified him. Late that afternoon he went into an inn and began to drink. When darkness fell he left with a bottle. He had only two coins left in his purse and had not eaten a bite. To make things worse, when he got back to his inn, he was apprehended by the innkeeper, a man half a head taller than himself, who said gruffly, "It's your last night here. I'll be putting you out come morning if I don't get paid."

Fowler wanted to smash the man's face, but the innkeeper was too burly for that. He ducked his head, mumbled in agreement, and stumbled to his room. For a long time he sat in the single chair trying desperately to think what to do. His only choice was to return to Bristol, where his brother had a small ironworks. He hated his brother, and the feeling was returned with interest, but he knew his brother would take him in for the simple pleasure of tormenting him. Undoubtedly he'd put him to the dirtiest work possible and force him to live in squalor.

He picked up the clay bottle and tilted it, but it was long

empty. He threw it across the room in a fit of anger and it smashed on the wall. *What else can I do? I'll starve if I stay in this cursed England.*

A knock sounded, and he looked up, startled and wary. He picked up a knife from the table and pulled it from the sheath. Opening the door, he peered out to see a well-dressed man standing in the dim hallway. "What is it? What do you want?"

"A matter of business," the man answered quietly. Fowler saw that his visitor was in his late twenties and had a pair of steady blue eyes. A thought crossed Fowler's mind. *Ives Hardcastle sent him. He's had a change of mind.* The finery the man wore signaled that he was someone high in the social realm. Fowler pulled the door back. "Come in," he said, and stepped back.

The tall man entered and waited as Fowler shut the door and walked over to the small table to set down the knife.

"What can I do for you?"

"It's a business matter."

"Business? Did Hardcastle send you?"

A smile touched the man's lips, and his eyes grew watchful. "You might say that," he said. There was something in the man's manner that baffled Fowler. He could not place him. Had never seen him as far as he knew.

"Well, what do you want? Is there a job in it?"

"You didn't do too well on your last venture with Ives Hardcastle, did you now, Jacob?"

Instantly Fowler grew wary. What's that to you?" he demanded.

"How much did he pay you for planting the evidence and testifying against Sir Edmund and his brother?"

Fowler's hand darted to the dagger. He had known when he had put the Bibles in the house and castle and then lied to the chief investigator that he was taking a chance, but Ives Hardcastle had assured him that there would be no defenders. "Get out of here," he said hoarsely. "I did my duty and that was all."

Jacob's visitor ignored the dagger in his hand. "Couldn't have been more than forty or fifty crowns for a job like that. Am I right, Jacob? And that's all been spent, hasn't it?"

"I don't know what you're going on about, man. Leave me," Fowler growled. He made his living by doing the bidding of those above him, usually doing the dirty jobs they didn't care to touch with their dainty white hands. Since he saw the man before him making no threat, Fowler began to wonder if there might be something in it. He demanded, "What do you want?"

"My name is Winslow."

He's come to kill me for lying about his father and uncle and putting them in the Tower!

Fowler slashed out with the knife, intending to land it against Winslow's throat. Two things happened. Fowler never actually saw either of them; he just saw the result. The man was holding a long, thin dagger in front of his face. Fowler had not even seen him move. Next he felt a powerful, sharp blow on his arm. His fingers went numb. His own knife fell to the floor. Then the cold steel of the man's blade was against his throat.

"Don't—kill me," he begged. "Please don't kill me."

"It would be easy enough to do, and to be honest, it was in my mind when I came here." But then the dagger disappeared. "It wouldn't profit me to see you dead, Jacob," Winslow said in a conversational tone. "So how would you like to make two hundred golden crowns?"

Jacob Fowler stopped breathing for a moment. Greed replaced his fear. "Two hundred golden crowns? For doing what?"

"Why, for helping me get my father and my uncle out of the Tower and back in their rightful places."

"I can't help you with that," Fowler whispered uncertainly.

"As a matter of fact, you are the only one who can. It was

your testimony that put them there along with your evidence. You did plant the evidence, didn't you, Jacob?"

"Never! It's a lie!"

"Oh, come now, Jacob. It's just the two of us here. No matter what you say, you can't be charged." Winslow leaned forward a little, and Jacob noted that his eyes were gleaming. "I could kill you. That's what many sons would do to a man who has done what you've done to my father. But I'd rather consider another route. Hardcastle didn't treat you too well, did he? Didn't pay you very much. Now it's all gone. There he is, the new master of one of the finest estates in the country, wearing gold rings, eating the best food, sleeping in a fine, soft bed. And you received a few measly coins while he gets all of that. There's no justice in it, is there, Jacob?"

Fowler was almost mesmerized by Winslow's reasoning and by the image of two hundred golden crowns. He looked around the room and then said, "All right. I'll say this here but nowhere else. Hardcastle hired me to do the job, but he told me that it wasn't all a lie. He said that the Winslows have some connection with William Tyndale, so I just fancied up the story a bit for the chief investigator."

"If my uncle and father should be released from prison and their property is returned to them, they could do a great deal for you."

"Yes, they could have me hanged!"

"But suppose I explain to them that it was due to Jacob Fowler that they had been released from the Tower and had regained their rightful places. That it all had been a terrible and honest mistake. My uncle might go even better than two hundred gold crowns—perhaps three or even four. And you're not getting any younger, Jacob. You're in need of a profession."

"What kind of a profession?" Jacob demanded.

"Oh, I would think perhaps marrying a wealthy widow might

be along your line. You're not a bad-looking fellow, but there's no courting a wealthy woman wearing those clothes and with your hair like that. A man must have an appearance to make an impression. I might even wager that you most likely know such a woman—do you now?"

As a matter of fact, Fowler did know such a woman. She'd had three husbands and was plain almost to the point of ugliness, but she had money, lots of it. Furthermore, she seemed to be open to a bit of romancing. Why, with a fine suit of clothes, maybe riding up on a fine horse, a little sweet talking—Widow Hoskins could be his! And after he married, there would be ready money for girls and drink, and the woman would just have to keep her mouth shut. That's how it was with wives. He had thought of Widow Hoskins more than once, but there seemed little chance of winning her, not when other suitors had so much more with which to tempt her.

Now he said craftily, "I might be knowing a woman such as that, but a lot of good it'll do me if I'm hanged for lying to the king's man."

Winslow smiled reassuringly and said, "Do as I say, Jacob. You'll be all right. You shall have your widow. I shall have my father and my uncle out, and we'll have Stoneybrook." Stuart paused, and Fowler watched the blue eyes narrow and turn ice-cold. "The only one who will lose will be Ives Hard-castle."

"I wouldn't mind that," Fowler said wolfishly. "Not a bit of it! Now, Master Winslow, you tell me all about this plan of yours."

⚜

The wind was shifting in the court of Henry VIII. Anne Boleyn had given birth to a daughter, whom she named Elizabeth, instead of the son Henry so ardently desired. "The king is no longer satisfied with Anne," many were saying. This would have been a dangerous thing to say during her pregnancy. Henry had

had laws passed that penalized anyone who spoke against the queen. But now he obviously had other interests. Henry had cast his eyes on a lady named Jane Seymour. Those who understood Henry the best whispered, "He'll be marrying her soon." When asked about Anne, "It's only a matter of time. The king will get himself out of that one."

Stuart listened to this talk as he moved around London, seeking a way to present the new evidence. He had Jacob Fowler primed, though he had paid him only a small portion of what he had promised. Fowler had been suspicious at first, but gradually had been won over as Stuart convinced him that the entire fee would be paid upon completion of the task. "But how will you keep me clear of it?" he kept asking. "How can we get them out unless I change my story? And if I should do that, they'd ask me why for certain."

Stuart was asking himself the same questions. He was struggling with the problem when a knock came at his door. He opened it, holding the hilt of his sword. "Orrick, what brings you here today?" He had informed Orrick of his whereabouts, and a couple of times Orrick had come to visit.

"I've come for you, sir. I ran into someone from Stoney-brook. Your mother, she's not doing well."

"She's ill?" Stuart demanded.

"Yes, sir, she's taken a bad turn, with the cold weather. I brought you a good horse, but we need to make haste."

At once Stuart pulled a cloak around his shoulders, and the two went out to the horses. Soon they arrived at the Murphy house, where his mother was staying.

The lady of the house met Stuart and led him to a room upstairs. Grace was propped up by pillows, and the covers were pulled high. A Bible in English was on her knees.

"Stuart!" she cried, her voice faint but her eyes alert. "You must be away from here. If you're found—"

"Shh, shh," he said. He sat down on the bed and kissed her

gently. "Never mind your fears for me. What's this I hear about you?"

"Oh, they say I'm ill, but it's nothing really. What are you doing in England? I've only gained a measure of peace through knowing you and Heather were safely away."

Stuart hesitated but then told her the whole story. When he got to Jacob Fowler, he said, "The man is ready to change his testimony, but only if he can escape the hangman, which is what I haven't figured out. He won't die for the money I promised him."

"Well, we shall pray about it and see what more has to be done. We need God's wisdom, of course."

Stuart gave Grace another kiss on the cheek and said, "I'll stay until you're better. Where is Quentin?"

"Away at Oxford. The Murphys saw him safely lodged there. He writes every day, pining for Stoneybrook. But I'm determined that he should see to his studies, even in the midst of such concern over . . . Your father would want him to carry on."

"Yes, he would. I'll stop by, check on him, as time allows, Mother."

Relief flooded her eyes. "I'd be so grateful." She swallowed and then coughed for several minutes. When she regained her breath, she said, "If you'll stay for but an hour, I might find a way to sleep."

Stuart understood then. She had slept little since Claiborn's arrest. How could she regain health if she did not sleep? "I'll be right here, Mother. Sleep now. I shall not leave you."

"Stuart, you'll never get your father's and your uncle's case reversed by yourself," Grace said from her bed. She looked better today after a week of rest. "Ives is too powerful, and even if it came to court, he could step in or have one of his hirelings do so."

Stuart nodded. He'd learned that Ives had survived Wolsey's dismissal and charge of treason—which arose after the cardinal failed to obtain Henry's desired annulment—and even absorbed a remnant of his power within the court. His stepbrother was a dangerous man in more ways than one. "But it has to be done before the judges. There's no other way to reverse what the chief investigator has set into motion."

"But the court can be swayed."

"It isn't supposed to be. It is supposed to be above influence and to mete out justice."

Grace held up her hand. "Right. There's only one man who can sway the court the way we wish it to go."

Stuart stared at her. "The king?"

"Yes, the king."

"But, Mother, that's impossible! Why should the king step in? He only does what's good for himself. He's the most selfish human being on the face of the earth."

"He has become that way, but he was not always so. Remember him as he used to be? As a young man, there was generosity in him and a desire for justice. The power of the throne has possessed him and corrupted him. But," she added spiritedly, "that which was in him as a young man may still be there, though buried and forgotten. You must go to Henry." She saw the objection forming on Stuart's lips. "I know he's surrounded by an army."

"And I am a wanted man."

"Yes. Let's set that aside for now."

"Set it aside? Mother, no one can get through Henry's guards."

"You'll never get to see the king as long as he is at court, but when he goes to hunt, he's not so well protected then, is he?"

Stuart lifted his head, his eyes alert. "Why, that's true. Many times he'll have only two or three men accompany him. Sometimes not even men of office. Just hunters or servants in charge of the dogs and birds."

"Then that's what you must do. Wait for him in the woods until you can speak to him."

"You realize, Mother, that he may simply call for my arrest. Then I will be with Father and Edmund in the Tower."

"We must leave that to God," Grace said. "God never contradicts himself, Stuart. If he's told you he will free Claiborn and Edmund, and if the only way is to gain the favor of the king, he will make a way for you to do so. It's his will that you speak to the king. Even if you go to the Tower for it, it's the right thing to do."

Stuart knew at that moment that there was no choice. "I'll be leaving then, Mother."

"God be with you, my dear. I'm a weak old woman. But in our weakness God is shown to be strong and all-powerful. As you go, I'll be praying for you."

Leaving his mother's room, Stuart went out of the house.

"Where ye going, sir?" a servant asked curiously.

"I'm going to borrow some of the birds from Stoneybrook."

"You mean Hardcastle birds?"

"Winslow birds," he corrected. "Come on."

※

Henry got out of his bed. It was early. The dawn had merely begun to appear, but a servant was ready.

"Sire?"

"What is it?"

"A message from the mews, sire."

"A message? What sort of message?"

"There's a gentleman there who wishes to give you a gift. Two gifts. A peregrine and a tercel."

Henry brightened. Surely this would be more interesting than listening to anyone in the palace! "Yes. I'll see the birds. No, I'll fly them." He dressed quickly. When he saw that the ulcer on his leg was bleeding again, he changed the dressing himself, stared at the raw wound, and wondered why God was allowing this to happen to him.

When he reached the mews, three young courtiers joined him. "No," he said. "Not this time. I want to be alone for a while." He had seen a tall, broad-shouldered man with white hair and a black eye patch.

"Yes, what's your name?"

"George Rochester, sire." This Rochester was a fine-looking man with a youthful face, despite the white hair, and a fit, strong body that Henry envied. *This young fellow looks as I did twenty years ago,* he thought almost resentfully. *But he's brought me some birds, so I'll not begrudge him.* "Rochester? Any relation to Sir Edward Rochester?"

"No, sir. I am not of that family. Only your humble servant."

"Nothing finer than a servant of the realm," Henry said heartily. "You have brought me a gift, I understand?"

"Yes, everyone knows Your Majesty's love of hunting birds. I do have two birds that I wish to give you, sire, should you find them acceptable."

"We'll go out and try them. There ought to be game stirring this morning. Let's have a look at them."

"Yes, Your Majesty."

Henry watched eagerly as the man opened one of the cages and thrust his arm in. "This one is simply called Lightning, Your Majesty. He's not as beautiful as some birds, but he seldom misses his strike."

Henry held up his arm and prodded the tercel's claw to make it step forward. The talons gripped Henry's gauntlet. "Looks aren't everything," Henry said. Just being in the mews and dealing with the birds had calmed his spirit. He expertly pointed out the good points of the tercel and handed him back.

"And this one is a bird almost worthy of Your Majesty's talent."

Henry stared at the peregrine and exclaimed, "Good heavens, I've never seen a finer bird! How is it that you have come by this bird, Rochester? You know, I suppose, that by law one must be at least an earl to fly a peregrine."

"Yes, sir, I know. I know also that that law is probably broken more than any law in your kingdom."

The king lifted an eyebrow and stared at the tall man, who said quickly, "Being an English servant, I decided to rescue this bird from a pernicious commoner who was breaking that noble law and present it to Your Majesty. I do not believe even an earl is deserving of this bird."

Henry laughed. "I can't argue that." He took the falcon and pulled out a couple of loose feathers. "I'm of a mind to try him, Rochester. Come along. You and I will have a hunt."

⚛

The two men had gone out alone, leaving even the grooms behind. The hawking went well, and the king was obviously delighted with both birds.

"Rochester, this is a magnificent gift! Seldom have I seen better. I accept them with pleasure." The wind was keening slightly, and the king's face was ruddy and filled with pleasure.

Stuart knew suddenly that he was at a turning point. Never again would there be such a moment. He breathed a quick prayer and said, "Your Majesty, my name is not Rochester."

Henry's eyes grew hard with suspicion. "What sort of trick is this?" He was always aware of the threat of assassination, and he darted a glance at his bodyguard, standing a hundred yards away.

"I am Stuart Winslow, Your Majesty."

Surprise washed across Henry's face. He obviously had been angered by the supposed treachery of Sir Edmund Winslow and his brother Claiborn. "You were a faithful servant, Stuart, but you became a traitor. You fled overseas."

"I stand ready to pay the penalty, but I ask Your Majesty one boon. Hear what I have to say before you call the guard."

At that instant a hare started. Henry whirled and threw the peregrine high into the air. The great bird's wings beat the air as it rose. The falcon wheeled sharply, spotted the feeding animal, and dropped like a stone. It struck, wings high, talons outstretched, and killed the hare instantly. Henry said, "Well, man, don't just stand there. Let's get the hare!"

The moment had broken Henry's severity. When he picked up the hare, he said, "I can hardly see you beneath that silly disguise you're wearing. " He took off his ermine cap. "Now, what's this all about, Stuart?"

"My father and uncle have been unjustly accused, Your Majesty. Your investigator," he added quickly, "was not at fault. He had improper evidence, and I've come to ask you to look into the matter once more."

"What improper evidence?"

Stuart told Henry the whole story, altering it to keep Jacob Fowler from being hanged. He told Henry that Fowler had been misled.

Henry listened shrewdly. "This fellow Jacob Fowler, he's ready to go before the judges and present new testimony?"

"He is, Your Majesty."

"He is a fine friend of justice, then," Henry said. "Does he realize that he could be hanged for perjury? Lying to my chief investigator is the same as lying in court."

"There are few men who seek justice fervently. I had to help him remember things. To take another look. And now he's ready to do it."

Henry was no fool. But he looked at the two birds and then grinned at Stuart, saying, "I shall see to the matter. Have your man at the palace tomorrow. I'll leave word that you are to be brought for a private hearing." Suddenly a wry grin touched his lips. "Am I allowed to keep the birds, Winslow, if I see that your father and uncle get a new chance?"

"Whatever you decide, the birds are yours, Your Majesty."

"Well, I'll take the birds."

"Your Majesty is merciful indeed and gracious and just."

"I'm so accustomed to hearing so much flattery that when an honest man speaks I hardly know how to respond." He turned suddenly and headed for the palace. Stuart watched him go with a heart alive with praise.

"Thank you, God, for preserving me! Now be my help and my father's friend."

⚭

As Jacob Fowler stood before the tiered row of judges with His Royal Majesty King Henry sitting on a throne to one side and his chief investigator beside him, he felt helpless. His legs were shaking so badly that he could hardly stand. He had just given his testimony, his voice had trembled, and now he stood enduring the heavy silence as the small eyes of the king seemed to bore deep into his very breast.

"And so you planted the evidence in the home of Sir Edmund Winslow and his brother. Why, you'll be hanged for that, you scurvy dog!"

"Oh, please, Your Majesty, it wasn't me that thought of it. Mr. Hardcastle, he told me that Sir Edmund was guilty and his brother too. That it was for you, Your Majesty. That's what he told me."

Henry glanced at Stuart and said, "Are you speaking for this man, Mr. Winslow?"

"The man has been dishonest, Your Majesty, but I feel he has learned his lesson. I pray you be merciful to him."

Henry glared ferociously at Fowler and then slowly nodded. "Very well, he shall have his back scratched and spend a few weeks in a cell."

"Oh, thank you, Your Majesty!" Fowler gasped in relief. He was seized and hurried out of the room by two guards.

Henry looked at the judges. "I see no profit in prolonging

this matter. It's plain to me that Sir Edmund and his brother have been falsely accused. Does anyone see the matter differently?" Henry did not even bother to look surprised when the judges all nodded.

Henry said, "Mr. Winslow, the court will give you the papers that will set your family free. I will have officers accompany you with authority for the arrest of Ives Hardcastle." Henry rose and faced Stuart. "I've two fine new birds that I'm anxious to try." The king of England winked at Stuart and left the room singing one of his own songs.

⚇

The darkness had become so familiar to Edmund and Claiborn that they paid no heed to it. They lay alone on their hard bunks. Claiborn thought of his early days when he was first married to Grace, of the birth of Stuart, then later, the birth of Quentin. And his heart was at peace, although he knew the shadow of the headsman was over him. Edmund was breathing heavily in a troubled sleep.

Suddenly the bar of the cell door screeched and the door swung open. The lamplight in the corridor was brilliant in comparison to their gloomy cell, and it hurt Claiborn's eyes.

"Is that you, Jennings?"

"Aye. It's me, sir."

"Time for a little exercise?"

"Not this time, sir. Get yourself cleaned up. You and Sir Edmund. Bring all your things with you."

Claiborn did as he was told, wondering about the strange instructions.

Edmund awakened. "What is it?" he mumbled. "Is this the end, Jennings? Have they dispensed with a trial?"

"The end? No, sir, indeed not. Come along. You don't have much time."

The guard led them outside and down a corridor, and

when they were put in a small cell with a window, Claiborn looked out to the courtyard. It was a beautiful day, but he could see no crowd collected for an execution as he might have expected.

His son walked into the room. "Stuart! Oh, Stuart, have they taken you too?"

"No. You're free, Father," Stuart said huskily. "You're going home, you and Uncle Edmund, to Stoneybrook."

Edmund rose to his feet. "How—how can that be? Tell us what happened!"

The two men, shaking, sat down, and Stuart went through the whole story, including the trial. He ended by saying, "Of course, when the king said he thought you were innocent, that ended it. No judges were going to go against him any more than they'd think about flying to the moon."

"And the verdict?"

"The verdict, Uncle Edmund, is that you are innocent of all charges, and Stoneybrook is restored to your hands."

"God has done this," Edmund said. "I didn't believe it could happen, but God himself has done it."

"You're right about that, Brother," Claiborn said.

"Yes, it's like coming out of hell itself."

The two men stumbled out, Sir Edmund being half carried by his brother and his nephew. There was a light on his face, and he said, "I can almost believe in God who has done this great miracle."

"I hope you do, Brother," Claiborn said heartily. "Now we'll get you home."

❦

Edith Hardcastle paused in front of the small mirror that adorned the east wall of the dining room. She admired the diamond brooch on her bosom as it glittered like a star. She had taken possession of all the personal things that had belonged to Edmund. Now she turned and said, "I think we must go to London this week, Ives. You've been away too long."

"You've bought enough clothes to last you a lifetime, Mother."

"Ah, my dear, there aren't enough clothes to last me a lifetime."

"Well, we're not made of money, you know," Ives said. He took another pull at his wine and shook his head. "The way you spend money, you'd think the Winslow money is endless."

Edith laughed. "I'll get a few trifling things, and you can buy that horse you wanted so much."

"Ah, yes, Lord Scourage's mare. Yes, I do—" He broke off, for the butler had burst into the room with a rather wild look on his thin face. "What is it, James?"

"Sir, you have—visitors."

"Visitors?" Ives's eyes met his mother's. "Did you invite someone?"

"No, not for this evening, Ives."

"Who is it?"

"Sir, you'd best come to see—" But James never finished his sentence. The large double doors swung open. Ives and Edith came to their feet.

"Well, Ives," Lord Edmund said, "I trust we don't come at an inconvenient moment." His face was thin and pale, but there was a bright glint in his eyes. Stuart stood to the right of Edmund, and his father was beside him.

Ives gasped, "What are you doing out of the Tower?"

"Oh, I've been released. A special trial, hadn't you heard? Would you believe it, Jacob Fowler is responsible for my release."

Ives saw the implication of that, but he did not speak, for another man had entered the room and stood waiting. Aaron Snyder, chief investigator. Snyder smiled wolfishly at him.

"There is an empty cell in the Tower, Mr. Hardcastle, which you will soon occupy."

"What are you talking about?"

"You are under arrest for treason," Snyder said. His yellow teeth gleamed as he grinned. He said, "Come in, fellows."

Two men bearing chains came in, and Ives cried out as they began to put them on him. "You can't do this!"

"The king has signed a warrant for your arrest. Take him to the Tower."

"To—the Tower?" Ives gasped. He looked at his mother and cried out, "Mother—"

Edith was fully expecting to be next. "It was Ives who did all this," she said to Edmund.

Ives stared at her, his chains rattled, and he screamed, "It was her! She put me up to it!"

"Take him away," Lord Edmund said, then turned to his wife. "You're not welcome to stay here, Edith. I will provide for you, but I want you out of my sight and out of my life. And leave those jewels that you're wearing."

The three men watched as Edith slowly took off the jewels and said, "I will get a few things."

"I will have a servant go with you to be sure you don't steal anything else."

Stuart felt a sudden pang of sorrow for the woman, as awful as she had always been to his family. "I'll take her and find her a place to stay, Uncle Edmund."

"Good. Don't tell me where it is. Just get her out of here."

As she left, Edmund faced his brother and memories came back to him, and he said in a broken voice, "I—know I've treated you badly, Claiborn."

"That's all in the past."

"No, it's here, and I want you to know that you will be my heir and this will be your property when I'm gone."

Claiborn said, "These things come and they go, but God is

eternal. Come. You need to rest." Edmund gave one glance at the door through which his wife and her son had vanished. "She never loved me, did she?"

"I don't think so, Edmund, but your Savior loves you. The Good Lord loves you. That should be enough for any one of us. Come, now. Let's put you to bed."

25

Stuart arrived in Brussels early in October 1536. He made his way to Vilvoorde, where Tyndale was awaiting execution. Much to his surprise he was taken at once to Tyndale's gloomy cell. A thin ray of light slanted down through the single window and lighted the face of the prisoner. Tyndale's face showed no sadness, although it was the day set for his execution. He had been sentenced to be burned. But as Stuart studied the lean face of the prisoner, he saw no sadness, only joy.

Clearing his throat, he said, "I am sorry it has come to this, Mr. Tyndale."

"Don't be sorry, my boy." Tyndale leaned forward and smiled slightly. "My work is done. It is time for me to go and be with him whom I love better than anyone in this world."

Mostly Tyndale spoke of the years that he had spent with Stuart getting the Word of God to England. It was three years since Edmund and Claiborn Winslow had been released, and William Tyndale had kept up with the family. He well knew that Edmund had died a year and a half after his release, that the heir of Stoneybrook was Claiborn Winslow, and that this, his son, would one day be lord of Stoneybrook.

"Your uncle went out to meet God in good fashion?"

"Yes, he did, sir. My father and he became very close. My

father led him to saving faith in Jesus. He was actually happy when he died. Ready to go."

"Well, things have changed since that time."

"Yes, sir, they have."

Indeed, Anne Boleyn had been executed on May 19 of that very year. Stuart had been there. He had liked her despite her many enemies and their comments about her.

Henry had married Jane Seymour in less than a week. Jane had borne a child, a boy, born in October, and the infant had been christened Edward.

"Well, Henry got his son and heir at last."

Stuart had little to say. He loved this man and honored him as he did no other. When Tyndale fell silent, he said, "Well, sir, the first time I saw you, you said you wanted to see every plowboy in England able to read the Word of God in his own language, and now many already are doing so. It's only a matter of time until all men will be able to do so. That's quite a legacy, sir."

"Well, we give God the glory, my son. He has opened up the doors."

There was the sound of voices.

"That is my call, I think." He embraced Stuart, saying, "Good-bye, my son—for now. But we shall meet again in a better world."

The guards came and took Tyndale. It was October. The air was crisp. The sun had barely risen above the horizon, and when he arrived at an open space, the crowd was jostling for a good view. A circle of stakes enclosed the place of execution and in the center was a large pillar of wood in the form of a cross. A strong chain hung from the top, and a noose of hemp was threaded through a hole in the upright. The prisoner was brought in. A final appeal was made, asking him to recant. Would he renounce the words that he had declared over the years?

Tyndale stood immovable, his keen eyes gazing at the common people. He met the cruel and merciless stare of his judges and doubtless pitied them. A silence fell over the crowd as they watched the lean form and thin, tired face of the prisoner.

Stuart was at the outer edge of the crowd, but he was tall enough to see clearly over the heads of the others. He saw the lips of his friend move in a final impassioned prayer. Then Tyndale cried out, "Lord, open the king of England's eyes."

Tyndale moved to the cross. His feet were bound to the stake, the iron chain was fastened around his neck, and the hemp noose was placed at his throat. Stuart was glad he would be hanged first and spared the ordeal of being burned alive. Piles of brushwood were heaped around him. The executioner came up behind the stake, and with all his force snapped down the noose. Within seconds Tyndale was dead. The wood was set afire. Stuart could not bear to stay. As he moved away, he thought of a different fire, the flames that Tyndale had set among the people, a burning to know more of their God, and his Word.

❊

Christmas had come. The skies of December had dumped blank carpets of snow. Stuart was sitting on the floor in front of the fire playing with his son, Brandon. He looked up at Heather, who was watching them with a smile on her lips. "Have you ever thought about how fortunate you are?"

"What do you mean?"

"To have such a handsome husband. Look. He's given you such a handsome son."

"I hope he's not as vain as his father!"

Since Stuart had come back from the execution of William Tyndale, he had been silent, but now his face was alight with joy. "Between Christmas and my beautiful wife and a fine son, I cannot wallow in sorrow."

"William would not have wanted us to be sad. He would want us to celebrate, be glad for him that he's free."

Stuart held Brandon high, and the child laughed and kicked his legs and waved his hands. "Full of life, aren't you?" When he put the boy down, Heather came to him, and he took her in his arms. "Well, another year is upon us. What will it be like? There's still trouble with the king."

"There will always be trouble with kings, but God is the King of Kings. Your father is hale and healthy, but one day you'll be Lord Stuart Winslow, master of Stoneybrook."

"No one but God knows our future. It's not something I crave. What I crave is for this house of Stuart Winslow, humble as it may be, to grow. For our love to grow."

"Oh, that it will, husband," she said, with a smile, "That it will."

Coming from Howard Books in May 2010,
the next installment in the Winslow Breed Series

When the Heavens Fall

BY GILBERT MORRIS

PART ONE: *The Bad Seed*

1

"Now, you just behave yourself, Master Brandon Winslow, and keep your bloomin' 'ands where they belong!"

"Why, Becky, they belong right *here*."

Becky Elwald slapped the hand that had been touching her, and tried unsuccessfully to frown. "You're a saucy one, you are! Tryin' to destroy a young woman's virtue, that's wot!"

At the age of sixteen Becky already had drawn many a young man's eye. She would be fat one day, no doubt, but at this stage in her life she had a figure that would have tempted a saint. She reluctantly accepted his kisses, and he whispered, "You're a lovely girl, Becky. And you're the one who agreed to meet me at such a late hour. Surely you knew what to expect." Perhaps she needed a few more minutes of sweet talk, and then he'd win her heart as well as her willing kisses—

Becky abruptly shoved Brandon back, and shook her head. "You said you'd read me poetry. I thought you had love, not lovin', on your mind. Get out of this barn! If my pa catches you, he'll skin you alive."

"He couldn't catch me if he tried. Come on, sweetheart, and give us another kiss." He caught her wrist and pulled it up to his lips.

She stilled. She was giving in. He could feel it. "You ain't but fourteen," she whispered, "too young for this sort of thing."

"I'm old enough. And you are too delectable to ignore."

Becky's lips parted as he leaned down, and he knew he had won. She wasn't the first girl who had caught his eye, and as the future Lord Brandon Winslow, Master of Stoneybrook, he certainly had his pick among the shire. But her hesitation had piqued his interest. That and the challenge of avoiding her antagonistic father—it was rather like plucking a ripe pear from the tree of a curmudeonly orchard owner. It had become a delightful game, finding a way to meet her alone, away from her father's squinted gaze.

Brandon ignored Becky's increasingly feeble protests. He had given little thought to girls until this year, giving all his time to hunting, learning how to be a knight, and mastering the weapons that his father provided for him. But now he wanted to know what the mystery was all about.

He lowered her to the straw and smiled as he felt her surrender beneath him. He ran his hand—

"What be you a'doin', girl? And you, boy, you got no right to be here!" Becky's father shouted. James Elwald had a staff in his hand, and his eyes were blazing.

"Brandon just came to—to visit, Pa!"

"You think I'm blind? Get you in the house while I deal with this rascal!"

Brandon rose and moved swiftly toward the barn door, but Elwald raised his staff and brought it down, striking Brandon hard on the shoulder. He raised it again, rage in his eyes, but Brandon was quick and strong for his age. He caught the staff as it came down and yanked it from Elwald's hand. Without a second's hesitation he swung the staff, and the blow struck the older man in the head.

Elwald crumpled to the ground, and Becky—who hadn't made it out the door—let out a scream. "You killed 'im, Brandon!"

Brandon's heart skipped a beat. He well knew what would happen to him if Elwald were dead; all his father's influence could not help him if he'd killed a man. He leaned over and put his hand on Elwald's chest.

He looked up at Becky with a reckless grin. "Why, he's all right, Becky. He'll have a headache, but he's too mean to die."

Becky was trembling, and her eyes were enormous. "'E's a vengeful man, Brandon. You'd better get out of 'ere!"

Brandon laughed and took her in his arms and kissed her. "I'll be back. We'll have to finish what we started."

But there was real fear in her eyes as she pushed him away again. "Stay away from 'ere if you know what's good for you! You don't know my pa."

Brandon laughed. Outside the barn door, a huge dog rose to greet him, and Brandon put a hand on his head. "Well, how about that, Eric?" he said lowly. "If the old man hadn't come in, I would have had Becky. What do you think of that?"

Eric barked and ran alongside Brandon. He was a large yellow dog, covered with scars from fights with other dogs, and even a few with wild pigs and their saber-like tusks.

"Ah well, there will come a day! Let's get back before Father finds out I'm missing."

Brandon broke into a loping run, and the dog came after him at a gallop. He wasn't even breathing hard when the shadow of Stoneybrook Castle rose before him twenty minutes later. A huge silver moon threw argent beams on the frozen earth, and a ghostly owl sailed overhead, hunting, as Brandon and his dog passed through the gate. There was no one stirring at this time of night, and Brandon loved the silence that held the castle as if in a spell. He'd taken more than one thrashing from his father for sneaking out on midnight forays, but he knew he would do it again. It was not that he did not love his father, but there was a wild longing that took him at times, driving him to find an adventure to break the monotony of daily life. He could bear a beating, but not boredom.

He whispered, "Come on, Eric. Let's go to bed."

Brandon moved across the stone floor toward a winding stair, making no more noise than one of the tiny mice that shared the castle with the Winslows. Stoneybrook was an ancient castle, but the walls were almost as strong now in 1546 as the year it took form. It was not as large as many others built during earlier days, but it was home to the Winslows, and something to be proud of.

Moving quietly, he made his way up the stairs and entered the room on the third floor that had been his place for as long as he could remember. Without bothering to undress, he threw himself on the bed, and the big dog whined and plopped down beside him. Brandon hugged Eric for warmth but was too excited for sleep. He relived the sweet kisses he'd stolen from Becky, and already was purposing in his mind how he would find her alone again—somewhere they wouldn't be interrupted.

"Get out of that bed!" Stuart Winslow grabbed his son's hair and pulled him up and out of his slumber.

Instinctively, Brandon launched a blow, and his fist hit Stuart in the chest.

"Why, you dare to strike your own father, do you?" Stuart shook him, realizing the boy was only half-awake.

Brandon looked up at him, his hair askew from deep dreams. "I'm sorry, sir. I didn't mean to hit you. You scared me."

"You were never scared of anything in your life, Brandon! I wish to heaven you were!" Stuart Winslow studied his son, thirty-four years younger. Would the boy ever grow up? Did he really want him to? "Get dressed!" he commanded.

"Where are we going?"

"You're probably going to jail," Stuart said grimly, pacing. He stared at his son a long moment, then said angrily, "What kind of blood has come down to you, Brandon? Some bloody Viking raider, if not worse." He watched, irritated it was taking the boy so long to dress. "Come. Quickly."

"Where are we going?"

"To face your sins," he said over his shoulder. Stuart left the room, closely followed by his son and the big dog. He moved down the stairs, taking them two at a time. On the ground foor, he found his wife, Heather, waiting for them. She was forty-one but could have passed for a woman ten years younger. She was a woman of quiet spirit, but now there was fear in her eyes. No doubt she saw the fury in his own. He looked away. They'd had a good marriage and still loved each other deeply, but Brandon had become a problem neither one of them could solve.

"Will you be able to make it right with James?" she asked, following them now.

"I doubt it." He stared at Brandon and asked harshly, "Didn't you know James Elwald would come for you, boy?"

Brandon looked surprised, caught, but not overly concerned. And no wonder. Stuart chastised himself for having always gotten the boy out of every scrape he'd gotten himself into. *But not this time,* he promised. This time, the boy would discover what it was to suffer the consequences of his actions.

As soon as the three entered the great hall, Stuart saw two female servants replacing the stale rushes on the floor with new ones. The women wore sly grins they didn't bother to conceal. *They well know what Brandon is—has he been sniffing around them, too?*

Up ahead, in the middle of the Great Hall, was Stuart's brother, Quentin Winslow. Quentin was thirty-three and bore a striking resemblance to Stuart, as well as Brandon—with the same blue eyes and auburn hair. He fell into step with Stuart and Brandon. "A little trouble, Stuart?"

"A little! This whelp tried lifting the skirts of Elwald's daughter."

Quentin had been a rough enough young man himself in his youth, but he had found God and was now preaching the gospel. He said nothing, but there was sorrow in his eyes as he looked at young Brandon. "I'm sorry to hear that, Brandon."

"Not as sorry as he'll be!" Stuart snapped. He grasped Brandon's arm and hauled him toward the two men waiting at the end of the Hall. "Here's the boy, Sheriff."

Albert Fortner, the local sheriff, was a rather small man, but well built. He had a smooth face and a pair of watchful gray eyes. "Sorry to disturb you over this problem, Master Winslow."

"A problem? You call it a *problem*?" James Elwald shouted. His face was flushed with anger, and he gestured toward Brandon. "That's him! He tried to rape my girl Becky, and when I tried to help her, he tried to kill me. Arrest him, Sheriff!"

"Be quiet, Elwald. I'll handle this," the sheriff said. He kept his voice soft and said, "As you just heard, Elwald wishes to press lust charges against your son, for certain advances upon his daughter and for attacking him as well."

"Don't you deny it either!" Elwald shouted. "You've ruined young girls in this county before!"

Stuart turned to stare at Brandon, his face set in a hard expression. "Did you try to rape that girl, boy?"

"No. I was just stealing a kiss." Brandon stared with impudence at Elwald. "And I'm not the first to have done it."

The sheriff had to hold James Elwald back. "Did you hit this man with a staff?" he asked.

"Yes, I did. I'd do it again too," Brandon said defiantly. "He hit me first!"

Stuart stared at his son and could feel his wife watching him. He knew she wanted him to protect Brandon, but there was only so much he could do—or wanted to do, this time. "Mr. Elwald, the boy's guilty. I'll let you decide what to do with him. You've always been a good man. I've been proud of you and your work, and if you want to charge him, I won't fight you in court, and there'll be no hard feelings on my part. But I see no reason for the court, or the sheriff, to be in the middle of this; if you want to settle this matter between the two of us, I'll see you get fair play."

James Elwald's face softened, and Stuart felt a sense of hope. James had worked for the Winslows for several years, and it was unlikely he would risk endangering that. Still, a man had to stand up for his daughter. Finally James said, "The boy deserves punishment, but I'd get no pleasure, sir, in seeing him in jail. You always treat a man fair. I think we can settle this between us, man to man, father to father."

Sheriff Fortner nodded. "Well, that's best, I think. I wish you good day."

James and Stuart left a moment later, leaving Brandon alone with his mother and his uncle.

"You've disappointed your father, and me too, Son," Heather said.

"Mother, it was nothing. I was just playing."

"I think it was more than that."

"Your mother's right, Brandon," Quentin said. "I think you've gone too far."

Brandon could rise to any challenge, but he did not want to hurt his mother. He dropped his head, unable to respond.

The three waited until the two men came back, and Stuart said, "Brandon, apologize to Mr. Elwald."

"No, sir, I won't do it. He hit me first."

Stuart stared at his son and shook his head. "Can you not see your own culpability? What about Becky? What about—" He paced away and ran a hand through his hair in frustration before turning back. "All right, then. It will have to be the hard way. I'm going to thrash you, and you're going to work for James for one month. If you take one step toward his daughter, or show any insolence to James, or cause him any other difficulty, I've ordered him to tell me. I'll thrash you again, and your thirty days' time will start again at day one. Now, come and take your beating."

James Elwald watched the two go, and then turned to face Lady Heather and Quentin. "I'm sorry it came to this. I've always gotten along well with your husband, and with you too, Reverend Winslow. But I got to look out for my daughter. She's got a wild streak in her, I'm afraid."

Heather whispered. "And so has my son." It hurt her to think of Stuart whipping Brandon. He had not done so for some time now—he had tried kindness and other methods, all to no avail.

Finally the two came back, and Brandon's face, Heather saw, was pale as paste, and he moved like an old man.

Stuart's face was set. "Take him, James. Bring him back in thirty days—not before."

The two left, and Quentin understood that Stuart and Heather needed no company at this time. "Come and get me if you need me."

After Quentin left, Stuart turned to Heather. "Do you hate me for whipping him?"

"No, I love you, husband, as I always have. We've tried everything else. Maybe this will change him," she said sadly.

Stuart chewed his lower lip, a nervous habit he had when he was disturbed. Finally he put his arm around Heather and led her away. As they moved out of the Great Hall, he said, "I thought having a son would be the joy of my life—and it was, when he was small and young—but he's a grief to us now."

Heather stopped and took his hands in hers. "I gave our son to God on the day he was born. We'll believe that God will bring him out of this. Brandon *will* find God! The good Lord will not let his gifts fall to the ground."

THE
Author, Book & Conversation

GILBERT MORRIS

I've had three careers: Baptist preacher, college professor, and novelist. All of these have been rewarding to me, but I sometimes think I've written too many books. Recently I counted the number of novels I've published and the number of years I've been writing, and was shocked to realize that I've published a book a month for the last 25 years. Sometimes I think I've written the same book 221 times! It doesn't seem fair somehow. The author of *Gone with the Wind* wrote one book and became rich and famous, while I've written more than 200 novels and am still poor and ugly!

When I get tired of writing, I go out to my woodwork shop and make things—mostly sawdust. When I get tired of that, I go to the Gulf, five miles away, sit on the white sand, and think. I have around 45 great ideas a day, with gusts up to 85, and around once every five years, one of them is worth something.

1) Why did you wait so long to begin writing?

I taught literature on all levels, but it never occurred to me that I could write a book. One day I read a bad book and thought, "I can write a better book than that." I did, and sent it off. It came back. I sent it off again. Twenty-seven rejections later, the novel was accepted. I was 55. Wish I'd started writing when I was 18!

2) What is your basic motive for writing novels?

A very difficult verse in the Bible says, "Whether ye eat or drink or whatsoever ye do, do all to the glory of God." I try to write books for the glory of God, but sometimes I fall. Got to keep trying, though!

3) What do you want your readers to get from your novels?

Entertainment, for if a sermon or a book or a movie isn't entertaining, you lose your audience. But of course, after you've got people caught up in your work, the thing I want to happen is for the reader to be encouraged. I want them to find Christ if they have not, and if they have, I want to encourage them to accept hardships and find ways to serve God where they are; and I want to dramatize the truths of Scripture.

4) What do you feel is the most important element in a novel?

A character. You can get by with weak plots, sloppy writing, inadequate research, or any other weakness—as long as the reader loves the character. Look at Dickens. He had enough bad literary elements in his novels to sink a ship, but those characters! Wow!

READER'S GROUP DISCUSSION QUESTIONS

1. Mark Twain once said, "If an individual needs to be cut down to size, there's nobody like a relative to do the job." Claiborn Winslow is treated abominably by his brother Edmund, yet he harbors no bitterness toward his brother. Can you think of a time when you were treated unjustly by a relative or close friend? Have you been able to put all bitterness toward that person away?

2. Early in the novel, Grace's family attempts to force her to marry a man she doesn't love. We all know the scripture that admonishes us to submit to our parents, and sometimes this is simple. But what do you do when, like Grace, you are forced to choose between obeying a parent and taking a course of action that seems wiser and more likely to work out in the long run?

3. Claiborn understood that, in asking her to marry him, he was asking Grace to face a difficult life rather than a comfortable one. Grace made her choice. But is there ever a time when we should refuse to lead a friend or a spouse out of a comfortable life into a difficult one? Under what circumstances would you strongly feel that you *should* suggest a more difficult life?

4. When Claiborn and his family are at the end of their rope, about to be evicted by their landlord and with no resources, Claiborn receives a letter from his grandmother informing him that God has revealed to her that Claiborn is to return to Stoneybrook, the family's estate. Most of us feel uncomfortable when someone tells us, "God told me to do this." Would you ever step out on faith if someone told you that he or she had received a promise from God? We know that situations like this occurred in Scripture, but do things like this happen in our day?

5. In the novel, Stuart "happens" to meet William Tyndale. It seems a chance meeting, but Stuart's relationship with Tyndale results in his giving his heart to God. Can you think of a time when you just "happened" to meet someone and, looking back later, you realize that God used that encounter to direct your life?

313

6. When Stuart goes to court, he has great admiration for King Henry, but in time he discovers that the king is a terrible man, not one to be admired. Have you ever discovered that someone you once admired and trusted is not the person you originally thought? Do you cut them out of your life—or do you attempt to change them?

7. Stuart is thrilled at first to join the court of Henry VIII, but over a period of time the immoralities of court life undermine his already shaky spiritual life. Knowing that he is being debased by his surroundings, Stuart realizes that he should heed the good advice he's gotten from his family. Most of us have found ourselves engaging in activities that we know do not honor God—but realizing this and finding the strength to free oneself from these activities are two different things. What do you do when you find yourself in this situation?

8. As a result of his lifestyle in Henry's court, Stuart hits bottom: imprisoned and facing execution. He has no resources and no one who will help except God. Have you ever been in a similarly hopeless situation? For Stuart, this terrible trial is what he needs to get him to surrender to Christ. But how much better not to wait until life collapses, but to seek God before we go down in flames! What things in your life, now or recently, may have been nudges to surrender your will to God's?

9. Stuart devotes his life to serving God by smuggling Bibles into England—in direct violation of Henry's law. Is it ever the right thing to break a law in order to do good? How do we decide?